FINDING ELIZA

Heather Whitford Roche lives in Ballarat, Victoria. She spent three decades working as a counsellor and family therapist. *Finding Eliza* is her first novel.

FINDING ELIZA

HEATHER WHITFORD ROCHE

AP

Allandow Press
heatherwhitfordroche.com

First published in 2018

Cover design by Alissa Dinallo
Typeset in Granjon by Alison Arnold

Printed by Ingram Spark

ISBN: 978-0-6482753-3-6 (paperback)
ISBN: 978-0-6482753-1-2 (epub)

A catalogue record for this
book is available from the
National Library of Australia

For Kevin, Andrew and Ben Roche,
and for my late mother and father,
Isabel and Ron Whitford

Prologue
1900

A contraction rips from within. Eliza can scarcely breathe before the next assault tears at her body. Her stomach tightens and a guttural sound escapes her. As the pain ebbs she imagines herself away for a short while; she floats above the bed and looks down. She can see the old midwife, Gertie, and the outline of her own body. Almost free. Then the pain surges again and she is back. She calls for help; no one answers.

Eliza gasps as the contraction rises in her body. Her tangled hair sticks against her face. When it ends, it is the curl of wallpaper she notices, where it is peeling away from the splintered window frame. Shabby lace curtains, pallid from exposure to the harsh Majorca weather, hang limp. In the corner of the modest room is a dresser with shaped legs and ornate handles. On it, Chinese teacups sit splendid in their vibrant blues and greens. They don't belong.

Another contraction gathers.

'Stop that noise! Do as I say and this baby will soon be out.'

Sympathy is not something Gertie gives willingly. Countless years of delivering babies have hardened her to the panicked cries of labouring women. There will be no hand-holding.

Eliza stares defiantly at her but waits for instructions. Fleetingly, her eyes rest on the floral pattern of her mother's apron as she hovers in the doorway. Then she arches her back as the rage within her body continues. Pain throbs at her stomach as Gertie roughly slaps her leg and yells at her to push, and push hard. Eliza sucks at the air around her and catches a whiff of the old woman's whisky breath.

'Big push, girl. The little bastard's coming!'

Her face crimson, she pushes with all she has left. Just as the pain begins to overwhelm her, she feels the baby swoosh from within. She falls back on the pillows. Flickering light from the kerosene lamp dances patterns across the wall and her eyes follow the movement. Slowly, Eliza raises herself in the bed and gazes at her son, ruddy and plump.

Outside, the afternoon light closes. Shadows of the day fall long across the familiar dirt road. The lofty cypress pines dwarf the row of timber houses as the evening hue descends on the country town. Chimney smoke puffs into the air at irregular intervals.

The town is quiet.

Part one
May 1921

1

The train pulls to a stop. I collect my overnight bag and drop from the carriage to the worn platform. The chill of the May evening hits me immediately. I nod to the signal-man and pull up my collar. There is no porter or trolley boy on Sunday nights – only the movement of a few alighting travellers. I'm in no hurry to get home. I know what's coming.

My mother will want to know everything about Will and Eugene: what we did, what we ate, who we saw. There will be endless questions until my father steps in and says, 'Give the boy a break, Rhoda.' And she will stop and I'll go to bed, thinking about the quiet talk at family gatherings when I was younger.

The shrill of the train whistle is piercing as I step through the swing doors into the night. I wave to the old men drinking and warming themselves by a blackened kerosene tin under the peppercorn tree. They huddle around the fire, their faces glowing ruby in the dark. The darkness behind them shifts and moves, and two men emerge from the shadows and saunter across to them. Old Harry reels back from the newcomers.

'Got a drink to share?' says one of the strangers.

'No bloody way, piss off, you mongrels,' says Harry, swaying and waving his hands in the air. He's a feisty old bugger who's fond of taking the piss and entertaining his mates.

'What's in the paper bag, old boy?'

'Fairy dust,' says Harry. His mates laugh.

'You're a lousy old geezer, didn't anyone teach you to share?'

'I'll share, all right. Come near me and you'll cop this on your bloody head.' Harry waves the bottle towards them.

'Dirty old tramp, you'll pay for that.'

The man leaps forward and grabs Harry by the front of his coat. Harry tries to pull away but the younger man has a firm hold. He lets go of the coat but puts his hands on Harry's shoulders and shoves him hard. The old man topples backward and hits the ground with a thump, backside first. The sound of shattered glass pierces the night air as his bottle of grog smashes beside him.

Harry is cursing from the ground and the others are hovering back under the peppercorn branches as I reach them.

'He's an old man. Leave him alone,' I say as I get between Harry and his attacker, using my weight to push the man away. But his mate is by my side in no time. A couple of the old men are shouting, 'Give it to 'em.'

I get a whiff of his alcohol breath as the bloke throws a quick unexpected punch in my direction. He catches me on my arm, a lucky strike. The stinging of it stops me momentarily. I turn and face him. He backs away from me this time. I can tell he's no fighter. But the one who knocked old Harry over is up for it. He's a mean-looking bastard, thin and wiry, with drink in his eyes. He comes at me hard, the old men are yelling, and it's all I can do to hold my ground. Ted used to say, 'Never pick a fight, Knill, but don't be scared to defend yourself.'

The man goes for my head, little punchy hits that jolt me, then he lurches back, corrects himself and comes at me again. Except this time I'm ready, and I punch him hard, right in the middle of his stomach. He bends over and curses, his breathing laboured. After a while, he straightens and throws one fist in the air. Then for some reason, he steps back, flicks his head to the side and spits at my feet. I wait to see if he's about to change his mind.

'You've done enough damage, just clear off,' I say.

The old men have stopped calling and the night is silent. The two invaders have moved back to the edge of the group.

'You heard me, move on.'

'Yeah and don't come back or you'll be sorry,' shouts one of Harry's blurry-eyed mates. They all laugh.

'Chink to the rescue,' says the quieter one.

The old men hush.

'What?' I say.

The other one takes over. It's not just drink in his eyes; they're filled with derision too. 'You heard, bloody do-gooder Chink.' The two men laugh and kick at the dirt.

'Don't worry about them, Knill.' Harry is still on the ground.

I go to him, ready to help him to his feet, and that's when I feel the whack on the back of my head.

I'm on the ground and a boot slams into the curve of my back. The pain shoots through my body and, for what seems a long time, I can't catch my breath. Another kick takes me by surprise. The old men are yelling.

'Leave him alone, you cowards,' says Harry.

The world darkens. I can smell the smoke from the coals in the drum. I can hear the heavy boots of my attackers scraping on the gravel as they run into the night. But I can't talk. And I can't get up.

'He needs help,' Harry calls. 'Somebody help, for God's sake.'

2

As I move, the pain in my back brings everything to a halt. Nurse Dancy is by my side, plumping pillows and smiling – a wicked smile that I remember from school, where she was a few years above me.

'You're black and blue all over,' she says.

'More black and white,' says a junior nurse, 'with those bandages against your hair.'

It takes me several attempts, accompanied by groans and grimaces, to raise myself to a sitting position. Outside it's light – early morning by the feel of it. How did I get here? Have I been here all night?

'We've just sent your mother and father home, Knill,' says Nurse Dancy. 'They've been here for most of the night. They said to tell you they'll be back in the afternoon.'

'It could have been a lot worse, Knill,' old Doctor Smithers says. 'But it's bad enough. You have nasty bruising, swelling and a cut to your head, though, fortunately, no broken bones. Right now, you need a bit of rest.'

'Thanks, Doctor.' My voice is shakier than I would like, and my head is swimming. I'm glad it's Smithers who's here. I've known him all my life.

'Who did this to you, Knill?'

'I went to help old Harry and his mates – two blokes were menacing them. And then…' I want to tell Smithers but there is nothing there to tell. What happened? I can't remember.

The doctor raises his eyebrows and touches my shoulder. 'Nasty types. And perhaps some things are best forgotten. Try not to worry. Nurse Dancy will tease you out of here in no time.' The nurses giggle and Smithers walks off.

I sleep often during the day, drifting into lengthy dreams that make little sense. The nurses wake me for meals. I find fruit and a couple of books from home on my bedside table, but I don't recall my parents' visit. The nurses continue to chatter above my head, always in good cheer and joking between themselves. There are times when I hear their voices and they become tangled up with the dreams. Sometimes I notice Nurse Dancy frowning at me; it's then I try to be a good patient and stay awake.

But when awake, I'm troubled. I want to remember. I recall leaving the station, going to help old Harry and his mates, and that is all. It is only as the sky outside turns to night that something else creeps to the edge of my memory. A word. Chink. Someone called me a Chink.

John Batten, the quietly spoken police sergeant, peers down from his six-foot advantage beside my bed the next morning, takes down my story.

'Old Harry and his mates corroborate your story,' he says. 'The man that hit you from behind was the one that pushed Harry. Then they both laid the boot in. When the old men shouted at them to stop kicking you, they ran off. It was the signalman who brought you in.'

'But Harry could give you a description of the men?'

'They were all pretty shaken and they were less than useful at remembering details. They claim it was too dark and it happened too quickly. Plus, they were drunk, Knill. Not reliable witnesses. Did the men say anything?'

'One of them called me a Chink.'

John Batten shrugs and doesn't meet my eye. 'We may never get to the bottom of this, Knill. Forget about the whole matter is my advice, and be careful in the future.' He flicks shut his notebook and nods to me, getting to his feet.

'They put me in hospital and you tell me to forget about it?'

'We'll make enquiries.'

Laurie Bench is brought in later that day and put in the bed next to mine. Nurse Dancy shoots me an apologetic smile when Laurie isn't looking.

'I've been along that track hundreds of times,' he says. 'Just bad luck, the horse rearing.'

'Bad luck happens,' I say, keeping my reply short to curtail what could be a lengthy conversation.

Laurie, who is a schoolteacher, pursues anyone who will listen to his endless chatter. He knows everyone in town. He keeps detailed lists of local soldiers lost in action and those returning home. He is also a keen horse breeder and rider. 'A broken leg and a few stitches in the head – won't be riding old Tappy for a while.'

'I imagine not.'

'And your situation – a funny sort of thing to happen in a town like ours, don't you think?'

'Sure was.'

'You know, Knill, people can be mean-spirited when they want to be – it's easy to look for what's different about others rather than what's the same.'

'I'm not sure what you mean…'

Laurie avoids my question. 'What does your father say about all this?'

I don't answer. What could I say? Obviously, he is upset.

Laurie's comment – it stirs something inside, unknown, uncertain, and then it's gone. I know what he's getting at, though – it's been hinted at before.

My cousins Will and Eugene saved me from an unbearably lonely childhood. I didn't have siblings, but they were like brothers. The three of us were inseparable. They always chose me first to be on their footy team, before anyone else got a look-in. Without them, I wouldn't have stood a chance. Some of the kids used to tease me and call me names. I had the burden of the blackest hair in the school and, unlike the other freckle-faced kids, I had pale skin and dark brown eyes. Luckily, my red-headed cousins were more than able to stand up for me, but it never took away my sense of being different.

Laurie Bench sits up higher in his bed when Rhoda and Ted, my parents, arrive.

'Knill, you look much better. You have more colour today. Hello, Laurie, lucky you're in here, the rain has almost soaked us to the skin. Ted, shake your hat out, it's still dripping wet. What did you do with Knill's clean pyjamas?'

Each day I wish that Laurie would disappear and that Rhoda would somehow be banned from entering the ward. They talk about the same things. At times, they talk over each other whilst Ted sits reading the paper. Each day I vow to be more patient. Each day I fail.

Hospital routines quickly become commonplace. Bed sponges, shaves, bed-making, meals on tray tables, nurse tidy rounds and the all-important doctor's visit with Sister. Nurses hurry around and there is the sameness of idle chat between the patients; the cumbersome green trolley with its large teapot and white cups and saucers standing in the middle of the ward, the tea lady coming and going between beds with cups in wobbly saucers. All markers in the busy day of a hospital ward. Laurie talks and talks. I try my best to be polite but when I tire of the avalanche of local history or gossip, I feign sleep.

'Won't be playing that violin of yours for a while, Knill,' Laurie says on my third day.

'I guess not, Laurie.'

Nurse Dancy is doing her rounds and arrives at his bed.

'Do you know that Knill here plays piano and violin?' Laurie says to her. 'Not a bad singer as well. Remember the school concerts?'

'Yep, every Christmas.' She winks at me. I shake my head.

Laurie barely draws breath before he asks her if she's any relation to Reverend Dancy from the Methodist Church. 'Let me see, probably twenty years ago, if I'm not wrong.'

'No connection.' Her smile is broad as she unwinds the bandage across Laurie's head. 'I'm Church of England.'

'He was well known in the district, very well respected. Used to organise the Harvest Festival each year. All the churches joined in. Biggest event in town.'

'Can't say I've ever heard of him.'

'Pity. He was a good man, always looking after people. He helped out many families – holidays for the poorer kids in town, young girls who found themselves in trouble, couples who couldn't have children.'

'You mean he found them babies?' Nurse Dancy looks at him instead of the bandage.

'Well, no, not exactly, families often approached him if they knew of a young lass who – how can I say this? – you know, wasn't married and needed to…anyway, he was a good man. And you – fancy having the same name, nurse.'

'Fancy. Okay, that's you all bandaged up again.' As she passes my bed she raises her eyebrows, nodding in Laurie's direction. I grin back at her.

The moment of silence in the ward is broken by the clatter of the afternoon tea trolley as it rolls its way along the squeaking linoleum hallway floor. Then I hear my mother's footsteps, the tap, tap, tap of her small feet as she arrives at the door of the ward. Rhoda is never late for visiting hour.

3

Ted and Rhoda follow as I manoeuvre the crutches through the door of the hospital ward. I hobble along the polished passageway. The crutches hinder me but I know hospital rules are to be obeyed. When home, things might be different.

I can sense Ted behind me and catch sight of his hand firmly on Rhoda's arm.

'Knill, be careful at the front step, you're wobbly on those things,' Rhoda says.

'I'll be fine, just need some time to get used to them.'

She breaks loose from Ted's arm and leaps forward, almost knocking one of the crutches from my hand. I sway but regain my balance as I gently push her hand away. Why does she always have to make a fuss?

The familiar grimace on Ted's face isn't lost on me. 'Rhoda, leave Knill to manage.'

Rhoda retreats one small step to the side of the hallway, but she's close to my elbow, waiting to pounce.

Rhoda insists that I recuperate in their room. She's moved their things to the spare bedroom at the back of the house. My own room is considered too poky for the needs of convalescence and it's pointless to argue. The front bedroom is the largest room in the house. The blue bedspread has been on the black, iron-framed bed forever. The fringe is beginning to fray and patches of thin cotton are showing through the rows of chenille. Two identical wardrobes stand side by side. The dark oak is streaked from years of diligently applied polish. A matching dressing table stands next to the door.

I know this room well. As a child, I liked to play with the crystal set on the dressing table, and I was fascinated by the collection of rhinestone brooches and hat pins stored in the oval bowl with its fancy lid. I loved the little ring holder and used to slide my small fingers along it, sometimes removing a small gold ring that Rhoda kept there. That was when I felt closest to her.

Sometimes, I'd look up to see her standing in the doorway, gazing towards the window, her head tilted, revealing the sharp part in her wavy hair, which was always held in place with bobby pins. It was as if she didn't see me until I spoke or made a sudden noise. Then she would turn her attention to me and gently scold me for touching her special things. Rhoda ran her house just as her mother and her grandmother had done before her. Everything in order, well polished and in its place. All her energy went into this pursuit. She wore freshly ironed aprons and tiny blue velvet house slippers that made a line across the front of her feet.

I'm relieved to lie down on the bed despite Rhoda's fussing and chatting. After a week in hospital I'm still weak. My eyes close to the welcome feeling of losing myself in sleep. At times, I'm vaguely aware of Rhoda sneaking in and out of the room, tiptoeing along the side of the bed, peering at my face. Ted's in the sitting room, reading quietly, leaving me be.

Later in the afternoon, they get ready to go to the shops.

'Fish for dinner?' says Rhoda.

'Sole for the soul,' says Ted.

Doors are closed, keys rattle, and finally they make it out the front door. I watch from the window as they leave. Ted, still fit-looking, waits for Rhoda at the gate and as he does he stretches up on the balls of his feet, a mannerism all the McMillans share. His spectacles perch on his nose as if about to fall off any second. He's wearing his suit jacket – navy with fine stripes, wide lapels – sharply pressed trousers and polished tan shoes. He taps his fingers on the fence post. Eventually Rhoda bustles past his outstretched arm. Her grey overcoat, thrown around her shoulders, threatens to fall to the ground as it flaps against her long skirt. A muted pink, floral blouse strains across her corseted body.

She heaves her coat further onto her shoulders, then firmly tucks the worn leather purse beneath her armpit.

Her voice gradually fades as they move further along the footpath. I know from experience that my mother will be breathless by the time they reach Main Street.

At last I'm alone. I lean back on the pillows and sigh as the peace in the house surrounds me. I'm not sorry to be out of the hospital. The days passed by in a fog-like blur.

In the still of the bedroom, a small spider climbs high on the wall, its spindly legs working frantically to bridge the distance from the doorframe to the wardrobe's edge. My eyes travel with the spider as it crawls across a cardboard shoe box on top of the robe and then disappears. As I watch for it to reappear from its hiding place, I wonder about the box. I've never seen it before.

Time moves so slowly when you are infirm. I'm not sure how many minutes have passed – five? twenty-five? – when my curiosity gets the better of me. Ignoring the soreness in my body, I get out of bed and limp to the wardrobe. I hook the box sideways until it's sitting on the front of the wardrobe lip, then carefully lower it and take it back to the bed. My legs are shaky. I catch my breath and wait for my body to settle.

The top of the box is covered with dust so I wipe it with yesterday's newspaper. The top is jammed firmly over the base. I pull hard and the lid flips off, showering more dust across the bed. A musty odour escapes from within.

There are several envelopes and a parcel wrapped in soft, yellowing poplin. One of the envelopes holds faded photos, the edges curled. In one, a young woman with long hair flowing across her shoulders looks directly, boldly, at the camera. She looks not yet my age. She appears in the other photos with an older couple, a young lad and two smaller children. I spread the images across the bed, her eyes catching my attention as I do so.

I lift the parcel out of the box. The fabric is easily unwrapped to reveal a china cup, octagonal in shape but thin to the point of transparency. The pattern is brilliant: swirling blues and greens with silhouettes of large dragon-flies dancing across the surface. The cup's handle is decorated with smooth gold edging. I gently rotate it in my hand, discovering two raised gold Chinese symbols on its base.

Why does Rhoda have a cup like this? It bears no resemblance to her sets of pretty English cups, saucers and plates, protected from harm in her china cabinet.

At the bottom of the box is a large brown envelope addressed to Ted and Rhoda. I know I'm prying but the urge to continue outweighs my conscience. Inside are two letters. The first is handwritten and dated 21st February 1900. Across the top of the page is the formal letterhead of the Methodist Church of Victoria.

Dear Mr and Mrs McMillan,

It was a pleasure to meet with you both last month. I always think it most important to get to know people before we offer to assist.

As I explained at our meeting, it might be some time before an opportunity presents, but you appear to be most suitable people. I pray that God will help us in our endeavour to fulfil your request. Be assured I will contact you when the time is right.

I'm trusting this matter can remain in confidence between your good selves and me.

Yours sincerely,
Reverend Charles Dancy

I read the letter again quickly, trying to grasp its meaning. I rub my forehead and my fingers come away wet with perspiration.

The second letter is a thin greying note with handwriting that runs off the page at the end.

To whom it may concern,

This baby boy comes from a good family. Under different circumstances we would raise him ourselves but he deserves a mother and a father who can provide him with a decent life.

The baby's name is 'Scarffe Knill' but you may choose your own name which is only to be expected. He was born on the Fourteenth of November 1900.

Please take good care of him.

My eyes are darting all over the paper. I read it again, slowly this time. I watch the paper shaking, then realise that it is my own fingers that are unstill. The air in the room is staler than before. My heart booms within my chest. I turn back to the first letter. Why did Reverend Dancy write to Ted and Rhoda?

When it hits me, I sit bolt upright, setting off a line of fire across my ribs. The familiar feeling is back; it's never far from me. It's as if I've always known. And now it's staring at me – the evidence of this feeling.

I stare at Rhoda's dressing table, my body reeling. The diamond pattern of her oval bowl blurring into the background. Breathless, I can barely move. My eyes wander back to the paper in my hand. *Scarffe Knill…Fourteenth of November 1900.* I read it over and over, again and again.

I'm not their son. That's why I'm different. That's why I don't look like them.

But who the hell am I? Scarffe Knill?

The old photos look up at me. I've never seen these people before. And yet, they have something to do with me. I pick up one of the photos and peer at the faces – the serious-looking older woman, the proud man beside her and the young woman with the challenging eyes.

Time has slowed, the stillness of the house smothers me. I dress with urgency, then sit on the bed to recover. Ted and Rhoda have the answers I need.

I wait.

4

How much time passes before I hear the front gate and their footsteps on the path and then the verandah? I don't know. It seems hours. Rhoda is talking and Ted laughs.

The front door opens and Rhoda bustles down the hallway into the kitchen, where I now am.

She stops when she sees me. 'What are you doing, Knill? Doctor Smithers said bed rest for a week and…'

Ted closes the door and walks in behind her.

'I'll put these parcels away and then—'

Rhoda sees the letters, photographs and cup on the kitchen table. She swings around to face Ted, who has also seen them. Ted's hat falls from his hands.

'You always told me to tell the truth.'

They both look at the table, the strange cup with the swirling patterns so different from everything else in the room, then at each other.

'Let us explain,' Ted says.

'When were you going to tell me?'

'Knill, we should have told you, but it never seemed like the right time,' Ted says.

'The right time! For who?'

Ted holds his hand towards me. His eyes meet mine and I glare at him. My throat tightens as I fight the urge to cry.

'I had a right to know about this, for Christ's sake.'

Rhoda moves towards me. I flinch; she stops.

'Don't touch me, I just want the truth.'

They're staring at me, eyes wide but not making a sound. I'm leaning on the back of a kitchen chair. I push it hard and surprise myself when it flips over. Rhoda backs away, hands to her face. Ted touches her arm but doesn't take his eyes from me.

The three of us stand in the small kitchen. It's as if they are in a distant shadow. Their mouths move as they voice their explanations, but I can't really hear them. I'm not their son and they deceived me. They made me part of their daily deceit. And they didn't even have the decency to let me in on the secret.

Ted's serious voice breaks through, though it still seems a long way away.

'We didn't want you to feel different from the other kids.'

'But I did! All the bloody time I felt different. I even looked different! Now I know why.' I can feel my face distorting as I fight to hold back the sobs rising in my chest.

'We treated you just the same. You were like our own child, no different.'

In the blur, I am aware of Rhoda by the sink. Standing taller than normal, she steps forward. 'Yes, we should have told you, it should never have happened like this.' She holds the fabric of her skirt tight in her hands. 'I'm sorry, Knill.'

The room is once again silent. Ted is closer to me now, but I don't want to make eye contact. He keeps talking, explaining. 'We wanted a child and when you arrived our family was complete. We took you on as our own. Knill, we love you, and it makes no difference.' Ted's voice falters and he turns his head away.

Rhoda is watching Ted. The expression on her face is resigned and there is something different about her; I've never seen her this way before. I feel a pang of concern for her as Ted continues. A pleading tone has entered his voice. Again, I've stopped listening. My thoughts are scattered and I float between the kitchen and a recurring childhood dream.

In the dream, I am looking through a window and my family and friends are all inside. The tinsel on the Christmas tree shines in the lamplight, the large table is set with coloured bon-bons, bowls of lollies and serviettes. They are laughing and singing but ignore my calls to open the door.

I hate that dream and curse when it becomes part of my waking thinking. I often feel that I'm out of kilter. Awkwardly aligned, block-shaped instead of round and smooth. Always different.

I want to get out of the kitchen, the house. Like a feral deer, I want to run away. The name flashes before me again: Scarffe Knill. Rhoda and Ted gave me my second name but not my first. Scarffe. And Scarffe Knill who? I feel as if I've been stripped of something. Even if my own name, Knill McMillan, was fake, it was all I knew. Scarffe Knill…Scarffe Knill. The name shifts about, refusing to settle.

I look around the neat kitchen with its floral curtains hanging each side of the small window. As a child, I used to climb on a chair and peer out. The yellow kitchen dresser was painted by Ted, with newspaper spread on the floor to catch spills. My eyes rest on the green-fronted wood stove, which I huddled next to on winter mornings.

Ted and Rhoda stand side by side watching me. Rhoda is quiet. I've never known her to be so silent. Ted's shoulders are slumped, he looks pale. I walk past them and go to my room.

My hospital bag is still partially packed. I push pyjamas and socks into it, stuff my wallet in my pocket and carefully attach my fob watch to my jacket.

I tell them I'm going. I'm aching and sore but I need to get away from this place. I need to be gone.

5

She has a recurring dream about a grand and imposing house, a staircase at its centre which she knows she must climb. It has polished banisters on each side. As she makes her way up it, her feet begin to slide on the shiny timber and her hands splay before her as she reaches to grip the rails. But already she is falling. In slow motion, she floats and falls, her gaze strained towards the balcony.

She can see the two baby cribs standing side by side. One draped in a pink shawl, the other in blue. The ornate bassinets rock slowly to an unfamiliar tune. A shrill violin plays as she claws her way towards the babies. She stumbles onto the landing to find the cribs empty and motionless. The coloured shawls lie scattered on the floor.

She wakes to the sound of her own sobbing.

She will not be consoled. Ted listens as she revisits the events of the last twenty-four hours. She speaks until she has little breath left.

'He deserved more. We should have told him.'

'Love, he just needs some time to get used to the idea.'

'Haven't I always told you there would be trouble over this? I know I'll never see him again.'

All these years she has known that the truth would eventually come out. Knill really belonging to someone else. And Ted never quite understanding what it's been like for her to raise someone else's child. No, she knew this would happen. Motherhood, despite her love for Knill, has been her silent burden.

Never has she been so distraught. She blames Ted. He should have stopped Knill from leaving. Instead, he simply asked him to keep in touch. She knew it would come down to this. She always knew.

Memories churn in her head. All those years of wanting a child, her child. Not feeling worthy, not being a real mother. Ted's family assumed it was her problem. They always think it's the woman's fault. 'Poor Rhoda, she can't have children.' Not that anyone talked to her about it. They had plenty of whispered conversations behind her back and gave her sympathetic looks when the subject of babies came up. Her fury rages as she thinks about the secrets she kept, to protect Ted's manliness. When Knill was growing up, there were more secrets – lies even – telling Knill he looked like his father.

Rhoda will not be silenced again, no more lies, no more pretence. In the end they all betrayed her, Ted, her parents, and now even Knill. And yet, somehow Rhoda knows she has no right to feel betrayed. No right at all.

6

Spencer Street Station stretches dark and lonely before me. I've been here countless times but tonight I have a sense of dread as I peer along the emptying platform. A large clock hangs from the metal ceiling. Nine-thirty. I follow the other travellers in a sheep-like procession as if I'm headed somewhere. I'm envious of them. They seem so sure, so certain of the next hour, the next day. I'm tired and aching. The anger that fired me into action has deserted me. I feel like a stupid kid who doesn't know what to do next.

An old man sleeps by a paper stand. His skinny-ribbed dog sits at his side, on guard. I pat the head of the mutt as I pass. Steam from a nearby train engine hisses into the still of the night.

I'm too late for the tram to Collingwood – to Will and Eugene's place. Could I walk? It's out of the question. My body's too sore and I crave sleep. I pick up my bag – it now feels like a burden to carry – pull my coat collar up against my neck and head towards the nearest station bench. The refreshment rooms are in darkness and closed for the night. I'm cold and shivering, but mostly my eyes won't stay open. I slump on the wooden seat. Weariness wins.

I wake in the semi-dark. My back and legs are stiff, my head is throbbing. I'm cold. The clock says six-fifteen and I've been on the station bench all night, like some hobo. I pull myself up to a sitting position. People are passing me now, some glance at me, others are too focused on their own business to be bothered. Spitting noises from the train engines provide a strange background, accentuating the feeling I have of being in a continuous dream.

The men's washroom is further down the platform. I've never liked going in there, often waiting until I get to Collingwood to use the lavatory. The stench of stale urine hits me as I enter. The old porcelain basins are chipped and grimy, and the concrete floor is damp and dirty. Treading carefully, I use the lavatory and then splash cold water on my face.

My reflection in the cracked mirror above the basin catches me unawares. Thick black hair parted sharply, dark, watchful eyes and, despite everything, a hint of a pleasing smile ready to appear.

'Such a good-looking lad,' people used to say. 'Tall and striking. Where did he get those looks from?' Now I know.

Not Ted or Rhoda, not my grandparents. And my musical ability? 'He doesn't get it from the McMillans, that's for sure.'

I'm hungry. I need to eat something.

The refreshment room, with its high ceilings and domed glass windows, is a welcome escape from the platform. The growing light is cast on the chequered tablecloths. Teapots and white cups and saucers are stacked at the end of the counter. I wait behind an elderly couple. For a second, they remind me of Rhoda and Ted. The woman fusses and changes her mind as her husband smiles politely at the attendant. When my turn comes, I order tea and toast, then sit at a small table by the window.

Immediately, the hot tea warms me. I gulp it down and pour another. Toast and jam have never tasted so good. I wish I'd ordered double but decide against going back for more. With the comforting food and tea inside me, my mind returns to Ted and Rhoda. Briefly, I consider going back home to have it out with them, to ask more questions. They should have told me; they had no right to let me think I was their son. But I'm not proud of the way I shouted at them. The concern I felt for Rhoda, for that uncharacteristic quietness, flares again, then dies down.

Why hadn't I guessed? Had others?

Did my cousins know? The kids I grew up alongside? The kids at school? In a town as small as Castlemaine, everyone knows everything about each other's families.

They think a kid doesn't hear the whisperings, but they do, even if they don't fully understand them. I felt sorry for Ted, always in the background making excuses for Rhoda's peculiar ways. Her fast-talking. The way she finishes people's sentences for them. Growing up, I pretended the comments about her didn't bother me, but they did. By the time I was twelve, I had begun to avoid being around her in company. I guess I was embarrassed, though I also felt protective of her. In later years, just like Ted, I learnt to nod and agree. I know she can't help it.

Who is my birth mother? Why has she never contacted me? Or was she glad to be rid of me? I realise that in my haste to be out of the house I didn't bring the letters and photos. I want to look at her again, the young woman with the long hair. Is it possible to find her, my mother, my *real* mother? Does she ever think about me? An unexpected sadness washes over me.

The trains hiss and spit outside the refreshment room window. Minutes pass. Longer. Train after train moves off. I watch until they disappear.

When I next take in the room, it is almost empty. The attendants behind the counter are stealing cautious glances at me. I check my watch and can't believe it's ten minutes to midday. I've been sitting here too long.

7

Eugene opens the door, his familiar smile fading as he takes me in.

'Christ! What the hell happened to you?'

The narrow hallway is laden with boxes, pieces of furniture, shoes and boots. Several old coats hang off brass hooks on the wall. The embossed wallpaper has seen better days and in places it curls and droops. We head to the kitchen. I'm accustomed to the run of this house and relieved to be back in a familiar place.

'Have you been in some sort of fight?'

'You could say that. I need to sit down for a while.'

I slump onto a kitchen chair as Eugene slides the kettle across the stovetop. He keeps looking at me and shaking his head.

I explain the attack at the station and my time in hospital. And the rest? I hesitate to tell him but decide that he should know. Eugene sits at the end of the old table, frowning. He looks just as he did when we were kids. His fingers drum continually on the table, and he glances towards the passageway from time to time. I know he's wishing Will would arrive home from work. He's not on his own there; I feel the same way. As the oldest, Will always takes charge. He'll know what to do.

'They weren't going to tell me,' I say. 'I had to find out by snooping in a box.'

Eugene stops tapping his fingers and lets out a loud sigh. The kettle is bubbling away behind him, but he ignores it. He glances again to the passageway.

'I guess they should have told you, mate. But would it have made any difference?'

'They lied to me. All my life they lied!'

'I don't really know what to say, Knill.' Eugene gets up abruptly and shoves the spitting kettle to the side of the stove, then sits back down. 'But they're still your parents. Funny, but we always envied you with your new cricket bat and train sets. We had the hand-me-down versions.'

'Cricket bats and train sets?'

'They tried so hard, Knill. They even let you call them by their names. We would have got a clip around the ears if we'd tried that with our parents.' Eugene runs his fingers through his hair and resumes finger-tapping.

I'm taken aback by what he said. Ever since I can remember, I've called Ted and Rhoda by their Christian names, not Mum and Dad like all the other kids. I think they thought it was both funny and clever when as a little bloke I first came out with it. They never corrected me, and the habit remained. I'm sure it had nothing to do with me being adopted. Or did it? Did I know somewhere deep inside?

'I'm not saying they were bad parents. The point is they should have told me.'

'They probably didn't know how you would take it, mate.'

'Did you and Will know?'

Eugene scratches his unshaven face and looks awkward. 'Well, there was a time when one of the O'Brian kids next door said you were adopted. Will punched him in the head and that was the end of it.'

'The family never talked about it?'

'No. They mainly talked about Aunty Rhoda's... nerves, I think they called it. I thought it was strange that you didn't have brothers or sisters, but I didn't think much more about it, Knill.'

'I have this feeling that everyone else knew, except me.'

'We just knew there was some sort of problem with Aunty Rhoda. Couldn't have kids or something. Didn't think about how come she had you. Well, seems she didn't have you, did she?'

The front door opens. We both look to the hallway as Will's footsteps grow louder. He stops when he sees me.

'Knill?'

'There's been a bit of trouble,' Eugene says to his brother.

'What sort of trouble? What happened to your head?' The kindness and concern in his voice get to me and my eyes moisten. Will is always there when the chips are down.

'It's a long story. Sorry I just landed here. Didn't know what else to do.'

As I tell the story again, I catch them glancing at each other across the table.

'Uncle Ted and Aunty Rhoda must be pretty shaken up,' Will says. 'We know how they dote on you.'

'I just need some time to sort this out for myself.'

'And your job at the railway station office?'

'I dropped a note under the stationmaster's door before I left.'

'You mean you're not going back?'

'No.'

Will scratches his head. 'Look, I can see this has knocked you about, Knill, but it doesn't make any difference to us, mate.'

'That's because you know who you are.'

'Well, you're still our cousin, adopted or not.'

They both grin at me.

'It makes sense now,' Will says. 'What with you playing piano and violin. The rest of us can't hold a note.'

Will and Eugene are both wiry, with thick ginger hair and blue-green eyes shaded by bushy eyebrows. They look alike, always have. Eugene is taller by a couple of inches. Brothers. They will always be brothers, even when they disagree, as they often do. They sit quietly now as if they have run out of words. The looks on their faces tell me they don't know what to do. For a minute, I feel a bit foolish. Perhaps, as they say, it doesn't matter. They are still my cousins.

It is only then that it becomes clearer. Will and Eugene are not really my cousins. I'm not related to anyone I know.

Eugene gets up to fill the teapot. The kettle clangs on the stovetop. Coming here was a big mistake. It isn't going to work; they can't possibly understand.

'I'm leaving,' I tell them. 'I need to think this whole thing through.'

'You can't go anywhere in the state you're in,' Will says.

They both step towards me but I already have my bag in my hand and I'm in the hallway.

'Wait. At least have a rest.' Will tries to grab my arm, but I'm already pushing through the front door.

'Bloody hell, Knill, you selfish, selfish bastard,' says Eugene. 'Where are you going to stay?'

'The Salvos. I don't know.'

'You're not a kid anymore, Knill. We won't be there to save your bacon,' Will calls after me.

My bag is hitting my legs. My heart thumps against my rib cage. At the end of the street I slow. It's colder now and afternoon rain threatens. A tram rumbles in the distance and I know my only option is to wait for it and get on board.

8

The blue chenille bedspread is crumpled where she lies. It's mid-afternoon and Rhoda has barely moved from her bed since Knill left last evening. Her cherished crystal set, a wedding present from Ted, sits on the neat dressing table by the door.

'Come out to the sitting room for a little while, love.' He is carrying tea and biscuits on a tray.

She turns her back to him and the room is silent. Ted watches her for some time, shrugs, and then walks from the room. In the kitchen, he flinches at the clunk of the china cup as it tumbles into the enamel sink. Her strange grief perplexes him, always has. He can understand her concern for Knill, though; he's also worried about the lad.

Knill has been the bright light in their relationship from the first time they set eyes on him as a baby. His chubby little legs as he used to follow them around the garden.

His first day at school with the oversized satchel strapped to his back. The warm pride Ted felt when he heard Knill practising his violin in the front room.

And there wasn't a moment when Ted felt that Knill wasn't his son, despite the boy's different blood.

She walks past the large hydrangea next to the shed wall and across to her rose garden. Each year, since they married, she's planted a new rose. The roses are her pride and there's not much Rhoda McMillan doesn't know about the glorious blooms. The lavender hedge along the edge of the garden is in full flower. Rhoda runs her hands along the purple tips, inhaling the familiar scent. The night dances a protective shadow across her cherished garden. Rhoda glides quietly down the path onto the street. It's still dark, but she pays no heed to time or place.

'She would never leave without telling me where she was going,' Ted tells his brother, Stan. When Ted woke this morning, still in the spare back room, Rhoda was nowhere to be found.

The two men stride towards Main Street. They pass the local bakery, with its steamy opaque windows and early morning waft of fresh baking. White's butcher shop is open for business and the neat concrete floor is still wet from the morning hose-down. There are a few people on

Main Street. A large woman wearing a black dress with an oversized collar is laboriously washing the drapery shop window. Both Ted and Stan wonder who she is – new in town, perhaps. The local pharmacy is still closed. There's no sign of Rhoda.

Ted struggles to explain his concerns to John Batten. He tells the policeman about Rhoda being concerned because Knill has gone.

'Is this anything to do with your son's attack at the station?' asks the sergeant, leaning his weight on the wooden counter between them.

'No. Well, not directly.'

'Problems at home, Ted?'

'I'm not sure what you mean…'

'Just that it seems a tad unusual for Rhoda to leave just because your son took off for Melbourne.'

'It's a bit tricky. You see, Knill found out some information about his birth. He was adopted and he didn't know. He discovered it himself and was pretty upset.'

'So he was adopted, he found out, then left town. Now your wife is missing, is that right, Ted?'

'That's about it.'

'I can understand Knill being a bit…surprised, but why would Rhoda disappear? Are you sure she didn't catch the train to Melbourne to follow your son?'

'We asked at the station. No one saw her and she never travels alone. No, she didn't do that.'

'Has she ever done this before?'

'Once before, a few years ago. She left one night, and I found her the next morning sitting on a bench in the park.'

'She was gone all night?'

'She wasn't well. She'd been in hospital. Nerves. It was her nerves playing up.'

'Is that what's happening this time, Ted?'

'Yes, probably, but I can't find her to get her to the doctor.' Ted places his head in his hands as Stan steps forward.

'We'll post a missing person's report.' John Batten straightens, shakes Ted's hand, and goes into the next office. Ted picks up his hat and lets out a sigh.

He doesn't look at Stan. He already knows what he's thinking from the set of his jaw. Bloody Rhoda and her nerves. Poor bloody Ted. Family business should be dealt with inside the family, not out in the open like this. Everyone knows that Rhoda has a few problems. This latest mess is certainly proof of it. Running off without a word to anyone.

All day Ted searches for Rhoda. He loves this town – so many comforting memories of his own childhood as he walks alongside the hospital, around the school and through the Main Street several times. He stops at the public gardens where Rhoda spent happy hours with other gardeners tending the roses and the beds of annuals. He half expects to see her, with her gardening gloves and hat, but today the stark emptiness of the place pulls him back to reality. It's late in the day when he sits at the kitchen table and peels the wax paper from the pasty his sister-in-law sent around with Stan. He has no appetite but makes a pot of tea. He thinks he should be doing more but has run out of ideas. All he can do is wait and hope.

9

I have no idea where I will go or what I'll do. Perhaps I should go home?

But I'm too tired, in both my body and mind. At the top end of Swanston Street, I pass a Salvation Army boarding house. If I lie down and recover, then I can make decisions about what to do next. The front door is heavy, and the entrance room I enter – grey and threadbare – does little to raise my spirits. But I know it will be cheap and I need to make my money spin out. From a room to the right of the hallway a voice calls.

'Looking for a room, son?' The Salvation Army officer behind the desk is a solid presence, a bear of a man, with a voice to match.

'Yes,' I say, standing in the doorway.

'Any idea how long you'll be here?'

'Maybe a couple of days, I'm unsure.'

'We can fix you up with a room on the first floor, looks like you need a good rest.'

'Thanks.'

'What's your name, lad?'

'Knill. Knill McMillan.'

'Welcome to Salvation Retreat. I'm Captain Gerry Waller.'

A sparse bed occupies most of the space in the room. A wooden wardrobe is squeezed between the foot of the bed and the door. It's now three o'clock in the afternoon. I shove my bag under the bed, kick off my boots and lower myself onto the neat blanket.

Will's words are ringing in my ears: 'We won't be there to save your bacon…'

…I get picked by Will. He's picked Eugene already. I smile with relief and line up behind my cousins. The two teams eye each other off as Will and another grade sixer hammer in the wickets. The cricket bats, balls and knee pads are unpacked from the bag on the ground. Will bats first and makes two runs. Eugene steps up to bat.

'Bowled!' comes the scream from Billy Stern. Eugene kicks the turf and walks to the side.

'Out for a duck, Gene. Quack, quack.'

'Your turn, McMillan.'

I see the 'don't you dare miss' look in Will's eyes at the end of the pitch. I wait for the ball, swing hard at the air to the right. The ball slams against the bails. The cheers from the fielders pierce my ears. Will swears and spits into the dust.

Mick Stern, Billy's older brother, runs up and laughs in my face. 'Dumb shit. It's a bat not a violin.'

I lunge at Mick with the bat and catch him on the side of the leg. He goes down and then everyone is swarming. Billy tackles me to the ground and is punching the hell out of me. Eugene is trying to drag the lump off me and Will is swearing and throwing punches at Mick. Then the bodies separate and Mr Marshall is towering over me.

'Who started this?' he says.

'He did, sir,' says Will, pointing to Mick Stern. Eugene backs Will up and Mick and Billy are marched away by Mr Marshall.

'You two as well,' the teacher calls to Will and Eugene over his shoulder. The other boys are silent. I stand up, grab my school satchel and run…

I wake, and for a few seconds I can't remember where I am. Then it all floods back. It's six o'clock in the morning and the early light is different in this room. My watch is my only reminder of normality. I look at its large ticking face. Without thinking, I wind it as I've done for the past five years. I feel the familiar spring firm between my thumb and forefinger, telling me that time is assured for another twenty-four hours.

The breakfast room is stuffy but warm. The walls are covered in faded striped wallpaper with yellow sprigs of roses dancing between the lines. Heavy curtains at one end of the room block out most of the natural light. Stale food odours hang in the air. The breakfast tables are close together and an odd array of chairs sit haphazardly around them. A few people wander in and help themselves to food and cups of stewed tea. They are a motley lot, and somewhat dishevelled. I'm relieved when they ignore me and make for their familiar spots. A trestle sits in the centre of the room laden with plates, cups, saucers and cutlery. Enormous metal teapots sit to one end. I glance around and hesitate before pouring myself a strong black tea. I sit at the nearest table. I know I should be hungry but I can't muster any enthusiasm for food. The hot brew is comforting and takes away a lingering, bilious sensation.

Gerry Waller walks amongst the tables, talking and joking with some of the boarders. Then he's by my side. He smiles as he shakes my hand.

'Did you sleep well? You sure looked exhausted.'

'Yes, thanks.'

'You from the country?'

'Castlemaine.'

Gerry Waller has the eyes of a man who's seen and heard just about everything under the sun. He asks if I'd mind some company, and an hour later I've purged myself of the whole story, beginning with the attack. I surprise myself when I tell him how angry I feel towards my parents.

'Well, not my real parents,' I scoff.

Gerry is a good listener. His cup of tea has been drained and refilled several times over that hour.

'I can see where you're coming from, Knill,' he says when I've finally finished. 'But I also think your parents might be worried about you. It wouldn't hurt to drop them a line and tell them you're okay.'

'I'll think about that.'

I can't tell him that at this moment I never want to see them again. I smile and thank him for listening.

'It makes good sense to talk things over. Come and see me again if you want. I'm here most days.' He shakes my hand with a strong confident grasp and gives me a reassuring nod as he leaves. The feeling of being a kid returns; I want to call out to Gerry and ask him to come back. I'm not ready to be on my own. Not yet.

But tiredness overcomes me and my body hurts. I head back to my room and lie down. The conversation with Gerry has left me feeling a bit confused. But he had a point – I should let Ted and Rhoda know where I am. I check my watch – I'll go to the post office and send a telegram soon. I pull the blankets over my aching body and succumb to sleep, dozing on and off for the rest of the day, until it's dark again.

10

The following day, Paddy Whelan, a local potato farmer, rides his horse a couple of miles to the north edge of his property off Shepherds Road. He checks the fencing a couple of times a year. It's a still winter morning and his horse is flighty, its ears forward.

'What is it, Gupa?' He pats the horse's neck and looks across the paddock to the dam. There is something bright on the water. Without seeming to make any decision, he adjusts the reins and is galloping towards it. There's movement in the old wooden rowing boat. He calls, and a woman stands unsteadily on her feet. She's wearing some sort of dressing-gown, is soaking wet and covered in mud.

'Rhoda? Rhoda McMillan, what are—?' Paddy jumps from his horse and runs to the edge of the dam. 'Don't move, Rhoda, I'll come in and get you.'

He can barely hear her reply.

'Leave me be. Go, go away, Paddy.'

He wades into the muddy water and grabs the side of the boat. He pulls it to the bank and puts his hand out to Rhoda, who is shivering and crying. Her arms stay slack at her sides.

'I was looking for her,' Rhoda says, as Paddy takes off his jacket and wraps it around her. Her blue slippers are caked with dirt and her hair is flat and pasted to her face.

'I couldn't find her. She's gone. They took her away.'

'Let's get you out of here, Rhoda.'

Paddy gently coaxes her from the boat and lowers her to the bank. He's known this woman all his life. Poor Rhoda. There's always been gossip about her, her constant talking, but he's found her to be a decent person. He's seen the flowers she puts on the children's graves at the cemetery. This will knock Ted for six.

Doctor Smithers looks down at Rhoda in the hospital bed. 'What started all this? Ted?'

'She was upset about Knill leaving. Then she disappeared. We looked everywhere...Paddy found her like this, wet and confused. In her nightclothes. How she got out to his property is anyone's guess.'

Rhoda's face is pale against the white of the hospital pillow. The two men watch her eyes flicker as she labours between consciousness and deeper sleep.

'What happens now?' Ted asks the doctor.

'It's serious. She has pneumonia.'

'She'll recover, won't she?'

'It's too early to tell. She's weak, Ted.' The old doctor places his hand on Ted's shoulder.

'You mean she might…die?' Ted stares at Smithers, hoping for reassurance. His body, which has felt so heavy and unfamiliar since Rhoda went missing, as if it doesn't belong to him, feels heavier still. Oh, Rhoda, how can this be happening?

'I'll be back later today, Ted. Let's see how she is then. But get your boy home. If you can.'

Ted sits by Rhoda's bed, his mind roaming over the times when the Rhoda he knew seemed to vanish and he couldn't understand where she had gone. When Knill was young and she took to her bed for a week, refusing to speak to him and ignoring all offers of support. Even Knill couldn't get her to respond. Not right that a child sees their mother like that. Then, as if nothing had happened, one morning Rhoda got up, dressed and carried on as normal. No one spoke about it, and life continued. This is one of those times, he knows, only more serious. Far more serious.

Millie Dancy comes with a bowl of water and gently sponges Rhoda's face and hands; Rhoda doesn't rouse. Rhoda gave Millie a bouquet of roses once, when the nurse was a little girl. Funny to think Millie is now looking after her.

Rhoda drifts between sleep and an agitated wakefulness as the nurses come and go.

'Tell her I'm sorry…tried to find her, I was lost.'

'You're in the hospital, Rhoda.' Ted strokes her cold arm.

'They took her from me. I begged and begged them…'

'No one is taking anyone away, Rhoda. Knill will be back, he just has to work a few things out.'

'Knill…I tried, I tried to be a good mother.'

'You're a good mother, Rhoda, and a good wife. Shh, just rest.'

'A fine boy. I didn't deserve him.'

'We both deserved to have him and we did our best, Rhoda.' Ted pulls out a perfectly ironed handkerchief, wipes his eyes and tucks it back in his pocket.

Where is Knill? Ted wishes, so much, that his son would walk through the door to the ward. Stan has sent a telegram to Will and Eugene asking them to find Knill and get him home quick. He needs to be here. To offer comfort. To be comforted. To say goodbye. Ted pats Rhoda's hand and wishes he could do more.

Rhoda talks less as the day goes on. Ted doesn't move from her bedside. Stan and Kate sit in the waiting area and bring him cups of tea that go cold on the side table.

When Doctor Smithers returns, he examines Rhoda, then pulls up a chair to sit with Ted.

'Ted, you must realise that Rhoda is dying. Her signs are very bad indeed. There is nothing else that we can do for her now.'

'Are you sure?'

'Yes. I'm sorry, Ted.'

Millie Dancy and the other nurses become quiet. Ted imagines his nephews scouring the city for Knill, all the places they might be looking for him. Each time the door of the ward opens, he is hopeful. But it is never Knill.

Less than an hour later, Rhoda takes her last breath, quietly and without fuss.

11

Through the night, I move from my bed and walk along the narrow passage. An old man slumps on the floor against the lavatory door. Stepping around him, I urinate into the toilet bowl. I don't bother closing the door. Back in the hallway I move past the drunk bloke and the associated stench of cheap liquor. I know I can't stay in this boarding house for long.

All I need is a job. I've got training and experience from my work as a clerk at the Castlemaine railway station for the last few years. That should count for something. I can get work in the city like Will and Eugene. I'm fascinated by the crowded row houses in Collingwood, with their tiny boxed gardens behind low fences. I love the thought that anyone can live behind those facades and do so with privacy and intrigue. In the city, you can be who you want to be, there's no one to watch every move.

But I know I've got to talk to Ted and Rhoda. My anger isn't so hot anymore. It's a dull ache, filled with a longing to know more. I decide to catch the twelve-fifteen train to Castlemaine. I know so little about why they adopted me and what happened at that time. For all I know they might have information about my real parents. I still can't imagine why they didn't tell me long ago; I still can't imagine how I never guessed. I feel a bit foolish for not questioning them more. If the last couple of days have given me anything, it's that I now know that I must make decisions for myself.

'Wait another year,' Rhoda said, when I told them I wanted to enlist in the army. 'You're too young and the war is near its end. Just you wait and see. You're our only child. If something happened to you we would have no one.'

Well, she was right: the war ended and the need for army recruits lessened, and my chance to go and fight for my country was lost forever. But I envied Will in his uniform and the sense of pride that accompanied him, despite the bayonet wound in Ypres that left him with a stiff arm. Eugene didn't see fighting action – he enlisted, but, due to chronic asthma, was never sent overseas to serve.

I now regret my obedience to my parents. Ted understood why I wanted to join, but in the end he went along with Rhoda. I should have put up a fight. Several lads in the town defied their families to join up. More guts than me, that's for sure. Not having done my bit, when others had been prepared to die, sits heavily with me. One more thing that sets me apart from the others. I should have gone and served my country. It makes my guts squirm if I think about it for too long.

I shave and dress with a bit more care than yesterday. I'm less sore today and deciding to go home has given me some purpose. In the breakfast room, Captain Gerry sees me, waves and comes quickly to me. I wait for him to sit down, but he asks me to follow him to his office. There, he closes the door behind us and tells me to sit in the chair at the end of his messy desk.

'Your cousins have been looking for you,' he says.

'Will and Eugene have been here?'

'Not exactly. It seems you mentioned staying with the Salvos, so the police came looking here.' His eyes are serious, troubled.

'The police!'

'Your cousins received a telegram, from your father…'

'I'll let him know where I am. I've already decided to go home.' I exhale. 'For a moment, I thought something bad had happened.'

Gerry Waller's hands still. 'Something bad has happened, Knill.'

My stomach lurches and I can feel my legs begin to shake on the edge of the chair.

'It's your mother. She died last evening.'

Then Gerry is standing beside me asking if I'm all right. He calls to someone for a cup of tea. Others come into the small office. They talk over my head. I hear one of them say something about Will and Eugene.

'She, she can't have…what happened?'

'We don't know, but your cousins will be here soon.' Then someone puts a blanket around my shoulders. I'm shivering, and I can hear my teeth chattering.

12

Ted pulls on his suit jacket for the funeral and feels something in the inside pocket. Pulling the envelope from its hiding place, he's startled by the familiar handwriting. Slowly, he opens the sealed flap. His hands shake as he lowers himself onto the blue bedspread.

Then he reads the last words from his wife.

13

The small church is full to overflowing. Ted and Rhoda are well known in the district and the locals have come out to pay their respects. I stand next to Ted in the front row and we stare at the mahogany coffin, with its wreath of roses from Rhoda's beloved garden layered along the casket. Ted is quiet, but his hands are trembling. I touch his arm and he nods in acknowledgement.

Since Will and Eugene brought me home there's been a steady stream of visitors at the house; the kitchen bench is overflowing with cakes and food boxes. Apart from sleeping, Aunty Kate and Uncle Stan have been with Ted ever since Rhoda died. Will and Eugene often joke about their parents' bossy ways but we all know that when there's a problem they're the first to help. They sit on the other side of Ted. My cousins are in the row behind us. I feel a comforting pat from Eugene on my shoulder.

I glance around the church to a sea of faces and a soft rumble of voices. Then the pianist starts and all falls quiet. The hymn 'Nearer, My God, to Thee' is one of Rhoda's favourites. I remember her asking me to practise this one. She would stand by the piano and hum – she never sang, even in church she mimed the words.

'Keep up the practice, Knill,' she'd say. 'You can play for the church one day, you're good enough.'

My throat constricts and I cough slightly. The minister takes his time to get to the lectern and go through the various readings and testaments that have been written for Rhoda. Stories about her garden, her expertise with roses, her cooking ability, her generosity towards the church and, of course, her role as a devoted mother and wife.

Finally, he nods for the coffin bearers to come forward. The McMillan men – Will, Eugene, Uncle Stan and Ted – step forward, dressed alike in their Sunday-best suits. Stocky and well groomed, they are men who can be relied upon. For the first time, I'm aware of the family resemblance between the two older men and my cousins. Rhoda's brother Angus and I join them. We shuffle around Rhoda's coffin and follow instructions from the undertaker. With the casket on our shoulders we begin the long walk down the aisle to the gentle sound of the Lord's Prayer. People are standing; Paddy Whelan's head is bowed. Doctor Smithers and Nurse Dancy stand side by side. Some of the women clutch handkerchiefs to their faces, others look straight ahead. I keep an eye on Ted, who is across from me at the front of the coffin. His face is pale but stoic. I breathe long and slow and follow his example.

As we near the door of the church I notice a woman in the back row, wearing a black lace scarf across her head. I've never seen her before. She's not a local. She turns towards the coffin procession as we shuffle past. In her hand she holds one single white rose.

We walk into the daylight, the congregation spilling out around us as we place Rhoda's casket and roses into the back of the waiting hearse. I look around for the stranger. She has left the churchyard. I catch sight of her on the other side of the street, her small frame, the white rose. Then she is gone.

We file in procession to the cemetery at the end of the block. The old wrought-iron gates are wide open in preparation for the burial. The path leading to the Presbyterian section is gravel. The sign is faded, a corner of the wooden frame missing, exposing the rotting grey timber, but the wording is still readable. I walk with Ted, Uncle Stan, Aunty Kate, Will and Eugene. People follow but I keep my eyes focused ahead of us; my mouth is dry.

'This will be over soon.' Will claps his hand on my shoulder.

I nod to him as I see the mound of freshly dug soil ahead.

'Three generations of McMillans in the place now. We'll be the fourth,' Will says.

'You will,' I say so quietly he can't hear me. 'I'm not so sure where I fit in…'

Lofty cypress trees line the distant fence. Rows of old gravestones sit in the crumbled earth as they have done for years. As a kid, I remember running along the edges, eager to get the flowers placed in vases and then off again.

'Careful! Don't step across the graves,' Rhoda said. Mother's Day, Father's Day, birthdays and Christmas Day, we would arrive at the cemetery, laden with flowers to place on the graves of those long gone. I know the place well.

The burial is swift. People come forward to shake our hands and offer condolences. I stand by Ted's side, relieved it is almost finished. Laurie Bench limps our way and shakes our hands.

'This is a sorry business. Who would have thought that just a couple of weeks ago we were all chatting in the hospital?'

'Thanks, Mr Bench.'

Then an old man I hardly recognise steps forward from the crowd of men in suits. A teacher from fourth grade. He was a pianist himself and took a real interest in my music.

'It's a sad day. A while since I've seen you, Knill.'

'Mr Lavery.' I shake the older man's hand.

'Call me Bill. School days are well past for both of us.'

Billy and Mick Stern wait quietly by the gate. Their mother and Rhoda were friends. As we leave the cemetery they come forward.

'Our condolences, Knill. You too, Mr McMillan.'

Billy was in my grade, Mick a class above. Mick was worse than Billy. He'd trip me up by the gate and hold me down whilst his mates watched and laughed. 'Ching Chong Chinaman,' he chanted at me once, in earshot of Mr Marshall, who grabbed him by his collar and hauled him to the headmaster's office. He never said it again.

Mick stands here now as if this kid stuff is history. I suppose it is.

14

At last we are alone at the kitchen table. Exhaustion accompanied by a strange relief that the funeral is over.

'And all those people came to pay their respects,' Ted says.

'She would have liked it,' I say, knowing we must talk about more difficult matters. Apart from conversations about the plans for the funeral, we haven't spoken in length about Rhoda's death.

Today the old house feels small and bereft in its silence: the kitchen, with its familiar benches, and the bread crock, with its sliding lid that doesn't quite shut. Even the furniture looks forlorn. The floral curtains hang limp.

'Was it because I went away?'

'She carried a burden.'

'About what?'

'You'll understand when you read the letter.'

'She left a letter?'

'Yes.'

Ted gets up from the table and shoves three logs of spliced wood into the square mouth of the stove. He juggles each piece to allow the next to fit. He pushes hard on the door and the metal catch clangs sharply. I can hear the crackling as the fire takes hold.

'Sorry I wasn't here.' My voice shakes as I try to stay in control. When I last saw Ted, he looked fit and strong. Today he has the appearance of an old man.

'It's okay, son. None of us expected things to turn out this way. I had no idea what your mother was going through. Not just because you left home but about things that happened in the past. Nothing can change it now. I still can't believe it myself.'

Ted leaves the kitchen and returns with an envelope. 'Read this, Knill.'

He hands the letter to me, then goes to the stove and pushes another piece of wood into the fire box. He checks the water level in the kettle, then fumbles amongst the crockery in the side dresser – Rhoda's blue floral cups and saucers. I almost expect her to come bustling in to take over. The water starts to hiss. The old black kettle has been on the stove for as long as I can remember. I wasn't allowed to touch it until I was ten, when Rhoda showed me how to lift it from the stove to the bench without spilling the boiling water.

Ted pretends not to watch me as I begin to read.

Dear Ted,

I was sixteen when I gave birth to a baby girl. My parents made sure that no one knew and they sent her away. Never have I been able to erase the memory of that tiny little baby, despite only seeing her for a few minutes. Every day I think of her.

When we married, I wanted nothing more than to have children. Imagine the anguish of discovering that we were sterile. Of course, Ted, I wasn't sterile, you were. It was God's way of punishing me for my previous sin.

After Knill arrived, I lived every day thinking that I didn't deserve to be his mother and that something bad would happen to him. How could I tell him he wasn't really our son? Imagine thinking that your own mother could give you up. Who would have thought that he would be so angry? Again, this is God's punishment for me.

Make sure that Knill gets the box with the photographs and letter, including the cup that arrived with him. It is my hope that in time he will understand and maybe even forgive the two mothers in his life.

You've been a good husband, Ted. If only I could have been a better wife and mother.

Rhoda

The knot in the middle of my stomach tightens. I re-read the letter and turn to him. 'A baby of her own?'

'I didn't know.'

'Why didn't she keep her baby?'

'How could she? She wasn't married.'

'She had family.'

'They probably thought it was for the best. Made the decision for her.'

Rhoda and her secret…She was such a stickler for doing the right thing, following the rules as if her life depended on it. Roast on Sundays after church, fish on Good Friday, washing on Monday, ironing on Wednesday. So perfect, so orderly and yet always talking, never able to find clarity. And always, always she carried her secret.

'She never mentioned it?'

'Never. That's how it was, Knill. It was meant to be forgotten.'

'Is that…is that what happened to me?'

'I don't know. More than likely.'

'What do you know about my mother…well, my other mother?'

'Nothing. Except that she was young and her family brought you to Rev Dancy.'

'And you knew I was coming?'

'Only the day before.'

'How old was I?'

'A few days old. Mrs Dancy used to care for the babies for a few days until the family was ready.'

'Did the Dancys know anything about my mother?'

'They never spoke to us about your mother. The unsigned note and the small parcel that accompanied you was the only information we had. The note said your name was Scarffe Knill. That's why we called you Knill – it seemed only right at the time. We had no idea about the cup except that it should be given to you as an adult.'

'They never told you anything else?'

'Secrecy, Knill. That's how it's done.'

I shake my head and try to make sense of all this. Ted's face is flushed and expectant. The kettle begins to boil and the lid rattles loudly before I get up and slide it to the side of the stove.

'And Rhoda? Somewhere there's a girl who is Rhoda's real daughter?'

'Yes, it seems that way. But there's no way of finding her.'

'What do you mean?'

'She will have another name. And now that Rhoda's… gone, there's no reason to find her.'

'But she might not know. I didn't know.'

'Knill, it's over. Anyway, we wouldn't know where to start.'

'So I probably won't be able to find my real mother?'

There is silence as Ted turns towards me. 'Do you want to find her?'

'Yes. If I'm to be honest, I do want to find her.'

'I see.' Ted goes silent and I sit down again, the tea forgotten.

I'm also thinking about Rhoda's daughter. I begin to realise how complicated Rhoda's life was. Her letter is wistful, rueful. Rhoda knew exactly what she wanted to say. It's as if she had been waiting for a long time to express herself.

Ted points to the parcel on the bench. 'The cup and the letters. You left them behind.'

Also sitting on the bench is a familiar brown case.

'And my violin?'

'Your violin probably belonged to your mother.'

'My real mother?'

'It was left on our verandah about a year after…after we adopted you. It had a note that said "For the boy".'

'Do you think my mother, my real mother, left it?'

'We don't know. It's been a mystery all these years. No one saw anything, it was just there early one morning. Anyway, Knill, you were obviously meant to have it, you're a natural. Your music teacher couldn't work out where your ability came from.'

Memories flood back. Learning to play the violin and piano at school and being teased for it. There were a couple of girls who learnt from the same visiting music teacher, but no other boys. Every second Friday afternoon we gathered in the small school hall, which boiled in summer and froze in winter. The three of us took it in turns to play from our homework sheets, quickly revealing who had practised over the fortnight.

'Rhoda wasn't musical and I can't sing in tune.' Ted smiles.

I don't know where to look, his face is too sad.

I feel inadequate and, if I'm truthful, bloody guilty for not being here when it happened. It's hard to believe that she is dead. All that hurt seems too much for one man to have to manage, and yet Ted's expected to.

I reach for the teapot and fill it. Ted's small frame is hunched over the table; I put my hand fleetingly on his shoulder as I place his tea in front of him.

'I'm sorry I wasn't here.'

I take a deep breath but can't trust myself to say anything else. I can't bear to think of Rhoda dying in the hospital bed, especially after reading her letter. I should have been there for her and for Ted.

'Not your fault, son.' He blinks back tears.

I turn towards the window. There is another thing I need to do.

15

The tea is hot and strong. After he drinks it Ted seems a bit more at ease. Or perhaps it is relief that I've read the letter.

'She meant to die, didn't she?'

'It seems that way, Knill.'

There is a long silence between us as Ted stares out the window.

'Does Uncle Stan or Aunty Kate know about the letter?'

'No.'

'Will you tell them?'

'I'm not sure Rhoda wrote it for other eyes.'

'Or maybe she did.'

'Best to keep it to ourselves,' says Ted.

I keep thinking about Rhoda's daughter and I'm not so sure keeping it quiet does anyone any good. But I respect Ted's decision for now.

The small single bed in my room is covered by the patchwork quilt Rhoda made when I was a kid. I reach out to the holland blind; it falls crooked when it reaches the ledge. I remember Rhoda's ambitious attempts to make the blind fall straight on the windowsill.

I can hear Ted fiddling around in the kitchen, the clunking of cups and the twang of spoons being put in the cutlery drawer. Sometime later, I hear him go to his room. The same room where I discovered the box. It seems so long ago now. Sitting on the edge of my bed, I pull off my boots and sink onto the soft mattress.

For a moment, I think I hear Rhoda, the sounds of her getting ready for bed. Then I'm jarred back to reality. I'll never hear her again.

All my resolve to be strong falls away. I roll onto my back and think of the woman who raised me. Her quirky, funny ways, which Ted and I laughed at sometimes. The special birthday cakes, iced to perfection, with my name written across the top in butter icing. Being on flower duty at the local show, with Rhoda insisting that all the exhibits be watered before opening time. I had to go around with a metal can and pour a little water on each display. As a small kid, I was proud to be Rhoda's son. She was respected in her role of head judge for the entire flower show. It wasn't until I was older that I noticed she sometimes overdid the fussiness and that people around her were raising their eyebrows.

Then there were the times when my elderly grandparents came to lunch on Sundays and I had to be on my best behaviour. Ted would wink at me across the table as Rhoda brought out the roast lunch. I spilled mint sauce on the tablecloth on one of these occasions but covered it with my napkin until after lunch. Rhoda saw me and quietly nodded her approval. She was always one for keeping up appearances, especially in front of her family. Rhoda's parents died weeks apart when I was about six. I sat between Rhoda and Ted in the front row of the church, peering at the coffin of my grandfather. Three weeks later, we returned to the church for my grandmother's funeral. Rhoda, on those occasions, held my hand so tight it hurt.

Outside, the night is light, casting shadowy patterns on the walls of my room. My anger is gone so completely it feels like it was never there. My adoption. My mother's smothering and fussing ways. No anger. Writing that letter wouldn't have been easy, especially at the time she wrote it. What gave her the courage to express what she really felt? Was it my discovery of the box and then leaving home? But was it courage or despair? In the letter, she sounded alone and without hope. The guilt visits me in the pit of my stomach, over and over. I try not to think about this but it's never far from my thoughts. If I hadn't responded with such anger, might she still be alive? How can Ted forgive me? How can I forgive myself?

What happened to Rhoda's daughter? Who raised her? Does she know she was adopted? After all, I didn't. Maybe somewhere out there, a woman is living the same false-hood that I lived.

16

We spend the morning outside; Ted insists on keeping Rhoda's garden perfectly tended. 'It's the least I can do,' he says as he gently clips a broken rose stem from its bush.

The two weeks we've spent together since the funeral have been good for both of us. It's as if we have begun to relate as adults not just father and son. Nothing will be the same again, but I've found some sort of inner strength that wasn't there before.

When I am not thinking of Rhoda and Ted, still listening for the sounds of Rhoda's preparing for sleep, my thoughts are often with the mother who gave me away as a baby. Did she suffer the same guilt as Rhoda? Where is the young girl in the photo? Does she ever think about me the way Rhoda thought about her daughter? I know it's probably too soon to be considering finding my real mother but I get butterflies in the stomach at the very thought.

We've arranged a headstone for Rhoda's grave and sorted through some of her gardening books. There's much more to be done but Ted wants to take his time with it. People visit and bring more food: endless bowls of soup, nut loaves, biscuits and sausage rolls. Ted is surrounded by generosity. He seems resigned to Uncle Stan and Aunty Kate being a constant presence in the house. Knowing that Ted is well supported makes it possible for me to make plans for myself.

'I'm thinking of going back to Melbourne,' I tell Ted the next morning at breakfast. I put down my knife and fork and wait for his reaction.

'No surprises about that, Knill.' Ted smiles at me. 'I've been wondering when you would head off.'

'Maybe next week. Will you be all right here on your own, Ted?'

'Right as rain.'

'I'll be back here some weekends, like Will and Eugene.'

'It's a good move, Knill, you need to find your feet.'

'I need to find a job.'

We both laugh and Ted pours himself another cup of tea. He is now using Rhoda's favourite cup. It seems to bring him comfort.

The Methodist Church is on the other side of Main Street. I'm hoping the minister is home. The neat house beside the redbrick church is devoid of garden except for a well-trimmed box hedge along the fence line. I can imagine what Rhoda would have thought of this wasted opportunity for a rose garden. A thin man on light feet answers the door quicker than I expect, and I introduce myself.

'I'm Reverend Johns,' he says. 'Sorry to hear about your mother.'

'Thank you.' Everyone in Castlemaine will have heard about Rhoda's death and the circumstances surrounding it. Of course, there will be various versions. Even if people don't know you in this town, they know about you.

'What can I do for you?'

'I'm making enquiries about church records.'

'You had better come inside.'

He's frowning as he ushers me to a front sitting room. It looks as if it doubles as his work room. He gestures for me to sit on a chair near his desk.

'What's this about church records?'

'Adoptions or boarding out.' I'm so nervous, I blurt it out.

His frown deepens. 'We don't have those records, Knill. We have nothing to do with that.'

'But you did. My parents had dealings with this church over twenty years ago.'

The reverend stiffens and becomes a little less obliging.

'Reverend Dancy was the minister,' I say.

'I see.' Reverend Johns places his hands behind his back, perches on his desk, and looks down at me.

'This is a bit tricky.' He scratches his chin. 'The Reverend Dancy, I believe, had some involvement in infant placement with families, but it was never an official part of his role.'

'But there is a letter from him on church letterhead—'

The minister cuts me off by waving his hands. 'Yes, yes, but that's part of the problem. He was never authorised by the church to do that work.'

'He just did it by himself?'

'He and his wife were well-meaning people – they thought they were doing the right thing. Except it wasn't authorised by the Methodist Church or by anyone.'

'What happened to the records?'

'There are no records. No church records at all. He and his family left town many years ago. He's not in the ministry now.'

'Do you know where he went?'

'No idea. What's all this about?'

'It's about me. I was adopted.'

'I see. But why do you want to find Reverend Dancy?'

'I thought he might know something or have records about my real mother.'

'That's a long bow. He'd be getting on now.'

'It sounds like you can't help me then.'

I stand to leave. He pushes himself from his desk, looking thoughtful.

'Hang on now…I remember someone telling me that he has a son living in Bendigo – quiet chap, they say. Theodore Dancy, something to do with a timber mill. You might find out more about Reverend Dancy from him.'

17

The parcel clerk at the Bendigo railway station tells me there are two timber mills in town. One close by and the other about a mile north.

'Who are you looking for?'

'Theodore Dancy.'

'Related to you?'

'No. Why do you ask?'

'He's a bit of a loner, doesn't have too many visitors.'

'Where will I find him?'

'He owns the mill at the end of Armstrong Street. A ten-minute walk.' He waves to the right.

'Thanks.'

'Good luck.' The clerk raises his eyebrows as he busies himself behind the small window of the parcel office.

From the outside of the timber mill, I can see wood stacks piled high, and large mounds of sawdust across the yard. The whine of the saws becomes louder as I walk through the gate. A couple of men notice me but keep working. Then a man appears from a doorway under a verandah of raw timber posts. It looks like some sort of office.

'Hello,' I call over the sound of the saws, 'I'm looking for Theodore Dancy.'

'What do you want? Not work, by the way you're dressed.'

I glance down at my clothes. I'm wearing my only suit, the one I wore to the funeral. My tan shoes are now covered in sawdust. I'm overdressed for a visit to a sawmill.

'Are you Theodore?'

'Theo.'

'I'm Knill McMillan.'

Theo shakes my hand; he's watching me in an unnerving way. I feel rough calluses and thick knuckles as he quickly pulls his hand from my grip.

'I haven't got all day,' he says.

'I'm from Castlemaine and I'm looking for Reverend Dancy.' I raise my voice above the noise. The saws moan from a buzz to a crescendo in the background.

Theo rubs his hand through his sandy hair, frowns, but beckons me to the doorway. We step inside; he closes the door. The relief from the noise is gratifying and we stand looking at each other.

'What's this about?'

'It's a bit of a story but—'

'I told you, I haven't got all day.'

He stands with his blackened thumbs hooked behind his trouser braces. His boots are enormous and covered with layers of grit and sawdust. This man knows hard work.

'Your father arranged my adoption. When I was a newborn.'

The sawmiller's hands move from his stomach and he straightens up.

'That's got nothing to do with me.'

'No, it's your father I'm looking for, Theo.'

He moves to an old stove across the room, removes a plate to reveal the glow of the fire and shoves a blackened kettle across the stovetop. The room is simply furnished. Chairs and a table. The stove. Not much else.

'Why are you looking for my father?'

'I thought he might have details about my real parents, especially my mother. He is the only person who had contact with her or her family at the time.'

'What's the point in dragging up old stuff?' He sits heavily in one of the chairs near the table and indicates for me to do the same.

I get a sense that Theo lives and works in the one place. The curtains that hang by the door are falling off their rods and the floor hasn't seen a broom recently. A marmalade cat with black ears sits curled up on an old footstool.

'He's dead.'

'Pardon?'

'My father, the mighty Reverend Dancy. He died last year.'

'Oh. Sorry...' I'm not sure who I'm sorriest for, me or Theo.

The kettle whistles and Theo heaves himself up, reaches for a teapot with a chipped handle, spoons some tea in and fills it to the brim with boiling water. He then plonks the pot in the middle of the table and hands me a cup.

He shrugs his shoulder and takes a slurp of the hot tea. 'We all gotta die sometime,' he says at last.

'And your—'

'My mother died two years ago, no Dancys left now.'

'Except you,' I say.

'Depends how you look at it.'

I watch the man across the table. Tough and resilient, but there's something else.

'You too?'

He nods and peers through the grubby window onto the sawmill. 'They were the champions of making everyone happy. The churchgoers, the people in need, the families without kids. They could soothe all wounds. Except their own. He was a strict old bastard and Mum had no say. She had to go along with what he wanted. Looking after newborn babies for farming out as well as looking after him and his godly ideas.'

'I'm sorry,' I whisper.

'When he died, it was a relief.'

A distant look drifts across his dusty face. For a moment, I feel like an intruder, like I shouldn't be meddling, but then he turns to me again. He takes a deep breath and I know we can talk.

'Did you know anything about your own, well, real parents?' I ask.

'Ha. It was forbidden talk. Found out at school – kids say stuff. When we asked the old bastard, he went berserk, belted us and told us to respect him and our mother, never talk about it again. Grateful, that's it, we were told to be grateful – ha.'

An awkward silence hangs in the room again. He rises slowly from his chair and moves across the room. It's as if he can't sit with the words we are speaking. His braces stretch across his well-muscled shoulders, developed from years of timber-yard work. The frayed neck of his shirt and overgrown hairline tell of a man not much fussed by social norms. He stands motionless, staring through the window into the distance, well beyond the timber yard, as if remembering too much. Then he shrugs and comes back to the table and lowers himself into the chair. He looks at me sheepishly as if he's revealed something he shouldn't have.

'Sorry,' I say. 'I didn't intend to pry.'

'Surprised myself a bit. Never talk about this stuff.' He looks to the side, then slurps his tea again.

'You never found out any details?'

'No, too scared after that. Then life rolls on, you grow up, move on. What's the point?'

We drink our tea in silence.

'You serious about finding your real mother?'

'If I can.'

'What difference will it make? Can't change things, can you?'

'Maybe not, but I just want to know. I have this…unfinished feeling. I should have guessed I wasn't their child, sure had enough hints along the way. My parents kept up the pretence, thinking it was the right thing, I guess. They were good people, though. They just should have told me.'

Theo nods and I know our talk has finished.

I tell him I should be going and thank him for the tea. He's looking thoughtful, his brow furrowed. As I push back my chair, the cat stretches and moves across to Theo's leg. He brushes his rough hand gently across its head.

'Wait up,' he says. 'There is something. I've got an old trunk that belonged to him. I've never opened it but I know it's his church papers. Took it with him whenever we moved.'

He looks at me and shakes his head. The cat slinks off.

'I might regret this, mate. I've been trying to put all this stuff behind me for years and now…' He smiles a nervous smile. I wait for this man with sawdust in his hair to make the next move.

The rusty trunk has a leather strap wound around its middle. We lift it to the table and I stand aside for Theo to open it. He sighs and unbuckles the catch, letting the belt fall with a thud to the tabletop. He quickly and roughly pulls at the lid. It's jammed hard but it's no match for Theo.

The top springs open to reveal books, papers and a smell of the past.

'Probably a good thing you turned up when you did. Been tempted to burn it many times,' says Theo.

I stand back, not sure what he wants to do now the trunk is open.

'You have a look. I'll be outside. Someone's got to do some work around here.'

The marmalade cat jumps onto the table and circles the trunk, sniffing and pawing at it, as curious as me. It then springs down to the floor and rubs against my leg before settling in front of the stove.

There is a leather-bound book on top of countless scrolls, papers and other books in the trunk. I lift out a folder embossed in faded gold letters. The Methodist Church of Victoria.

It's dark when I leave the timber mill. I farewell Theo before heading off to catch the last train back to Castlemaine. I've spent most of the afternoon flicking through notebooks about church meetings, choir practice dates and years of Sunday sermons. There were a few loose notes in a folder with names and addresses that didn't seem to relate to any of the more formal church functions, but nothing that suggested adoption records. I was beginning to think that Reverend Dancy had destroyed the evidence when I found an old Bible with a false back. Inside the Bible were entries of names, dates and addresses. I scanned the list for 1900.

An entry at the bottom of the page caught my eye.

16th November 1900
Baby boy, Scarffe Knill, healthy, two days old. Born 14th November 1900. Mother: Eliza O'Dare. Unmarried, from Majorca. Father: Unknown. Brought to Manse by Gertie Williams, midwife. Taken to new parents Mr and Mrs Ted McMillan, Castlemaine.

And then later, I found something else, my fingers trembling as they traced the faded ink.

18

The next morning, rugged in our winter coats, we walk to the cemetery. I tell Ted about my visit to Bendigo. He wasn't happy about me going; he thought I was chasing shadows. But he was curious about what I'd discovered from Theo Dancy.

'Majorca, that's not too far from here,' says Ted. 'About twenty miles, I'd say.'

'You know it then?'

'Never been there, but I know it used to be a big gold fever town. Not anymore, though. The gold ran out and the prospectors moved on. Probably still got a few hundred residents. Old Tom Geary used to work at the bank there, he often talked about Majorca.'

'Makes sense then, doesn't it? Only an hour or so away.'

I'm already thinking about a trip to Majorca.

'Reverend Dancy told us it was best we know nothing about your circumstances. He kept saying, "Make a fresh start." Well, I'll be.'

'Did you know any O'Dares in the district?'

'Never heard the name, until now.'

My suitcase is packed and I'm ready to leave the next morning. But I don't want to go if this new information has unsettled Ted. He looks thoughtful but says nothing as he places pink tea-roses and blue hydrangeas on Rhoda's grave. Is he thinking about her daughter? About how she might be twenty miles away too?

Will and Eugene are hard workers, but having fun is high on their agenda. Twice a week after work and on Saturdays they go to the Grace Darling Hotel in Collingwood. They laugh and joke their way through the rest of the week. Sometimes I go along to the pub with them and one Saturday afternoon they talk me into playing the piano. I'd forgotten how good it was to hammer out a few Ragtime tunes. The publican asks me to play on a regular basis. I tell him I'll play Saturdays if he gets the piano tuned.

Sometimes at night when I'm alone, I allow my thoughts to wander back to Rhoda and her troubles and to the O'Dare family in Majorca. There are times when the two stories play tricks on me and merge. Rhoda and her lost daughter and me and my lost mother. I have some searching to do, but I also need a job. I've got to pay for my keep, otherwise living in Collingwood won't be a reality for long.

But I'm lucky. I hear about a clerk's job at Flinders Street Station and go for an interview. Afterwards, I'm told to start the following Monday, the eleventh of July.

I'll remember my first day at Flinders Street Station for a long time. As I leave after my shift at six in the evening – my head full of new information, new systems and a hundred other details – someone calls out to me.

'Excuse me.'

I swing around in the direction of the voice. A man of Chinese appearance walks towards me. He looks flushed, as if he's been hurrying. I stop, not sure for a moment if he was calling me or someone nearby, but he comes directly to me.

'Are you Mr McMillan?'

'Yes.'

'At last I find you.'

'Pardon?'

'I've been looking for you. I made enquiries at the Castlemaine railway station. They said you were starting work here today. You fit the description.'

'What description?'

'I'm looking for Scarffe Knill O'Dare. No, sorry, I mean Knill McMillan.'

'What? How do you know…who are you?'

'Let me introduce myself, I'm Joseph Ah Sing. I'm a lawyer.'

We shake hands.

'You called me Scarffe O'Dare?'

The man shifts from foot to foot. 'Well, let's not worry about that now.'

'But why did you call me Scarffe O'Dare?'

'You look like the young man I'm looking for.'

'I look like…what's this about?'

Is this a joke? Only a few people know about my adoption. People are pushing past us and in the background is the noise of an approaching train grinding to a halt.

'Yes, a young man about your age, a certain appearance.'

'I'm not sure what you are talking about.' My feet haven't moved, I'm looking hard at the man.

'Don't worry about that, I can explain. Are you Knill?'

'I'm Knill McMillan. What do you know about Scarffe O'Dare?'

I look around to see if anyone is watching us. Are there others involved in this strange encounter?

'It's a long story. I need to talk to you.'

'You have my ear,' I say.

'We could have tea in the refreshment room? Yes?'

As we walk, I sneak glances at the man beside me wearing the crisp shirt and the tailored suit, but he gives nothing away. The refreshment room, with ornate glass cake stands and trays of cups lined along the countertop, is quiet. We sit near the window at a table with four high-backed chairs. Shortly, one of the waitresses comes to our table.

'Tea, please,' he says to her. He then turns to me. His face is no longer flushed and his breath is even. He runs his hand across the back of his cropped grey hair. I figure he's about Ted's age or perhaps a few years younger, about fifty. The sound of the waitress's footsteps on the timber floor breaks an awkward moment between us.

'You will probably be wondering why I have approached you?' he says. 'Please let me explain.' He pauses for a moment. 'Scarffe, I'm a lawyer for the Chinese community. I have many Chinese clients, both here in Australia and in China. One of my long-term clients from China is a man called Fong Choon.' His voice is low, his tone serious. I can tell he senses my apprehension.

'Sorry, but I'm not sure what this is all about.' How does this man know my birth name?

Joseph Ah Sing smiles and leans towards me slightly. 'Fong Choon came to Australia many years ago from Canton in China. He worked for the Chinese Protectorate in Melbourne before going to Central Victoria.'

'But what does this man, Fong…whoever…have to do with me?'

'Yes, I'll get to that soon, this is very important for you to hear.'

The tea tray arrives, and the girl lingers a bit too long before leaving us alone at the table.

'Fong Choon looked after many of his countrymen in the goldfields…'

A train whistles out in the station and begins to pull slowly away from the platform.

'Look, I don't want to be rude about this, but can you get to the point? So far it's not making much sense.'

'Wait, wait. I'll get to the point.' He looks me directly in the eye and holds up his hands. 'Fong Choon is your father.'

There is a long silence before I laugh at him across the table.

'You really think I'm daft? I've never laid eyes on you before and you expect me to believe that?'

I stand up to leave and, as I do, Ah Sing quickly responds.

'You need to hear me out, Scarffe. I know it sounds unbelievable, but please listen to me. There is much at stake for you.'

I walk to the door, but he's beside me in a flash.

'Here is my address card – call on me. I have more to tell you. That is, if you want to know about your father.'

I run down the steps and onto the footpath. My hands are shaking as I tuck the card in my coat pocket. I know the lawyer is watching me.

I don't remember the walk to Collingwood. I must have crossed roads and turned corners but it's all a blur. I can only hear Ah Sing saying 'Fong Choon is your father.'

Is the lawyer a little crazy? Perhaps he does this to others, stops them and tells them ludicrous stories. Is he really a lawyer? But very few people know my real name – how does he know it?

I arrive home to hear Will singing in the kitchen. *'It's a long way to Tipperary...la la la...'*

Domestic normality and Will's bad singing are both a comfort and a distraction. I tell myself to be calm, to not worry about the Chinese lawyer. I'll probably never see him again. I smell Will's famous sausages, head down the hallway and join in the singing. I love the simplicity of living in this house and its single rule: whoever gets home first starts cooking tea.

The next afternoon, Joseph Ah Sing is waiting for me again after I finish work. I swing around in the other direction, fasten my pace. He catches up and offers me an envelope.

'At least read this, Scarffe.'

I say nothing but take the envelope from him. I feel the smooth paper in the palm of my hand and rub my fingers along its surface. Then I shove it into my bag. I don't look back.

That night, in my room, I pull out the letter from the unsealed envelope. The handwriting is neat, precise.

Dear Scarffe,

I give this letter to my friend and countryman, Mr Joseph Ah Sing. My hope is for him to find you one day.

I met your mother, Eliza O'Dare, in Majorca, a long time ago. She was very young and our love was forbidden by her mother. Of course, my Chinese heritage was not seen in a favourable light, despite my being educated and in a position of good monetary status at the time.

Before returning to China, I tried to see Eliza many times. Her family turned me away. There was nothing I could do but return to my own life.

You must ask how I discovered that Eliza had a child? I returned to Australia on Protectorate business several years later. A Chinese gentleman in Maryborough told me of a rumour suggesting that Eliza had given birth to a child.

Once again, I could not find Eliza, but I did have contact with her mother, Mrs O'Dare. She reluctantly told me that Eliza gave birth to a baby boy, Scarffe Knill, in 1900 and that he was given to a good family.

I believe that you are Eliza's son and I am your father.

It is my wish for you to speak further to Mr Joseph Ah Sing as there are matters that he will arrange for you.

Yours sincerely,
Fong Choon

P.S. Mrs O'Dare told me that Eliza left items with you that will prove your identity.

19

Lying on my bed the next morning, I stare at the high ceiling and think that someone must have made a hurried attempt to paint it. Streaks of green sneak through the cream colour of the surface. The painter either ran out of paint or went to war, perhaps. My eyes move to the letter on the dresser.

I would like to tell someone about Ah Sing and the letter. To watch someone else look surprised and question its validity. Something, however, cautions me to keep it to myself. I'm sure most people would view the letter with scepticism. Will and Eugene would laugh and say it's rubbish, and I can't worry Ted about it.

As I shave I take in my shiny black hair, square jawline, and chocolate-brown eyes with renewed interest. I consider the idea that I have a Chinese father. Comments have been made about my Chinese appearance over the years, especially at school, but whenever I told my parents about it they were quick to say the remarks was nonsense. But, now that I have the truth, if they didn't know who my father and mother were...? I button my shirt and finish dressing. This 'What if it's true' thinking is not something to get caught up in. It can't be true, anyway. Or can it? I step outside the gate and onto the footpath, my mind as untuned as Will's singing voice. Deep down, however, I know there is something about this letter that can't be ignored.

More than ever, I think about Majorca. I've been biding my time, considering a trip to the small town, but now it seems that there is another reason to go. Both for Eliza O'Dare and this new possibility of a Chinese father who worked and had connections there. But I'm not ready yet.

I throw all my energy into my new job. I'm a quick learner and enjoy the challenge of the daily routines. My co-worker, Artie, many years my senior, has welcomed me and mentored me in the job. Every Friday, we work towards the weekly collation of ticket sales and a revenue count. The completion of this task signals the start of the weekend, and our moods lighten as we prepare for a couple of days off.

Flinders Street Station swells with people as they hurry and bustle along to catch trains and head home.

A young paperboy calls, '*Herald! Herald!* Get the latest.'

I take a copy from his outstretched hand and flip him a coin.

'Thanks, mate,' he says.

The headline on the back page is *Coventry to miss match against Richmond*. I know what the conversation will be over tea tonight. Will and Eugene are staunch Collingwood supporters.

'Scarffe, Scarffe!'

It's been two weeks since my first encounter with Joseph Ah Sing but I recognise the precise sound of his voice. Turning, I find him almost by my side, immaculately dressed as usual.

'I saw you as I crossed the street, Scarffe. I had to hurry to catch you.'

'I don't have anything to discuss with you, and my name is Knill.'

The lawyer stiffens. 'Suit yourself, Knill, but you can't run away forever. Make your mind up when you have the facts.'

'I'm not sure I want to know any more facts.'

'I'm not going to chase you again, Knill. If you want to talk to me, you know where to find me.' He abruptly turns and walks in the other direction.

I'm surprised at this. Ah Sing didn't strike me as someone who would give up. I watch him as he walks briskly away. Soon he becomes a distant figure partially hidden amongst the crowd. I catch a glimpse of him as he turns the corner onto Collins Street. People are flowing around me, and Joseph has gone, and I feel…what is it that I feel? Let down? Disappointed? Incomplete? All of those things. And frustrated. It's at this moment that something shifts for me. I will contact Joseph Ah Sing after the weekend. This matter must be dealt with, once and for all, I tell myself.

Monday morning lasts forever. I keep glancing at the clock on the counter wall. One o'clock is my lunch hour and I'm planning to visit Ah Sing in Collins Street. I'm nervous about going and keep telling myself that I'm being foolish. There is no reason to trust him. But then, I consider after a moment, there is no reason not to.

'Must have been a full moon last night,' says Artie. He's in good spirits and jokes with me about the difficult customers during the morning. I grin with him and enjoy his humour. The office we share is divided by two large desks. Artie, like me, respects a tidy workplace. Timber files and boxes line the wall, neatly labelled and dated. I take comfort in being able to look along the wall and know that men before me have handled tickets and dockets in the very same manner. I like the sense of contentment that being part of a workplace brings. There's security in contributing to a system, even if it is only stacked boxes with dates.

I climb the steps of the building and open the solid timber door at 652 Collins Street. A slight Chinese woman turns her head to me as I step inside. She's about my age with long black hair and dark eyes. She wears a fine cream silk blouse with a collar high under her chin. The minute buttons on her bodice catch my eye; they cascade down from her neck, past her slim waist, before disappearing under the ugly brown desk where she sits. 'Can I help you, sir?'

Her voice pulls me from my thoughts and I realise I've been staring at her.

'I've come to see Mr Joseph Ah Sing.'

Immediately, her eyes flicker to a large book on her desk. She looks up. 'You have no appointment, sir. I'm afraid my father...Mr Ah Sing is very busy. Will you call again when he is expecting you?'

'Well, how do I know when he is expecting me?' I reply, finding my voice and smiling.

'Oh, yes, of course, you can make an appointment.' She points again to the large book on her desk.

The high walls and the elaborate ceiling roses of the outer office dwarf the mahogany desk where she sits. Straight-backed chairs, stained in clear black lacquer and boasting ornate carvings, stand in a neat row next to the wall. Behind the chairs are three large wall hangings with gold-thread fringes. Chinese characters are woven across the bright red and gold fabric. I am looking at these spectacular adornments when the inner door opens.

The lawyer stops abruptly when he sees me, then he recovers and slowly smiles. 'So, Scarffe, you have changed your mind. Very wise.'

'It's Knill, and I was just about to make an appointment with…your daughter.'

The young woman's eyes flash between me and her father. She quickly lowers them when she sees me looking at her.

'No need to make an appointment. I can see you now.'

Ah Sing nods to his daughter and ushers me to the next room, which is also lush, its matching ceiling rose painted in the same colours. Several more of the black lacquered chairs line the wall. The lawyer scrutinises me. There is no doubt he is surprised to see me.

'We have much to talk about, Scarffe.'

'Let's get one thing right, Mr Ah Sing. My name isn't Scarffe, it's Knill, and I would appreciate it if you call me by my own name.'

The lawyer watches me with what appears to be an air of superiority. To be honest, it unnerves me. But, nodding, as if agreeing to my request, he invites me to call him Joseph, and gestures for me to take a seat. I move to the large leather armchair opposite the desk and wait for him to sit down.

I already have the impression that he is a man who works hard at having people listen to him and that he doesn't take kindly to what he might perceive as a lack of respect.

'Did you read the letter, Knill?'

'Yes, but I'm not sure that it has anything to do with me. There is no real evidence to suggest that my father is Fong Choon. What makes you so sure he is?'

'Some years ago, when I started to look for you, I made enquiries in Central Victoria.'

'You've been looking for years?'

'Yes. I had to make enquiries to all the small towns in a reasonable radius from Majorca. I had many unsuccessful attempts. When I moved my attention to Castlemaine, Mr Bench's name came up.'

'Laurie Bench?' I can't believe that he has anything to do with this.

'A Chinese person in Maryborough told me about Mr Bench. He knew of him, said Mr Bench was involved with local history and knew a lot about the local families. I called on him first.'

'You went to Castlemaine?'

'Yes.'

'What did he have to say?' I dread the thought of Laurie gossiping to this man.

'Mr Bench was reluctant to talk to me. He said I should seek out the Methodist Church; he thought they might be able to tell me more.' Joseph looks a little uncomfortable. 'He also told me that there was a young man in town who looked a bit Chinese.'

'What…?'

'Yes, well…after a few discreet enquiries your name emerged as a likely possibility.'

'A likely possibility?'

'Knill, it's almost certain that you are my client's biological son. You are the son of Fong Choon.'

I stare at Joseph. He seems far away as he speaks, full of certainty, from the other side of his large desk.

'There could be some mistake. Sure, I'm adopted, but my mother was Australian. My father's identity is unknown.'

'Just because your mother didn't name your father at the time doesn't mean she, and others, didn't know who he was, Knill.'

There is a knock at the door and Joseph's daughter appears, an apologetic smile at her lips. 'Father, excuse me, your next appointment is early…'

Joseph gets to his feet, replying rapidly in…Cantonese? Then he turns to me. 'I'm sorry, Knill. I must ask you to excuse me. My daughter will make another appointment for you.'

20

The winter sunlight in Collins Street washes over me as I stand on the bluestone steps, grappling with everything Joseph told me. There's nothing conclusive; it could all be a case of mistaken identity.

I hurry back towards the railway station. I know Artie will be wondering where I am by now; I've taken longer than I should have. Then, despite the sunshine, it starts to rain, a light drizzle that dampens my hair and jacket.

The afternoon passes and I'm deep in my own thoughts, an uneasy feeling within me. I'm considering sending Joseph a message, cancelling the agreement to meet again, when I notice Artie watching me.

'Is everything all right with you, Knill? You're not yourself today.'

'Yeah, I'm fine. I need to think through a few family things, that's all.'

Could I confide in Artie? Where would I even begin?

After work, I head to Collingwood. A wave of exhaustion hits me as soon as I arrive at the house. I fall onto my bed and look at the now familiar ceiling, my mind foggy and confused. I consider writing to Laurie Bench; it can't do any harm. The front door opens – Will and Eugene coming in from work.

'Knill, coming to the pub?' Eugene calls. 'Have to hurry, only half an hour till closing.'

'Not today.' My mind is confused enough without adding pints of beer to the mix.

I hear them leave, eager not to miss the six o'clock swill.

A week later I arrive at Joseph's office. His daughter welcomes me with less formality than the first visit.

'I'm Li Ling, but call me Lily.'

Her voice is beautiful to listen to – lilting and soft. I am sure that she can sing. For a long moment I wish I could stay and talk with her instead of entering the inner office, but Lily informs her father that I've arrived, and I feel the dampness of my hands and the quickening of my heartbeat.

'I've decided to listen to what you have to say, but I'm still not convinced I'm the person you think I am.' The desk between us seems larger than before.

'Knill, do you know who your real mother is?'

This is the first time anyone has asked about her. It jolts me. 'Yes.' I can feel myself welling up with resentment towards this man who assumes he knows more than I do.

Knowing so little about my own beginnings makes me vulnerable and then angry. Why should others have more information about me than I have myself?

'You know that your mother was very young when she gave birth to you and that you were adopted by the McMillans when you were a few days old?'

'Yes.'

'Your mother and my client Fong Choon both lived in Majorca. They became friends and even hoped to marry at some stage. Of course, it would have been almost impossible for them to do so. In Australia the marriage between a Chinese man and an Australian woman was frowned on, still is to this day,' says Joseph, watching me intently.

The door opens, and Lily comes through holding a tray laden with tea things. She places it on her father's desk, smiles and turns to leave. His face softens as he nods to her. He turns back to me.

'When it was discovered that your mother and Fong Choon were meeting in secret, your grandmother forbade them to continue seeing each other. Fong Choon then returned to mainland China to attend to his business and family affairs.' The lawyer watches for my reaction.

'How do you know this is true?' I'm suspicious: the facts could be wrong or even invented.

'In China, Fong Choon is a very wealthy man. He is also an honourable and well-educated person. He never forgot Eliza.'

'In his letter, it says he tried to find her?'

'Her family in Majorca hid her from him and her brother threatened him.'

'That was years ago – he's taken his time!' My head throbs with this new information. 'And where do you fit in all of this, Joseph?'

'I knew Fong Choon in Canton, many years ago. He hired my legal firm to see if his son could be found. He has a family of his own in Shanghai but expresses a wish to meet his Australian child before his time runs out.'

'Before his time runs out? Is he sick?'

'Yes, he has a heart condition and he's getting older. He's worried that he may die and the opportunity to meet will be lost for you both.'

Joseph is watching me. It's all feasible, but my head swirls as I lean back in my chair. Fifteen minutes ago, my plan was to hear the lawyer out. I thought it would become clear that he had made a mistake and I would be on my way. Now the possibility is more than likely. My mother and Fong Choon…hidden from him by her family… another family in China. All of this may be possible, except how can any of it be proven? I try to stay clear-headed.

'Eliza O'Dare may have had other children.'

'Your birthdate, Knill. It's several months after Fong Choon was barred from seeing Eliza. Also, there is likely something in your possession that will prove you are the son of Fong Choon.'

'What's that?'

'That's not for me to discuss. But if you meet Fong Choon he will explain.'

'Meet him?'

'Yes, he would like to meet you, Knill.'

'Look, I'm not yet fully convinced I have any connection to Fong Choon. It all sounds a bit, well, far-fetched, if you ask me.'

'Of course, there is one other clue, not so conclusive, but...' The lawyer smiles broadly.

'And what's that?'

'You have Chinese resemblance.'

I sit back and muse...here it is again! Mick Stern's Ching Chong Chinaman.

'Do you think I look Chinese?'

'A little, Knill. You are tall, which is unusual for a Chinese person. But you have straight black hair – very Chinese. But most of all it is your hands. They are Chinese hands.'

I look at my sinewy hands. I have always liked my hands, enjoyed watching them at work: knotting, tying, writing, playing the violin and piano. Are they Chinese hands? My throat burns. I sit perfectly still. Completely lost.

'Chink, Chink, Chink.' The words echo around me.

21

When I found the information in Reverend Dancy's old trunk, that was all I thought I was searching for. My birth mother. Her name and where she came from and maybe a sense of what happened at the time. Eliza O'Dare. This hasn't changed.

The idea of Fong Choon refuses to properly take hold. And I'm not sure I want to meet him. The man who returned to China, the man who didn't hang around.

But I give my word to Joseph that I will return in three months. He isn't happy but agrees to my request. What I need is time. Lily stands up as I leave the office, I nod in her direction, hesitate, then push open the large doors into the busy street. There are other matters on my mind before I can turn my attention to the possibility of meeting a man who claims to be my father.

Opening the mailbox, I pull out three letters and unlock the front door with my other hand. It's quiet – my cousins must have gone out again after work – and I'm glad. I like the transition from work to home. Enjoying the stillness, I go to the kitchen and throw the envelopes on the bench. I turn my thoughts to preparing some food. I pull out potatoes and carrots and dunk them in the sink. One of the pleasures of living here is being able to decide what to eat each day. Lamb chops and vegies – tea will be ready when the boys arrive from the pub. I open the drawer, pull out a tablecloth that could do with a wash, and take it to the table. Glancing sideways at the letters, I realise that one is addressed to me.

It has a Castlemaine postmark. I don't recognise the writing.

Dear Knill,

I was surprised to receive your letter last week. I am well recovered from my accident and I sincerely hope you are also on the mend.

Please accept my condolences on the passing of your good mother. A most unfortunate event.

Knill, I have very little knowledge of the matters you raise in your letter regarding your adoption. There were rumours about Chinese bloodlines and a young girl from Majorca; however, I doubt the credibility of such gossip.

It is often wise to let 'sleeping dogs lie' as nothing good can come from raking up the past. You were lucky to have been taken in by such a good family.

I believe you now have an excellent job with the Victorian Railways. My best regards to you.

Yours sincerely,

Laurie Bench

Let sleeping dogs lie? Who does he think he is?

I fling the letter down on the table, then swiftly retrieve it, not wanting Eugene or Will to find it. I read it again, slower this time. I focus on the line in the letter 'a young girl from Majorca'. Tucking the letter in my coat pocket, I know what I need to do.

I'm surprised by the size of the Maryborough station, with its wide platform, wrought-iron lattice and fancy tea rooms. There are rumours that it was built in the wrong place – I'm not sure about that but it is impressive. More like a city station than that of a country town. I button my coat against the bitter August wind and head out onto the street. An old man wearing a bunched-up overcoat that falls almost to his feet is feeding two scraggy horses from nosebags. His coach has seen better days, but I figure it doesn't matter. I don't have much choice. The man nods to me without much interest until he realises that I want to pay for a trip.

'I want to go to Majorca. I believe it's a few miles out of town?'

'That's right, about six miles from here.'

'Can you take me there?'

'I can surely do that, lad.' The driver removes the nosebags from the horses and I sidle up to them. Two old mares, gentle and sturdy, they snuggle my hand as I reach out to rub their foreheads.

'What do you want at Majorca?'

'Oh, just visiting.' I look away, not wanting to reveal anything about my visit. I can tell the man doesn't believe me, but he nods anyway. I check the photo of Eliza inside my coat pocket.

'Where are you staying?'

'Wherever I can get a bed for the night – a boarding house or a hotel.'

Does this man know the O'Dares? Should I ask him?

'The Harp of Erin, they'll have a room.'

'The Harp of Erin it is then.' I slap the rump of the horse, pull myself into the coach and place my bag beside me.

The man heaves himself into the driver seat, taps the reins on the horses' flanks and the coach moves slowly eastward away from the town.

A hint of blue sky appears from behind the grey clouds as a southerly wind whips across the old coach. The two hacks canter their way towards the nearby township of Craigie. We pass small homesteads on both sides of the road. A few sheep are grazing along the fences, keen to reach the lusher grass on the outside. The paddocks here are scrub-like, with bushland bordering the fences. The driver leans to the side and points out the Craigie school. A bluestone building, surrounded by well-groomed gardens and large trees.

'Cricket ground, to the right. Near the school,' he says above the plodding of the horses. I nod as he lightly flicks the whip.

'Do you know much about Majorca, lad?'

'Only what I've read on the railway maps.'

'In its heyday, it was a bloody big town. Men, some of them fools, flocked here in search of fortune...Ha, not many found it. Most of them moved on to the next town promising gold when they failed to find a wealthy reef. There's no such thing as a quick fortune.'

'You're right about that.'

'Many of the young lads went off to war, of course. The place was like a ghost town for a few years. Some of them are back now but a bloody lot didn't return.'

'I know.'

'Did you go yourself?'

'No.'

A silence falls between us. We cross a narrow bridge over a flowing creek.

'McCallum's Creek,' says the driver. 'Not far now.'

The horses slow as their hooves hit the timber planks. In the distance, I can see the outline of another town.

'That's Majorca ahead,' says the driver.

The township is set amongst mullock heaps, poppet heads and tall ghost gums. Across to the west, beyond the gum-tree horizon, the blue Pyrenees Mountains meet the skyline. Leaning forward, I take in every detail. Then my eyes wander across the gold-fossicked paddocks as our coach makes its way towards the town centre. For the first time in months, it occurs to me, I'm relaxed.

The horses slow as we take the bend into Talbot Street. The houses and buildings are mostly timber, but there are several sturdy brick dwellings in a cluster. The varying sizes and shapes of the buildings reflect the architecture of a hastily built township during the gold rush. Some of the storefronts sit empty. From my vantage point, I watch the townspeople going about their daily business. There is a group of older men and a couple of blokes in army uniform talking together outside the general store. They look up as they hear the coach. The driver waves to them as we pass.

I have a rising expectation about this place. Somehow, I know it's a good decision. We pull up at a drinking trough across from a low-fronted hotel.

'That's it, my lad, the Harp of Erin.'

I step down to the footpath and pay the driver.

'Is there another coach I can take back in a couple of days?'

'There's one that goes to Maryborough most mornings – ask at the general store.'

I can feel the driver watching me as I walk off, wearing my city clothes, bringing my smell of city with me.

The Harp of Erin has seen better days. The enormous door creaks as I push it open. The place smells of coals and stale food. Striped gold and brown wallpaper frames the room; a few chairs and a sunken couch with horsehair stuffing poking out suggest grander times. A blackened fireplace, with its built-up ashtray, sits at one end of the parlour. A woman wearing gold-rimmed spectacles is standing behind a counter. She looks up as I enter. I step around a tall hatstand with umbrellas and felt hats at odd angles.

'Looking for a room?' she calls.

'Yes.'

'One minute.'

She pushes the pile of invoices aside and pulls out a large red book, runs her fingers across the blank squares and looks up. 'Room five's vacant. How long are you staying?'

'One, maybe two nights.'

'Business in town, have you?' She drops the key on top of the open book.

'Not sure yet.'

As I take the key, she smiles for the first time and nods to indicate where my room is.

It's mid-morning, but I waste no time. Leaving my bag in my room, I head out. The cold late-winter air bites at my face as I sink my hands further into the pockets of my coat. All that has taken place in the past months fades now. It's as if I'm on the cusp of something new. Of course, Eliza's family could have been amongst the people who moved on in search of riches elsewhere. But I have a good feeling about being here. I walk towards the centre of town. The general store seems the right place to start.

Beneath the large verandah, I peer through the glass window, with its advertising signs and handwritten church notices. A Bushells Tea poster obscures the counter and a display of cast-iron pots lines the floor just inside the door. What am I waiting for? Go in, Knill.

A large bell clatters as I enter. The man at the counter, who is not much older than me, looks up and nods. When he finishes with the customer he's serving, he flashes a friendly grin my way.

'I'm not sure if you can help me. Just making a few enquiries.'

'Fire away.'

'Do you happen to know the O'Dare family?' I'm conscious of lowering my voice, though it is just us now in the store.

The man thinks for a short while. 'Can't say I know the name, mate. But that's not surprising – I've only been here a few months.'

I nod and turn to go.

'You could ask at the post office. They know just about everyone in town. It's just around the corner, you can't miss it.'

I turn right and see a solid redbrick building with timber windows and a stylish slate roof. Inside, several people are waiting for mail, posting letters and parcels.

'I'm looking for a family by the name of O'Dare.' I speak quietly to the attendant but I'm aware of others in the small room listening.

The woman helping me wrinkles her brow in response to my question. 'They did live in Majorca. Across the road from the school. Old Mrs O'Dare died. About two years ago now.'

'I thought there might be other O'Dares still living here?'

'No other O'Dares left now.'

I thank her and move from the counter, walk slowly out the door.

Was old Mrs O'Dare Eliza's mother? How can I go about finding someone who knows more?

'Excuse me,' a soft voice calls from behind me.

I swing around to face a woman carrying a cane basket over her arm. In the basket are loose lemons, small bunches of parsley and several letters. She is in her late thirties, perhaps early forties. Her hat covers a mass of red ringlets that fly out at all angles around her face and neck. She looks kind and unassuming, almost shy. I can tell she would normally not talk to strangers.

'I overheard you asking about the O'Dares.'

'Do you know them?' I blurt out a little too eagerly.

'I was friendly with the family, but I'm afraid the information given to you by the postmistress is correct.' She watches me with her head to one side.

Others are moving past us as they leave the post office. A rough-looking character on horseback stops and tethers his animal to the fence. We move a few feet along the gravel footpath. There is a slight breeze, which carries the shrill voices of the children playing in the schoolyard up the hill.

'Exactly who are you looking for?' she asks.

I sense her reserve, but also her curiosity. Hope flares within me.

'Eliza O'Dare.'

Her eyes flicker and her mouth twitches slightly, but other-wise she remains composed.

'Why are you looking for Eliza?' She takes a small step to the side and moves her basket to the other arm.

'I would rather not say – that is, unless you knew her?'

'Yes, I knew Eliza O'Dare.'

The horse tied to the fence languidly flicks its tail. My hands are damp with sweat. The woman standing in front of me knew my mother.

I take too long to answer and then she softly asks, 'And what is your name?'

'I'm – I'm Knill McMillan…but I have another name. It's Scarffe Knill O'Dare.'

She closes her eyes for a moment before speaking. 'I think we need to talk. But not here, not now. Maybe…maybe you could come to my home this afternoon. At three o'clock. My name is Robina Smyth. I live at 24 Gully Street.'

I can barely get the words out. 'Thank you. I'll be there.' I shiver as she walks away. She has only gone a few paces when she hesitates and looks back.

'I always knew someone would look for her one day.'

22

I wash in the hotel room, and slide the photo of Eliza into my pocket. A half mile away, Gully Street is a quiet thoroughfare behind the main street, with small weatherboard houses huddled close to an unpaved footpath.

Corroded metal numbers on the wooden door tell me I've arrived at number 24. It's larger than the other houses in the street, but in need of a good coat of paint. However, the garden is lush and well tended. Rhoda would approve. I walk up the redbrick path, step onto the verandah and knock.

Robina opens the door quickly and ushers me into her front parlour. I wait until she takes a seat on the low sofa before I choose a floral chair across from her. A teapot and cups sit on the small table in front of her. They remind me immediately of Rhoda's special teacups. She pours the tea; we drink it slowly and make small talk about the weather and my trip from Melbourne. I carefully place my cup and saucer back on the table in front of me and Robina puts a couple of logs in the fire grate. We both know it's time to talk.

This woman has trusted me enough to invite me into her home, so I trust her enough to tell her my story, only leaving out the part about Joseph Ah Sing and Fong Choon. Robina listens, her head to one side. 'That is a terrible thing for you to have lost both your mothers,' she says when I have finished talking. 'I can understand you wanting to find Eliza.'

I show her the old photo. 'This is most likely my mother, well, my real mother. My father, Ted, said it came with a few other items when they adopted me.'

A smile flickers across her face. She peers at the photo for some time. 'That's Eliza, all right. The others in the photo are her parents and brothers.'

She looks from the photo to me, watches me intently. Her eyes are a soft grey. After a moment, she closes them and takes a long deep breath. Opens them again.

'I will tell you about Eliza. You of all people have the right to know.'

23

'So much time has passed since that night, but after meeting you this morning, it's all I can think about. I'll try my best to recall the details.' Robina leans back in her chair. The room is still around us.

'It was November 1900. We were just young girls, eighteen and seventeen. Eliza came to my house early one morning; it was still dark. There was tapping at the window. I thought I'd imagined it. Then it came again, louder this time. I crept to the window and I could see her huddled against the verandah post. When I opened the window she hushed me to be quiet, not wanting my parents to wake. She told me she had given birth to a baby the night before. For a moment, I didn't believe her, then she handed a warm bundle through the window. Of course, that was you, wasn't it? Eliza told me her mother and old Gertie wanted to give you away.'

'Who was Gertie?' I ask.

'The local midwife – had her nose in everyone's business.'

The clock on the mantelpiece chimes. I wait.

'She begged me for help. She wanted to go to the edge of town to meet her friend, Fong Choon. She said he would know what to do. I didn't suspect that Fong Choon was the father of her child; Eliza never spoke to me about it. I wanted to help her but I was concerned that my parents would discover her and you in the house. You see, they didn't like Eliza and didn't agree with our friendship. They thought she was too brash. Of course, that was the very thing that I admired about her – she wasn't frightened to speak her mind. Foolishly, I tried to convince her to go home and that her mother would understand. Eliza got angry. She had a mind of her own at the best of times. She said she knew what would happen and she wasn't going back. She cried then, saying that if her dad was still alive things would be different. Her older brother Magnus – a pig of a man, if you ask me – had accused her of bringing shame to the family. So, you see, she had no support to keep a baby, and her mother still had two younger sons to raise as well. The family was also worried about what other people would think. Gossip and rumour were rife in Majorca and no one wanted it to be about them.'

Robina places another log on the grate. Her grey eyes are serious and the curls are dancing on her forehead.

'What was Eliza like?'

'She was a bit unusual, really. She wasn't one to go along with what was expected of young ladies – she always wanted to have her say. She had a determined nature. She was loyal, though, loyal to her friends and family. And funny – always laughing and joking. That's why I loved being around her, she made me feel good. Of course, she attracted attention from the young men in town. She was a good-looker, long hair and a flashing smile.' Robina pauses for a moment. 'There was a restlessness about her too. She was never content to follow convention – it's as if there was something missing and she was driven to pursue it. Apparently, her father was similar, always dreaming of life beyond here. Mind you, they were a talented lot, the O'Dares. Mr O'Dare played violin and piano. They had a strong bond, those two. He taught Eliza to play. They sang together at concerts in the town hall, especially at Christmas and New Year. Anyway, I digress. I need to get on with the story.

'Eliza met Fong Choon through Maryanne O'Connor. The three of us had been schoolfriends. Maryanne worked at Lugg's bakery, which was next door to the Chinese tearooms. She got to know some of the Chinese residents in the district. They were mainly well-educated merchants and mine owners, all gone now. Fong Choon was a patron of the tearooms. Eliza often met Maryanne there after she finished her work as a housemaid at Doctor McCracken's house. Maryanne was high-spirited, just like Eliza, and the two of them were often subject to a bit of local gossip. Mind you, the locals loved talking about others, still do. The locals shunned the Chinese – associating with them was taboo. After Maryanne left the district to work in Ballarat, Eliza continued to meet with Fong Choon. He was unusually tall for a Chinese man, handsome, I suppose you could say. He was well educated, with a polite, shy manner about him. I imagine that Eliza became fond of him…well, these things happen, I guess. No one suspected Eliza was having a baby, least of all me. How she hid her condition, I'll never understand.

'We waited until just before daybreak before we headed off towards the west of town. Eliza was tired and weak but insisted on carrying you. She shouldn't have been walking anywhere, but, as I said, she was determined. I remember being frightened – we had been constantly warned off about going to the Chinese quarters. There had also recently been some unrest and fighting there amongst the old coolies. Many of the younger Chinese men had returned home to China but the older, less able men stayed on.'

Robina turns to the fire but she's not really seeing it.

'The morning was very still. I was nervous, but Eliza looked straight ahead, holding you close to her. I can't imagine what it must have been like for her. She was tough – I'll always remember that. And me? Well, I was immature and still under the influence of my family. My biggest fear was that I would be found out by my parents.'

The afternoon sun fades and a shadow falls across the small sitting room. The log in the grate is starting to burn low and the room is losing its warmth. I place another log on the fire. Robina doesn't seem to notice.

'I was shocked by the poverty and squalor of the Chinese quarters. I'd heard all sorts of stories about it being a shanty town, but nothing prepared me for the reality. Eliza kept a steady pace. She was pale but determined. I protested, saying we should go back but she ignored me and kept walking.

'There were a few old men sitting around the huts, smoking – opium pipes, though I didn't know it then. They watched us as we approached.

'"Bah, you not welcome here…go away!" one of them said.

'We quickened our step, and on the other side of the old huts we came to a clearing and a small solid house.'

Robina pauses for a moment. What is she about to tell me? All this while, I have done nothing but listen to her. Now I feel how tense I am, how stiff my body is. The room is silent and Robina takes a deep breath before she continues.

'Eliza called out to Fong Choon. She knocked on the door. I wasn't much help to her. I was a foolish young thing back then. Not at all like Eliza. She'd had to fend for herself and help raise the younger ones after her father died. She had grit. Anyway, where was I? Yes, she was knocking at the door and calling out. There was no answer. She went around to the back of the house looking for him. She was weakening then. She tried to open the front door and luckily it was unlocked. I was wishing I hadn't come, but I followed her inside.

'There was no one there. The furnishings were both English and Chinese in style. The bedroom had a large bed and Eliza placed you in the middle of it. You looked so tiny, bundled up on those soft exotic covers. In the kitchen, the shelves were stacked with decorated pots, cups and bowls. So much colour. I'd never seen such unusual and ornate finery. The house was nothing like the shanties we had passed on our way there.

'There was a large cast-iron stove with a metal frame looped across its top in the middle of the room. It was cold, and we could tell that a fire hadn't been lit recently. There were no signs of Fong Choon, no clothes and no personal items. I watched Eliza, not sure what she would do next. She was clearly shaken.'

Robina is remembering that day as if it happened yesterday. She continues in a trancelike manner.

'I helped her to the bed, where she lay next to you. It was obvious that she wouldn't be able to walk any further without rest. I decided to let her sleep for a couple of hours, thinking we would have to return to town and Eliza would have to face her family. My own situation didn't bear thinking about. My parents would have discovered my absence and there would be all manner of fury unleashed.'

I get up to stoke the fire and stretch my legs.

'Then an old Chinese man arrived at the door. Not the one who'd shouted at us. Someone else. I jumped back, telling him to leave. He indicated that he wasn't going to hurt me and told me that Fong Choon had gone back to China.

He shuffled away as quietly as he arrived. You know, that old man lived a long life on the edge of town. I used to see him occasionally, walking around the outskirts. He died about five years ago.

'Anyway, that's not what you want to hear. When Eliza woke, I told her about the old man's visit and the news about Fong Choon. There was no consoling her. Later, the old man returned. Eliza spoke to him and heard again that Fong Choon was in China on family business. Before the old man left, he placed a metal container full to the brim with Chinese soup on the doorstep. He was a kind person.

'It was the best soup I have ever tasted, I was ravenous. Eliza could only sip from hers. A while later a ruckus started outside the house. We both jumped up. Eliza ran to the bedroom and picked you up from the bed. I saw Magnus, her brother, on horseback, and my father in the old jinker. I knew we were in big trouble. There was a dreadful scene. My father shoved me outside. I remember begging him to forgive me. Magnus and Eliza had a terrible row.

'Magnus yelled at her and swore shamelessly. She held her ground and refused to leave but eventually she was no match for his violent temper. She got into the jinker beside me. Amazingly, you slept through all of this. Eliza was quiet as we travelled. I suspect she was trying to work out what to do when she got home. I remember it as if it was only yesterday. I cried all the way, and my father kept shouting at me.

'When the jinker pulled up at the O'Dares, Eliza handed you to me whilst she stepped down. Then she took you back and clutched you tight. She cursed at Magnus as he tied his horse to the fence. There was no love lost between them. She went into the house, and I was sent packing to stay with relatives in Maryborough for a month. My parents forbade me to have contact with Eliza. It was a couple of months before I spoke to her again. By this time, she had returned to work as a housemaid with the McCrackens. She didn't want to talk about what happened. But I knew that you had been taken from her. From then on, Eliza was a different person. She withdrew from her friends in the town. Then, suddenly, she just left.

'There was a circus in town about the time she disappeared. Some people say she left with it. Someone said that Eliza was working for a circus in Sydney, but it was never proven. There were other silly rumours saying she went to China looking for Fong Choon. Apparently, her family tried to find her but couldn't.

'Two years ago, Eliza's mother died. She was a harsh woman, but she'd had her share of difficulty to contend with in her life. I hoped that Eliza would appear at the funeral. She never did.'

'Did Eliza's brothers come to the funeral?' I ask.

'No, it was a very small affair. It was Mrs O'Dare's wish to be buried privately without announcements.'

'So none of her children attended?'

'No. I went to the cemetery in the hope that Eliza might have shown up, but there was no family.'

'Do you know where her brothers are now?'

'Magnus died in a mine accident, a long time ago, and the younger ones left town as soon as they were old enough. I have no idea where they live.'

I look down at my hands, my 'Chinese' hands, and notice my fingers are trembling. Poor, poor Eliza.

'Knill, I don't have anything else to tell you about Eliza. However, I do have something that you might like to keep. As we were leaving Fong Choon's house that day I took a piece of china. I must have lost my mind for a moment. The colours were so beautiful. I believe that Eliza also had similar pieces given to her by Fong Choon.'

24

My room in the Collingwood house is plainly furnished –
a bed, a small dressing table and a chair. It is at the front of
the house, where dappled light from the tree in the small
garden filters through the window.

Will and Eugene are in the hallway, laughing and joking
around and making plans to go to the pub. As always, they
are scurrying to get there well before closing time. The
scraping of boots being pulled on, and then footsteps in the
hallway past my closed door.

'You there, Knill? We're off to the pub. Coming?'

'Not tonight.'

There is a moment of hesitancy before the front door
opens and they are gone. I know my cousins are thinking I'm spending too much time alone; Will said as much
last night when I got home from Majorca. I'm not good
company right now.

I like the silence of the house. Growing up alone gave me plenty of practice at being content with my own company, so much so that I often seek out time alone. I haven't opened the parcel Robina gave me. It's time.

The neat paper package holds a cup identical to the one in the box left with me when I was adopted. As I hold the two dragonfly-adorned cups there is a strange comfort in the idea that Eliza also once held them, that she may have sipped tea from them. They are my only link to her.

Knowing Eliza's story – my story – is unsettling, but hopeful as well. I like knowing how hard Eliza fought to keep me with her. I like knowing that Eliza and her father played violin and enjoyed singing – somehow that makes a difference. For the first time since finding out about my adoption I feel some sort of connection to someone. I need to find her, except I don't know where to start. How dare they do that to her…and me? And who left the violin on my doorstep? Did she do that, hoping I would learn to play like her and her father? It warms me, the knowledge that the O'Dares' violin was left for me when I was a baby. Someone must know where she is.

Melbourne's cold late-August weather dampens my enthusiasm for anything other than work but I find myself going over and over Robina's story until it settles and finds a place of its own. A faint memory teases me. It flickers and then retreats so quickly that I can't grasp it. Violin music, floating softly, then gone. When it comes, I remain still, desperately trying to capture it, but each time it eludes me. The mind can do strange things to a man.

Something else nags at me: Robina's remark about the circus. Maybe Eliza did leave Majorca to work for a circus? It's my only clue, this thin rumour. I ponder the idiocy of investigating it. I've heard that Ashton's Circus – the only circus I know about – is playing in St Kilda. The flyers are up all over Melbourne. There is a half-page advertisement in the *Herald* – a bold announcement. A photograph of two trapeze artists smiling and laughing for the camera.

I was three years old when a circus – my first and last – came to town. Its huge tent erected on the old cricket field. Ted and Rhoda took me. My eyes were like saucers as we came through the doorway, which was edged with red and orange braid. A woman with exaggerated rouge and red lipstick handed us tickets. As I stepped past her, she patted me on the top of my head. I moved away, not liking her touching me. We sat in the front row, very close to the ring – wherever we went, Ted always insisted on being early to get good seats.

Soon the circus began and the animals paraded around in a circle. We were so close that I pulled back in fear as they brushed past. I was frightened of the large elephant; it dwarfed all others. Rhoda and Ted also seemed a bit apprehensive. They told me afterwards that it was the first time they'd seen an elephant. The creature was led along by a small attendant wearing white trousers and a purple and black satin shirt that ballooned on his body and looked too large for him. The elephant wore a giant red and pink feathered headdress which flopped from side to side, a sparkling blue saddlecloth across its huge back and gold fringe around its neck. The elephant swayed to the music as it was led around the ring. The clowns were playing alongside the animals, throwing coloured balls in the air and making piercing siren noises. The band played loudly, drowning out the raucous clowns. My eyes darted from the performers to the elephant, the band and the keepers. I loved the crazy clowns, throwing their balls high enough to touch the roof, teasing the band by running up behind them and stealing their hats. The crowd applauded and laughed. We were almost as loud as the circus.

At interval, Ted bought me a stick of pink and green fairy floss. Sweet spun sugar, which wobbled as I licked it.

The circus eventually came to its grand finale with all manner of noise, music and applause. Then the circus folk lined the arena and bowed to the audience. My face was covered with fairy floss, my hands sticky as I clapped and laughed. I didn't want it to be over…it was a wonderful childhood memory. A memory that I'd forgotten, until now.

I smell the salt air as I step from the cable car. Will and Eugene have often talked about going on the Scenic Railway at Luna Park and swimming in the St Kilda Sea Baths. I walk until I glimpse the top of the big tent and then I know I'm in the right place. It's five-fifteen in the afternoon. The performance isn't due to start until seven o'clock. A few people are walking around caravans which are parked in a semicircle behind an impressive tent. It's quiet; I suspect the circus people are resting before the show.

A young man with tattoos across his forehead calls to me. 'Who you looking for, mate? No jobs, if that's your business.'

'I want to speak to the boss or someone who's been around for a long time.'

'As I said, mate, what's your business?'

'I'm making enquiries about someone who might have worked for the circus about twenty years ago.'

'Me old man might know.'

I follow him down a row of tents and caravans. We stop outside a worn tent. A grey mongrel is tied to a tent pole. The pole leans precariously towards the ground and looks like it could fall over the moment the dog barks.

'Dad, someone here wants to know something.'

There's no answer. The young man continues to look me up and down but says nothing. The dog follows suit. Eventually the flap of the tent is pulled back to reveal an older version of the man beside me.

'Yeah, what do you want?'

The old bloke eyes me with caution as I explain, nodding when I wrap up.

'If she worked here I'd probably remember. I've been working with the circus for thirty years. Don't recall any Elizas, though. Haven't got much to go on, have you?'

I haven't. I feel like a fool, but the man's eyes tell me I shouldn't. He seems to know what I'm looking for. I thank the two of them, and head off.

An animal handler is feeding a cage of greedy monkeys roughly chopped carrots and turnips from a bucket. It's a welcome distraction and I watch for a few minutes. I'm about to leave when the young man turns up.

'Wait up, mate. The old man's been thinking. He says you ought to talk with Queenie. She knows everything. Been here forever.'

Again, I follow him. This time to a caravan, where he knocks. After a moment, the door flies open. The woman – Queenie, I presume – scowls when she sees the messenger, but immediately flashes a large smile when she notices me. She wears a flowing red robe that reveals the same colour petticoats beneath. Her blonde hair is piled high on her head, so high it wobbles.

She invites me into the cramped van, which is decorated from floor to ceiling with gaudy posters and photographs. Stale food odours mixed with cigarette smoke waft around the poky space. Queenie seems pleased to have a visitor. I sit awkwardly on a small wooden stool. My knees come close to my chin as I explain my mission.

'Eliza O'Dare, Eliza O'Dare. Hang on a minute, lovey, there was a Lizzy O'Dare.'

'How long ago?'

'Let me see, that would be going back to about 1901, or maybe a little later.'

'Do you remember much about her?'

'She didn't stay long. A pretty young woman, long thick hair. From memory, she worked the ticket boxes and assisted the seamstress.'

'Any idea where she went?'

'It's a long time ago, but Tilly might remember. She's the head seamstress and costume maker. Come on, we'll see if she's busy.'

Queenie leads me through the camp, her flowing robe rustling as she strides. I feel a flutter of anticipation.

Tilly – Queenie's opposite in terms of shape and personality – is not pleased with the interruption to her day. She remembers no Elizas, but she does remember Lizzy O'Dare. I show Queenie and Tilly the old photo I have in my wallet. They both stare at the faded photo.

'It looks a bit like her,' Tilly says. 'But I can't be sure. She was a good seamstress. I was sorry she left. Always kept to herself, no one got to know much about her, except I think she joined us in either Talbot or Majorca. Small towns on the goldfields.' Tilly hesitates as she straightens. She looks long and hard at Queenie, and a message seems to pass between them. Finally, she shrugs her thin shoulders and turns back to me. 'I did hear something else about Lizzy. I heard that she was working for Wirth's Circus about the time of that bad fire. It happened up near The Rocks in Sydney. Horrible business that was, people died. But you know, love, she might not have been there at all, you know what circus gossip's like.'

25

Am I chasing shadows to think about going to Sydney? To The Rocks? I can almost smell the circus fire as I head home. It's unbearable to think that Eliza…that Lizzy…I'm not sure about this anymore.

I could go to the library, maybe the hospitals, and seek out records of admissions around the time of the circus fire. Working for the railways entitles me to one free interstate train ticket a year. Should I take a few days off work?

It's early September and I still don't go. I'm finding it difficult to take the next step. Ted writes to me every week. Whenever I see his handwriting on the envelope I feel both love and a tight constriction across my chest. Guilt for even wanting to search for Eliza in the face of what happened to Rhoda. Then, one afternoon, I arrive home and find a letter from Robina.

Dear Knill,

I hope this letter finds you in good health. Since meeting you, I have gone over our conversation many times. It was indeed a pleasure to make your acquaintance and to share details about Eliza. I often wonder what happened to my good friend. I do know, however, that she would have been proud of you.

There is news that I feel obliged to share with you. It was passed on to me from one of our local townsfolk, Ida Milligan, who travels to Melbourne a couple of times each year. Last week she reported running in to Michael O'Dare at the Methodist Church in Richmond.

This is the first time I've heard of Eliza's brother for at least ten years. Michael was Eliza's youngest brother. He was a quiet lad who always kept to himself.

Knill, I'm not sure if this information is of interest to you but I thought I should pass it on.

I trust you are well.

Yours faithfully,
Miss Robina Smyth

The Methodist Church in Richmond is easy to find. Alongside it, a narrow path leads to a redbrick cottage. I tap the brass handle a couple of times and step back. A thin man wearing a clerical collar opens the door. He peers at me over the top of his glasses and I explain I'm trying to find a member of his congregation.'

'Who would that be?'

'Mr Michael O'Dare.'

The minister cocks his head to the side. 'What's your name?'

'Knill McMillan.'

'You say he's a relative of yours?'

'Michael O'Dare is my mother's brother.'

The man hasn't moved and I'm blurting out things I shouldn't be talking about on the front step of a minister's cottage.

'What is it you want with Mr O'Dare?'

'I just want to meet him,' I say. 'I'm really looking for my mother.'

Then, to my surprise, the minister's face softens and he invites me into his front room and asks me to explain myself further. We sit on the hard chairs that I imagine he uses for chats with troubled parishioners. He listens courteously, without surprise or judgement. What family secrets he must have heard…

'I was told by a family friend that Michael O'Dare is one of your parishioners and it's the only link I have to my mother. I won't persist if he refuses to have contact with me. I just want one chance to meet with him.'

I hope I'm convincing this man that I'm worthy of his help. I hope I'm convincing myself. Since talking to Robina,

I have mixed feelings about Eliza's family. After all, they are the reason she gave me away. If I'm honest, I don't want to meet her family only to be rejected all over again. I'm not even sure I want to meet any of them except Eliza. Yet Michael was young at the time. How could he have been part of it? And he may know something about his sister's whereabouts.

'That sounds reasonable. You're right, Michael is a member of our church, but I can't be sure that he will agree to meet you.'

'I understand that.'

'I'll inform Mr O'Dare of your request and he can decide.'

'Thank you.' As I exhale, I realise how much I really want this to happen. To meet with my…uncle. How strange that sounds and feels.

The minister shakes my hand and ushers me to the front door. 'Return here next Sunday at twelve-thirty, after our church service.'

The week passes slowly. I'm as unsettled as the spring weather. What if Michael is angry or dismissive? What if he's like his brother Magnus? But I won't back out. No, I will see this through regardless of the outcome.

On Sunday, I dress carefully in pressed trousers, white shirt, firmly knotted tie and suit jacket.

'Look at you, dressed to kill. What's the occasion?' Will is up earlier than usual, in the kitchen making tea.

'Just going to Richmond,' I lie. 'A workmate's birthday.'

'What's her name?' He grins.

I've said nothing about Majorca, about Michael, about the circus, though I know they are worried. I heard my cousins talking a few nights ago.

'Shouldn't he be getting through this by now?'

'Give him more time. We can't imagine it – what he's going through.'

I know I should explain more. After today I'll talk to them.

On board the train to Richmond, I catch a glimpse of myself reflected in the window of the carriage: tall, with straight, dark hair crowning my face. A Chinese face? I arrive a few minutes early and sit on a bench in a small park nearby. It's quiet. The trains and trams are only half full and parts of the city look deserted. I don't like this feeling of emptiness, I like to feel part of something. Then I remember why I'm in Richmond and dawdle towards the church. I want to give Michael time to leave if he doesn't want to see me.

When I arrive, the churchgoers have almost dissipated. I hesitate for a moment when I see the minister appear in the church doorway. Standing beside him is a tall, heavy-set man, immaculately dressed in a well-fitting suit. His receding hair is combed high across his forehead and he carries a Bible in his left hand. He looks up as I wait by the gate. The minister notices me and beckons me to come forward.

'Michael, this is Knill McMillan.'

Eliza's brother shakes my hand as the minister makes his way back to the cottage. He is waiting for me to speak.

'Thanks for meeting with me, I wasn't sure—'

'Can you tell me what this is all about?'

'I think you may be my mother's brother.' My voice is shaking as I study his face. Do we look anything alike? I'm too nervous to judge.

'I'm not sure I understand.'

The minister hasn't told Michael why I want to meet him. Hell.

'My mother is Eliza O'Dare from Majorca. She gave birth to me in November 1900. I was then given out for adoption.'

I hold Michael's gaze. He coughs nervously and looks unsure of what to do next. 'How do you know all of this?'

'I have letters, documentation from the minister who arranged the adoption, and I've also confirmed the story with Robina Smyth at Majorca. Robina was with Eliza the day she tried to escape with me.' My voice is stronger now.

I'm aware of Michael stalling for time. I pull out the faded photo from my jacket pocket and show it to him.

'Um, I don't know what to say.' His eyes are riveted on my face.

'I don't want anything from you, Michael. I just thought you might have some idea where my mother is or what happened to her.'

We are still standing on the path leading to the door of the church.

'I think we need to sit down and discuss this. I'm sorry, you caught me off guard just then.'

Michael suggests we go into the church. I draw a deep breath and follow him.

There is a chill the moment we enter the arched doorway. Rows of maroon-covered songbooks line each pew and a large wooden collection bowl rests on the edge of the back seat. I follow Michael to a pew at the side of the church. The sunlight shines through a window above the bench where he indicates we sit. I watch the puzzled but gentle face of the man sitting alongside me. We hesitate to start the conversation.

I speak first. 'There was no other way to do this. I had to meet you.'

'How did you find me?'

'A friend of Robina's from Majorca met you recently, I believe, by chance.'

'Oh, you mean Ida.' He smiles for the first time.

Michael has a shyness about him which I immediately like. He gives the impression that he keeps to himself. He is polite and well mannered but not one to engage in personal talk. It can't be easy for him, speaking with someone who claims to be his nephew.

'I'm not sure I can help you. Eliza's been out of my life for a long time.'

'I really have to find her.' I try to check the unexpected emotion that rises in my voice.

'Tell me, why are you looking for her after all this time? You look like a lad who's made a good life for yourself.'

I bite my bottom lip as Michael's question hits hard. He watches me.

'I guess it's difficult for others to understand why I need to know who I really am.'

The light streaming through the stained-glass window creeps further towards the narrow aisle.

'But you had your family, the people who adopted you.'

'You know, Michael, you're the first blood relative I've ever met.'

We hold each other's gaze for a few seconds, then I look away. I can feel the sting in my throat and I don't want to make a fool of myself in front of this man despite the fact that he's my uncle. A living link to my real mother.

He nods and I can feel my chest relaxing. It's as if some sort of truce has been declared. He places his Bible on the pew beside him and turns to face me, begins to tell me the family history.

His oldest brother, Magnus, was killed in a mine accident a couple of years after Eliza disappeared.

'I was only a kid but I remember it, all right. Three young blokes killed in a shaft collapse, Magnus was the last to be pulled out. It was a bad time for the family and my mother, as if she hadn't already had enough.'

There is a reverent silence between us until I speak. 'And your other brother, what happened to him?'

'Hugh moved to Canada, let's see, a good five years ago. Always good with his hands – set up a successful building business. He's married with four children. I miss Hugh, we were good mates when we were kids. We send cards at Christmas. You can tell that the O'Dares are not much good at keeping in touch.' He smiles sheepishly.

Michael is a bachelor and works as a bank manager in Richmond. His life is one of predictable daily routine. He had enough turmoil when he was growing up, he tells me.

'Times were difficult for the family once our dad died. Eliza, particularly, missed him. She became what the family termed "a bit wayward" after his death.' He rests his hand on the bench, in a shaft of sunlight.

'Eliza was a lot like Dad – they had a love of music and would play and sing for hours. Dad learnt to play violin from his mother in England. He could also play piano. Dad taught Eliza to play the violin from when she was a little tot.'

Michael stops abruptly and for a moment I think he is about to cry. He then coughs and moves forward in the wooden pew.

'Eliza looked after us kids most of the time. She was three years older than me and two years older than Hugh. She was good fun, a bit wild, didn't care much about what others thought. Yes, she was headstrong and stubborn, all right.' He pauses. 'She and Magnus never got along, especially after Dad died.'

'And your mother, what was she like?' I can't believe I'm hearing about Eliza's family.

Michael smiles. 'Mum was a stern woman at the best of times, but underneath her toughness she was caring and wanted the best for us kids. She took no nonsense from anyone. When it was discovered that Eliza was…well, expecting you, she took charge. It was a big secret.'

'What happened when I was born?' I can feel my throat constrict but I know I've got to ask.

'No one was permitted to talk about it, and when the baby…when you were born, you were to be given out to a family wanting to adopt a child. Hugh and I didn't know too much about it at the time, but we knew there was a big problem and that Eliza was in trouble. This must be hard for you to hear, I'm sorry.' He sighs and pulls out his handkerchief.

No one has said sorry to me before. I blink back the tears welling in my eyes but I don't move.

'Why did Magnus have so much control over what happened?' I ask.

'With Dad gone, he assumed the role of head of the family. He had a frightful temper and made things worse. Mum went along with it because she was afraid of his outbursts as well. It was a terrible time.' Michael pauses again. 'In the end, Eliza wasn't able to stand up to Magnus and our mother. Without Dad, everything started to go awry. Things would have been different if he'd been alive.'

'Sounds like you all missed him.'

'Mum was different when he was alive – she was happier. Sure, she was bossy but she also relied on Dad. He was a gentle man. We loved him.' Michael wipes the back of his hand across his face. 'You had a good grandfather, Knill. A Londoner. Came out looking for gold, never found any, met Mum and ended up staying in Majorca. Eliza named you after him. His name was Scarffe Knill O'Dare.'

'So that's where it came from.'

'Eliza insisted that Mum include your name on the note that went with you. There was a big to-do over that.'

He smiles awkwardly at me as if he's said too much.

We sit silently for what seems minutes. I think about the man from London, the man whose name I was supposed to have.

'And the violin. Do you know who left a violin at my doorstep when I was a baby?'

'Do you play?' he asks.

'Yes.'

His eyes glaze over as he reaches to touch my arm then pulls back. 'My mother left my father's violin with the minister's wife, the one who arranged your adoption. I didn't know until years later when I asked my mother what had happened to it. The minister's wife promised she would make sure you got it.'

'But your mother wanted nothing to do with me?'

'She did what she thought was best at the time, but I think she always felt guilty about insisting you go to another home. Remember, she also lost her daughter because of it.'

'Eliza never forgave her?'

'No, and she never saw her daughter or her grandson again.'

'Did she look for Eliza?'

'When Eliza left, she put missing notices in Melbourne papers – not that she could afford the money. She also sent letters to hospitals and churches. Mum tried her best to find out what happened to her. Then, after Magnus was killed, she became withdrawn and rarely went outside the house. When Hugh and I left Majorca to find work she refused to answer our letters. Eventually none of us had any contact with her. She even arranged for her own funeral to be held in secrecy and without a church service. I didn't know she had passed away until last year.'

'I'm sorry, it's not been easy.'

'Life can be cruel to all involved, Knill.'

We are both drained and exhausted. Michael pulls out a small notebook and pencil from his pocket, quickly writes his address and hands it to me. I tuck it inside my jacket pocket next to Eliza's photo.

An hour and a half has passed when we finally shake hands, and our visit ends as abruptly as it started.

'Keep in touch, Knill.'

I walk back to the railway station, my head swimming.

26

Sydney is noisier than Melbourne, that's the first thing I notice. In Macquarie Street, impressive buildings tower above me as I head towards the busy centre of town. At school, I remember learning about the parade that was held in Sydney to commemorate Australian Federation. From photos of the parade, I recognise some of the buildings, especially the pink sandstone Treasury, which has an arched entry and columned balcony. Eliza would have been here the year of Federation, if she really was here. Meandering along, I can picture the mayhem on that day.

A group of women are laughing and joking ahead of me, their flimsy dresses swishing from side to side as they head towards the tram stop. They have haircuts I've never seen before, short and cropped like boys', but shiny and sleek. The men are wearing smart suits with wide lapels and dapper hats with contrasting bands.

Sydney has a way of its own – bustling, fashionable, relaxed and free.

It's two weeks since I met Michael in Richmond, and Eliza's never far from my thoughts; it is as if I will discover her around the next corner. Surely a person can't just disappear without trace?

There are, however, so many unanswered questions. Did she flee to Sydney to be away from her troubles? Why did she leave the circus in Melbourne, providing Eliza really was Lizzy O'Dare? Somehow, I want to believe she was. Today I have the same sort of feeling I had when I went to Majorca. A sense of finding out more about Eliza. Today I feel strong and energised.

I imagine her, all those years ago, walking these busy streets. Trams clanging and people milling around, as they do today. Perhaps she stopped to peer into shop windows, under ornate lacework awnings, as I do now. Catching her breath when she spots the harbour – its glistening water the deepest of blues. Anchored boats rocking in the breeze. Did she also squint as the sun shone through white clouds? Was she alone or did she meet someone from the circus? I picture the young girl in my photo, her long thick hair falling down her back, striding towards The Rocks. I can see her as she looks at the street signs: Elizabeth Street, George Street; she hesitates and then continues.

With my hat shielding my face from the early October sun, I find the Sydney Hospital without difficulty. It is a handsome sandstone building, more than a hundred years old. A steep flight of external steps lead me to heavy doors with long brass handles. Inside, at the office, I ask for help. I'm directed down a narrow corridor with dark wood panelling along each side, and I tap hesitantly at the door marked 'Records'.

'Come in,' a gruff voice calls.

I open the door and peer into the face of a man who looks like he's been at his desk forever.

'I am wondering if you can help me with some details of someone who may have been a patient?'

The clerk looks at me without moving a muscle in his face. 'Young man, we are not at liberty to give details to anyone but relatives.'

'I am a relative. She may have been my mother.'

I watch him, hoping he will be sympathetic. Slowly, after a lengthy pause, he heaves himself from his comfortable, well-worn chair. He moves to a wall of narrow timber drawers. Moving along the wall, he contemplates the marked dates on the small square labels.

'What year?'

I can't believe my luck.

'Anywhere from nineteen one to nineteen four.' I make a calculated guess.

'You don't want much, do you, lad?' The clerk smiles and I realise he is about to check the records.

'What was your mother's name?'

'Lizzy O'Dare or Eliza O'Dare.'

I watch patiently as he opens and closes several drawers before pulling out a set of cards starting with *O*, which he meticulously flicks through, one by one.

'A Mary O'Laughlin, she was forty-six years of age. Elizabeth O'Toole, thirty years and a Florence O'Leary, seventeen years. Two died in 1902, one in 1904 and they all had husbands or family to sign for them.'

'What about patients that didn't die?'

'That would take me all day, lad. After all, I'm doing you a favour checking the deaths, seeing I really shouldn't. No sign of your Eliza or Lizzy O'Dare – no one going by those names died here.'

I'm relieved and I think she's probably still alive. Tilly's story about the fire and Eliza being up here in Sydney may only be rumour.

I walk swiftly down the steps of the hospital into Macquarie Street. Looking for Eliza makes me feel purposeful, as if I'm on the brink of discovering a new person, a different Knill McMillan, or is it Scarffe O'Dare? For the first time, I fantasise what it might be like to be Scarffe O'Dare. I smile and dip my hat politely to a couple of stylish women as they pass. They flash broad smiles my way. The warm sun settles on my shoulders as I join the Sydney bustle.

At the State Library, I request the *Sydney Morning Herald* clippings for 1901, the time of the Wirth's Circus fire. If Lizzy or Eliza had been in the fire, it might have been reported. I wait for them in the reading room, daunted when a librarian drops two heavy volumes in front of me.

I begin turning the brittle pages. A stale odour accompanies the volumes; these pages are not often opened. Month by month the reports go on. Some of the articles are intriguing and I find I've half-read them before I even notice: the first federal election, the Parliament opening in the Royal Exhibition Buildings in Melbourne. I berate myself for time-wasting.

I'm starting to doubt that the fire happened when I see it. August 1901.

CIRCUS FIRE KILLS EIGHT PEOPLE
17th August 1901

A fire broke out in the main tent of Wirth's Circus yesterday. Some of the animals were rescued by circus staff but many perished. Eight people were burnt to death. Three bodies are still unidentified. The people who died were: Joe Spelding, Fred Leonard, Johnny Wheeler, Susannah Stippling and Sally Farquharson, all part of the travelling circus acts. Not all circus employees have been accounted for. Two young seamstresses who recently joined Wirth's are still missing.

Two young seamstresses…I read the record several times. On the next page, there is another entry with a photo of the charred circus site and its stony-faced owner standing beside a burnt-out animal cage.

CIRCUS FIRE ARREST
23rd August 1901

A local man has been charged over the Wirth's
Circus fire. Police report that the man admitted to
deliberately lighting the fire after a dispute with the
circus owners over wages. Eight people perished,
three of whom are still unidentified. The man will
appear before the magistrate's court later this week.

The circus has ceased to operate for the time being
and many of the staff have moved on or have not
been seen since the fire.

I don't want to know any more. Was Eliza one of the unidentified people who died in the fire? Was she one of the
seamstresses? I don't want to believe it. I close the heavy
folder and slide from the wooden chair. My gut feels heavy
and there's a tightening in my chest. My hands are shaking as I push the door, and I almost lose my balance as it
swings open suddenly. Glancing back, I see the librarian
standing by the volumes I've left, hands on hips and glar-
ing after me as if I've committed some sort of crime by
leaving so abruptly.

Outside, the fresh air washes across my face. I bump
into a woman about to enter the library. I apologise quickly
and stand aside for her to pass, then hurry on. I am not
walking; my feet are colliding with the footpath. How can
I stay upright? Eliza was one of those three unidentified
people. She has to be. It makes sense – no one has heard of

her in all these years. She would have been only nineteen years old.

It starts to rain, a lightly falling shower. I stop in a small park and let the soft spring rain wash over me. I have a very profound sense of having lost the mother I've never known.

27

Back home, tired after the long journey, two letters are waiting for me on the kitchen table: one from Ted, the other from Joseph Ah Sing. Ted's letter is short and contains snippets of local news. There is also a timid enquiry about when I'm coming home for another visit. I've visited twice since Rhoda's funeral. On those occasions, he cooked roast lamb and made quite a show of how domesticated he has become. He puts on a good front when I'm with him but it can't be easy for him, adjusting to living alone after all these years. I will write and let him know that I'll be home for Christmas.

I'm curious as I open the letter from Joseph. He wants me to meet him this Friday at one o'clock. My three months aren't quite up. But he writes that there has been an important development that must be discussed.

I have already decided not to discuss my Sydney visit with Will and Eugene. They think I went there on railway business. I want to tell them about my search for Eliza, my meeting with Michael and even Joseph. I meant to, after meeting my uncle, but I didn't. I'm not ready to talk yet.

I know my quest to find Eliza has stopped. I thought about it all the way home. Before, I believed I could find her if she was somewhere to be found. Now all of that seems useless. I'm aware of numbness settling over me, slowing me down, but I know I've got to fight that as well. I should write to Robina Smyth; she would want to know what I've found out. Would Michael? Just now I can't bear to tell them about the two seamstresses who probably perished in the fire.

I pick up my violin, my mother's violin and, before her, my grandfather's. I never tire of the smooth surface as I place my hands on the familiar bridge, silken and worn. As I play, the vibration on my jaw is soothing. Magically, the strings and bow become an extension of my inner self. The external world disappears; it's as if I'm in another place. Even as a kid I had this feeling. When I place the violin on the bed beside me I'm surprised to see that two hours have passed.

Music drifts into my sleep, too, seducing me to follow it. I strain to hear it; it teases from a distance. I call out… Don't leave, stay, show me your face, don't go, come back…

I wake abruptly; the house is silent except for the remnants of chords. Then the soft sounds fade away. I want so much to follow them.

28

The grey October afternoon reflects my mood. Today I confess to indulging in self-pity. It soothes me to feel sorry for myself, although I know I must soon snap out of it and get on with living my life. I'm ready to abandon any further idea of knowing about the past. With my real mother dead, what's the point? I also want to be free of my constant nagging thoughts about who I really am. Searching for Eliza has kept me in a suspended state of hope. I'm craving a normal life like my cousins': work, pubs, dances and girls.

Seeing Lily Ah Sing takes away some of this grey feeling.

'Knill.' Her smile is sweet when I come in. 'We are expecting you. My father will be with you soon.' Lily is wearing a white blouse with small blue flowers. Her hair is held back off her face and knotted intricately behind her ears.

'Hello, Lily.' If I'm honest, the thought of seeing Lily was one of the reasons I decided to come. She is reading a thick volume of something; it looks like one of her father's law books. She pushes it aside.

'Right on time, it's my father who is running late,' she says.

'I didn't expect to be back here so soon.' I hover around her desk.

'No, but it's important that you came, Knill. My father is anxious to see you.'

'Do you work every day, Lily?'

'Yes, it's my job.'

'I'm not sure I'd like to work for my father. He lets me get away with too much.'

We laugh together.

'That's not the case here. My father is a good boss but has high standards.'

We both swing around as a door opens. Joseph looks serious as he beckons me into his office. I wink at Lily as I follow him.

'I'm very pleased you could come today. I have more news for you.'

'Three months isn't up yet,' I say.

'Almost.'

He picks up files, taps them sharply and replaces them on his desk. He clears his throat and looks directly at me.

'I have received another letter from Fong Choon. He is impatient to see you, Knill.'

'He's coming here to see me?'

'No.'

'I'm not following you.'

'He sends money to pay for your journey to China.'

'To China! He wants me to go to China?' I place my hand on Joseph's desk and laugh. 'Good joke…'

I scan his face. It's serious; he isn't laughing with me.

'Fong Choon worries that time is passing.'

'But that's crazy. I have a job. I can't just go halfway around the world to meet someone I don't know.'

How can I think clearly? My mind refuses to work. I take in the minute detail of my shoes – the laces tied firmly, the brogue leather punch marks distributed evenly, the rich brown glow, the result of nugget meticulously applied each morning. I shake my head. I could never have imagined such an outlandish proposal.

Then Lily appears at the door. She glances at me before passing a folder to her father. As she steps to the side of the office, she smiles and gives a small shrug of her shoulders.

Joseph is on his feet. 'Knill, this envelope contains tickets on the *Castlefield*. The ship leaves for China in two weeks, November fifteenth.'

'First you tell me he wants me to go to China, then you tell me I have to leave in two weeks. No, this is madness.'

Lily watches me with her kind eyes.

'All the necessary arrangements are made for you,' says Joseph. 'All you need to do is say yes.'

I sit quietly for what seems a long time. How can I confess to Joseph, with Lily listening, that the idea of travelling to a foreign country petrifies me? That I've never travelled further than Sydney, and that was only last week?

'I have to think about this. It's too sudden.' I catch the concern on Lily's face.

'You need to decide in the next two days, Knill.'

Then the biggest surprise of all – Joseph says that Lily and his friend and assistant An Meng will accompany me to China. Instantly, my worries about the language difference and my lack of travel experience are relieved. I've never met An Meng, but I could easily imagine looking at the endless seas by Lily's side.

As I leave, I shake Joseph's hand. I hesitate and then nod to Lily. I can feel them watching me as I depart the building. I don't quite understand the expression in Lily's eyes. Is it a longing? A wishing? I get a sense that my decision is important to them, very important.

I walk into the warm afternoon air of Collins Street. The traffic rumbles past and people stride alongside me, all going about their normal business. A shiver of excitement – or fear – passes through me. I can't believe what I've just heard. China. Go to China to meet my father! This seems like a dream; I know it's not.

What is Fong Choon really like? And why has he gone to such lengths to find me? This, Lily's eyes, my own excitement: it all puzzles me. What does it mean? Fong Choon has his own family in China, and it's been a long time since he was in Australia. He could just forget Eliza…forget me. Why doesn't he?

29

Will and Eugene arrive home to the unfamiliar sight of me drinking beer at the kitchen table. Not managing to hide their surprise, they sit down. Something's wrong, says their quick glance to each other. I can't contain myself any longer and tell them everything. Words are tripping out of my mouth, stammering, disordered. I leave nothing out: the letters, meetings and the China proposal.

They gape, mouths open. I can see the humour in the situation, my boisterous, funny cousins, lost for words. Eugene finds his voice first.

'So you really are half-Chinese then?'

'Looks that way!' Relaxed by the beer, I grin from Eugene to Will.

'I can't believe this person, Fong Choon, wants you to go to China,' Will says.

'I've decided to go.' I surprise myself with my conviction. I hadn't quite realised I'd made that decision.

'What! You're going to bloody China. The bloke might be some sort of drongo!' Will is on his feet now.

'I have to do this. Otherwise I'll never know the truth.'

'What about Uncle Ted? How is he going to feel, with you miles away and not knowing what's happening?'

'I'll go home and talk to him before I go. I'm not going forever – just to meet Fong Choon and then I'll be home.' I'm making it up as I go along.

'What about your job,' Eugene says. 'You've got a damn good job, you can't just throw that away.'

Neither of them are convinced the story has credibility. They want to accompany me to Joseph's office on Wednesday. I laugh at the prospect of my cousins interrogating Joseph. I also cringe when I think of the polite and well-mannered Lily being subjected to my outspoken cousins.

'Knill, it's something you have to think about. A bit of time isn't too much to ask?'

'I'm grateful for your concern, but I don't have much time.'

It's strange but this conversation is helping me make up my mind.

Will paces the kitchen behind me.

'I have to do this,' I say again, though I'm rattled by their response and far from sure that I'm making the right decision. It would be so easy to let them talk me out of it. But I won't let that happen.

'Well, it seems like there's nothing we can say to change your mind. Do you think Fong Choon will pay for us to come too?' Eugene's grin is wide as he reaches for the beer. We all laugh and the tension in the room eases.

We drink more beer and talk well into the night. About when we were kids, about our jobs and about our cricket days in Castlemaine, but we always return to my journey ahead. I hold firm on my decision where once I would have relied on Will and Eugene for affirmation. This is one time when I must back myself.

I toss and turn until the first light of day edges around the blind. Thankful for morning, I pull off the covers and dress quickly. The comforting hiss of the kettle interrupts my thinking – the logic of agreeing to take an uncertain journey halfway around the world. Has my conviction gone? 'Think clearly,' I whisper to myself. I keep hearing a voice saying, Why not take the risk? What is there to lose? Then I think of Ted and wonder how he will take the news. I feel a pang of guilt and know what he will say. He'll counsel me to be cautious and want me to think about it. But this isn't Ted, this is me, I tell myself. I've got to make my own decisions and live with them. I'm muttering to myself when Will appears in the doorway.

'Listen, Knill, you sure that you want to go on with this China business?'

'Yes, yes, I am.'

'You know they say that China's the arse end of the world? You don't have to go, Knill. You could just say no and that would be the end of it.'

'If I don't go, I'll never understand or know what happened when I was born.'

'You know what happened. Ted and Rhoda adopted you. They made you who you are.'

I nod and Will shrugs. I don't expect him to understand but at some level I want him to respect my decision.

Lily isn't there. In her place is a man who introduces himself as An Meng.

'Mr Ah Sing is out, he back soon. You please wait.'

So, this is the man who is accompanying us to China. I smile and try to initiate a conversation, but he busies himself behind the desk. I'm intrigued by his unusual appearance. His dark brown suit jacket is two sizes too large for him. His white shirt is buttoned high under his chin. As he turns sideways, I see a long thin pigtail hanging down his back.

I settle myself on one of the chairs against the wall. The room is dark, relying only on light from the front window. I fiddle with my felt hat, placing it on the chair next to me and then picking it up again. I knead the brim between my thumb and forefinger, then put it down again. As I do so, I catch sight of a smudge on the tip of my right shoe, and try to rub it away. I know without turning that An Meng is watching me. I cough and straighten.

I'm about to ask how long I'll have to wait when the door opens. Father and daughter hurry in. They are talking and laughing together until they notice me, and contain themselves at once. Joseph apologises for being late and escorts me to his office. Lily steps aside and throws me a beaming smile as I pass her. At her side, she clutches brown parcels tied with shopkeeper's string.

I follow Joseph into his office and take my usual chair. He fiddles with papers on his desk whilst muttering regret for his lateness. He sits, coughs, moves more papers, then looks up at me.

'Well, Knill, tell me. What is your final decision?'

'I will go to China.'

'Good, then all we need to do is make the final arrangements,' says Joseph, with the broadest smile I've ever seen on his face. He claps his hands together, rises from his chair and calls to Lily.

'Before we discuss my arrangements,' I say, 'there is a matter I would like to ask you to handle for me whilst I'm away.'

Joseph lowers himself in his chair and looks down his glasses at me. 'And that being, Knill?'

'I would like you to make some confidential enquiries for me in the town of Maryborough.'

Part two
November 1921

30

The ocean spans ahead like a country sky on a summer's day. Familiar as I am with a landscape that stretches forever, I've never seen water so bountiful that it fills the entire horizon. Since leaving dock in Melbourne three days ago I've marvelled at this amazing sight. The vessel sways as the water nurses the ship out to sea. The black funnel spits its choking white steam, which floats lazily above the mast line and eventually fades into the distance. Light-footed crew scurry on deck, shouting to each other as they carry out practised tasks. They're a mottled lot: faces and bodies tanned and weathered from sea, salt and sun, but it's their swarthiness and seamanship that gives the passengers confidence. I can scarcely believe that I stand on board a ship that will dock in Hong Kong in nine weeks.

Telling Ted was the hardest part. I didn't feel good about worrying him, after all he'd been through with Rhoda.

'China!'

'I know it's sudden but—'

'You don't know these people. This Joseph Ah…it could be a hoax.'

'The information adds up.'

'Are you sure?'

'I've struggled with the decision, Ted.'

I told him about meeting Joseph Ah Sing and the letter from Fong Choon.

'How long?'

'A few months maybe.'

We were sitting at the kitchen table and ignoring the hissing kettle on the stove. I noticed a tray with Ted's cup, plate and bowl and a new, smaller teapot standing on the bench. Ted was quiet, looking out the window. Then he turned to me. 'You've never been one to take the easy course, Knill. This is no different.' He slapped me on the shoulder.

We walked the familiar path to Rhoda's grave, carrying lilies, roses and hydrangeas from her garden. Ted removed dead flowers from the pots before we placed the fresh ones in water.

'You come often?' I ask.

'Every Friday.'

'Is it hard without her?'

'I've been thinking about Rhoda – what she'd make of all this. China!'

'It wouldn't have been an easy conversation,' I say.

'She planted that over there. Did you know? A Chinese flowering plum. Tended it carefully, said it was fragile. I don't know, Knill. The thought of you getting on a boat would have terrified her. But I keep thinking of her giving her baby away and maybe the child wondering about her mother. I think it's right that you go. I'll be here when you get back.'

He wished me a happy twenty-first birthday and extracted a promise from me to write often. I spent less than twenty-four hours with him on that quick trip to Castlemaine two days before my departure date. I felt guilty as we shook hands.

'Get a move on,' he said. 'The train won't wait all day.'

I didn't look back.

Will continued to talk up the negative aspects of what might happen and how bad Ted would feel. 'You must be stark raving mad to even be thinking about going to China,' he said a week before my departure.

'Let's give Knill a break,' Eugene said.

'Someone has to talk some sense around here.'

'It's his life and he has a right to do what he likes. I admit to being sceptical, but Knill has given it a heap of thought. Downright gutsy, if you ask me.' Eugene glowered at his brother.

'I appreciate your concern, but I'll be fine. I have to do this and the last thing I want is for the two of you to be arguing over it. It's my decision.'

Eugene put his arm around my shoulder. 'The sooner you go, the sooner you get back, mate.' He gave a playful punch to my arm.

'I know it doesn't make sense to you. You know where you belong. You have each other, you are brothers. I have no one. That's why I want to go to China. When you look at your parents you see bits of yourselves – I can't do the same. This is a chance I must take. I just want you to understand that.'

'You have Ted, and I thought we might have mattered just a bit,' said Will.

'Yes, of course Ted is important to me and the two of you have been like brothers to me. But I must do this. I'll be fine and I promise I'll keep in touch.'

The two weeks between deciding to go and leaving passed quickly, between Will, Eugene, Ted, leaving work, and Joseph. His insistence on new clothes and personal items for the journey overwhelmed me. I've been groomed and prepared to look my best, even if it does feel unnecessary and overdone.

There is still an edge of fear to what I'm doing. I try to push the concerns from my mind – I have a right to meet this Fong Choon person who claims me as his son.

I would like to have a clearer idea about how it will all happen, though. The journey plans, although explained to me, seem vague. I've had to put my trust in Joseph – he has a good reputation, according to Lily, for organising travel to China. What I do know is that I am to travel to Hong

Kong, Canton, and then up to Shanghai, where I will meet Fong Choon. When I asked for more details about meeting my father, Joseph brushed aside my concerns and requests for more information.

'It's all taken care of, Knill. You just need to be ready to leave. It is my job to make the arrangements. Family in China will look after you. Trust me.'

I never tire of the magnificent ocean, and the sound of it lapping at the underbelly of the ship brings me a calmness I've never felt before. But my tranquillity is interrupted.

'You come now, Mr Knill,' calls An Meng. 'Ready for the dinner.'

It is becoming evident to me that An Meng is on the voyage to accompany and look after Lily and me. His role is loosely one of companion and organiser. Unaccustomed to having others looking after me, I am awkward and not sure how to treat him. But his serene manner interests me, and I find myself watching him as he moves about the ship. Since coming aboard, he has taken to dressing in Chinese tunics, high to the neck and long over his hips. His trousers fall softly and broadly above his ankles. His shoes are made of cowhide and are flat without heels. He looks comfortable in these clothes.

I follow An Meng along the outer deck and notice that he is hunched over in a way that wasn't obvious in Melbourne.

As we walk, the boat begins to rock more acutely. The sky is becoming darker to the north and the wind is strong and gusty. The crew are moving ropes and equipment alongside the mast. A sailor on the deck calls out to the quartermaster. 'There's a swell coming across and a northerly whipping up fast.'

We climb down the wooden steps to the dining saloon. An Meng ushers me into the saloon where other people are gathering. Lily waves shyly from across the room and indicates for me to sit beside her. There are other people at the table – a Eurasian woman called Molly Lau Hong, Prudence Talbot-Hamilton, an English woman with a welcoming smile, an old Chinese couple, Wong Bao and his wife, Lam Ming. Lily speaks in English as if she senses my nervousness. The others chat amongst themselves. I have no idea what they are talking about, although they smile and nod to me as if I do. Wong Bao and Lam Ming are returning home after twenty-five years in Australia, Lily tells me. Wong Bao is a successful mine owner. He switches to English, to tell us he made a promise to his wife many years ago that they would eventually return to their homeland. Both are concerned about the long sea journey and the effect it might have on their failing health.

'We like Australia but belong in China. We are going home now,' Wong Bao says.

I look at these people and for the first time I see my own features in theirs – it's odd to step into this aspect of myself. I think about home and belonging and can understand why this elderly couple needs to make the journey. I smile at the weathered faces watching me from across the table. They nod politely.

Molly speaks fluent Cantonese, Mandarin and English. Her black hair reminds me of the styles in Sydney – it's cut sleek and straight across her neckline with a short fringe over her eyes. Strands of pearls strung with large red diamante stones swing loosely around her neck and down the front of her peacock-blue dress. She is by far the most elaborately dressed person in the dining room.

'I have been married twice. Yes, but…bad luck for me as both husbands died.'

Lily is curious, and asks where Molly grew up.

'I was born in Australia to an English mother and a merchant Chinese father so my schooling was mostly in Sydney. But, luckily, I also spent time in mainland China and England.'

Molly, clearly enjoying the limelight, waits until there is a lull in the conversation before she turns to me. 'What's the purpose of your journey, Knill?'

'I'm travelling to China to meet, um, relatives…first to Canton, then Shanghai.'

'You have relatives in China?'

'Sort of, or should I say…I'm going to meet my father for the first time.'

'Well, that sounds like a story I'd be interested in, you'll have to tell me sometime.'

The person on the other side of Molly claims her attention and Lily turns to me. Her presence on the journey is reassuring, partly because she's done this trip before, but there is something else…I like her and find excuses to be in her company. In her father's office. Onboard the ship. I am lucky to have someone here who I consider a friend.

The dining saloon is lined with tables and chairs with a runner of carpet between each section. The walls are papered in a design of ivy leaves and berries in between carved panels of exotic fauna. Old seafaring photographs hang from a high picture rail. Trolleys with napkins and cutlery are parked under a nearby stairway, rattling from time to time to remind us of the movements of the sea below. The food arrives quickly – clear onion soup, corned beef with mustard, carrots and potatoes, followed by a sticky version of lemon sago pudding. I clean my plate with enthusiasm, but the others eat sparingly, pushing their food around their plates without interest. I gather they are complaining about the food.

'They are not happy with the food.' Lily brings her face close to mine and whispers.

'What's wrong with it?' I whisper back.

'Too English…'

I laugh at Lily as she giggles quietly behind her hand.

'They are saying they can't wait until they reach China so that they can eat well again.'

My cabin is decorated in yellows and creams and boasts all the amenities of first-class travel. The travelling trunk that Lily's father purchased on my behalf sits to one side underneath the porthole. When I first saw the shiny black metal box I was bewildered.

'Why will I need such a large trunk?'

'Oh, you have to take gifts for family in China. It is expected of you. Otherwise they'll think you don't respect them.'

An inexplicable feeling floats across my body when I think about meeting my mysterious father, and how quickly all this has happened. I should pinch myself to test the reality of it all. Knill McMillan, a country lad from Castlemaine, on his way to China to meet his father, a man he knows nothing about…

I take off my jacket and drape it over the padded chair in the cabin. My shoes, more expensive than I can believe, I place by my bed. I only wish Will and Eugene were here to witness the scene at dinner, to listen to Molly's stories of her life in Shanghai. I was fascinated by her ramblings, seeing her as someone who wavers between cultures, despite being very familiar with both worlds. I wasn't sure how the other diners felt about her, though. They mostly ate in silence, smiling politely from time to time. Are Lily and An Meng as intrigued by Molly as I am? There are so many aspects of this journey that are new to me. It's as if I really am Scarffe O'Dare. The life I lived as Knill McMillan is fading. Am I on the edge of becoming someone else?

The northerly wind is making its presence felt. As my cabin begins to lurch, nausea churns at my stomach. Breathing long and slow, I place my hands on each side of the mattress. The buffeting is relentless. The small lamp blew out earlier and the only light gracing the room is the lightning flashing intermittently through the small porthole. It is followed shortly after by crackling thunder. I shudder at the continuous loud clapping and hope the ship is strong enough to stay afloat.

Is Lily all right? She is four doors down from me. The door of my cabin is jammed shut and each time I try to lever it open the ship lurches and I'm flung back into the room. Finally, I manage to open it and move into the passageway. The wind catches the door and slams it shut behind me. The noise of the sea is magnified out here and salt water is spraying along the walls and across the floorboards. I snake along, stopping only when the boat rocks furiously as the swell hits hard against its bow. The noise is something I've never experienced before. I call for Lily several times, but I know she can't hear me. I hammer on her door until I can see the handle moving. Like me, she has trouble opening it. I push hard from the outside and the door springs open.

'Are you all right?' I shout.

Lily looks dishevelled in her nightclothes and her belongings are scattered across the floor.

'I tried to get out of the cabin but the door wouldn't budge.' Her long hair is falling across her face and she looks pale.

'You look unwell.'

'I'm seasick,' she says as she sits on the bed, pulling her dressing-gown around her.

'The storm will end soon. Best to stay put for a while.' I sit beside her and slowly the colour returns to her face.

'Do you think we should try to get to An Meng? He may not be doing so well.' Lily's concern for the old man is as if she is looking after him rather than the other way around.

'Where's his cabin?'

'Number five on the next deck.'

'As soon as the storm eases I'll go and check on him.'

The storm rages and we talk. Lily tells me about her life in Australia and how hard her father works to be successful. Her mother died many years ago; Lily has photographs of her and keeps in touch with relatives in China.

I notice, as she speaks of her mother, the quietness of her voice. I touch her lightly on the arm; she turns her head and smiles.

'It's like I have two lives. One in Australia and another that is connected to China.'

'Does it get complicated?'

'Yes, sometimes. Two cultures, trying to fit into both can be a bit daunting, but it's lucky as well. I have the best of both worlds. Well, I try to think of it like that, Knill.' Her beautiful oval face breaks into a glowing smile.

I want the storm to last all night. It feels like a long time since I've been able to break out of my own thoughts, to listen to the stories of someone else's life.

She asks about Castlemaine and I tell her what it was like to live in a country town. She laughs when I describe Will and Eugene and the things we got up to as kids.

'I think I would like your cousins. They sound fun.'

'They would like you too, but they would tease you to see if you have a sense of humour.'

We laugh and talk our way through the storm, our friendship growing. I know that I shouldn't be in here alone with Lily. Rhoda would be horrified, I think with a smile. But, given the circumstances, it somehow seems acceptable. And it is not as if I feel that way about her.

The gale keeps on, the swell shaking the ship's contents and occupants for hours. Just when the motion slows and it seems the worst is over a huge wave tosses the vessel yet again. Gradually the rocking slows and the boat calms to a steady movement.

'I should go and check on An Meng now,' I say.

Lily jumps up, as if she had forgotten about him, and gives me a guilty look.

'I'll come back and tell you how he is.'

I make my way down to the second-class area. The door of number five opens easily. I find An Meng asleep on his bunk and apart from the items flung across his floor all seems fine. I touch him on the arm. He rouses and immediately tries to get out of bed.

'No, stay there and rest. I just came to see that you are all right after the big storm. Lily was worried about you.'

'Miss Lily, is she in her cabin?'

'Yes,' I say, without telling him that I've been there too. 'And she's fine.'

The weeks pass slowly in this ocean of blue. Christmas comes and is a low-key affair with a lunch of salty pork roast and vegetables, a pudding and custard, and then it's all over. My thoughts are mostly about what the family will be doing in Castlemaine and a pang of homesickness hits me. But the novelty of being on this strange journey keeps me buoyant. Each day, An Meng teaches me some Cantonese words.

'*Néih hóu*, Knill.'

'*Néih hóu, sing muk lou si*.' We both laugh and I tell An Meng that Lily taught me to say 'clever teacher' as a surprise.

'*Gaau siu*,' says An Meng. *Funny*. 'You have a good sense of humour.' I've passed some sort of test.

He is a very good teacher and my respect for him grows and grows. Being born of Chinese heritage does not seem so strange now. So unusual. I find myself observing Lily and An Meng. I like their courteous manners, their quiet yet intelligent disposition, and their gentle way of being in the world.

My worries come at night, when I am alone in my cabin. They must slip in, uninvited, through the porthole. I don't like living off someone else's fortune. Lily's father has arranged travelling money and a bank account for my use in China, telling me that Fong Choon has sent money for the purpose. My expenses for the journey are paid for, all first class. I have never accepted money without working for it. I settle my uneasiness by promising myself that I'll repay the debt when I return to Melbourne. My new clothes were expensive, hardly what I am accustomed to or can afford. Joseph explained that a good impression is very important.

'Your family, and Fong Choon, will expect it.'

But what if I am not who Joseph thinks I am? What if I'm not the son of Fong Choon or the son he wants me to be? At these times, an image of Ted making tea or Rhoda in the garden pruning her roses will come to me, and I curl up in my bed, missing them dreadfully.

'Tell me about when you grew up in China,' I ask An Meng as we sit together one morning. The deck is still drying from its morning hose-down and the sky above is cloudless.

'That is a long time ago for an old man to remember, but they were good days. I was lucky, I had a good family.'

'Brothers and sisters?'

'Five brothers and two sisters. Lots of cousins and we knew everyone in Hiyang. High in the hills, the clouds met the mountains some days.' An Meng laughs fondly but as he does he coughs and holds his chest.

'That cough, it's not so good,' I say.

Not long after we boarded the ship, An Meng developed a hacking cough. He tries to hide it and waves away any concern from Lily or me.

'I'll be pleased to get back to China,' he says, ignoring my comment.

'Do you miss it?'

'Oh, yes, Mr Knill. I miss my mother country.'

'Even though you've been in Australia for a long time?'

'Yes, a long time, but now I must go to my home place. To know who you are and where you come from is the most important thing in the world.'

We move our chairs to follow the small strip of shade as the suns creeps across the deck. For weeks now we have travelled beneath this cloudless sky. A slight breeze breaks the heat and from time to time a fine spray of seawater gently cools the deck. I'm deep in thought when An Meng speaks again. 'You are troubled, Mr Knill?'

'It's just that I'm not sure where I belong.'

'One day you will understand. You have plenty of time to learn about your Chinese roots. Trouble might be how you fit it all together.'

'You understand, An Meng.'

'We can't change the past, Mr Knill, just have to live with the future.'

'Is that a Chinese proverb?'

'No, just a truth.' He grins and we laugh.

31

Molly's often on deck, wandering from group to group, chatting to the other passengers. Sometimes she sits with me on one of the blue canvas chairs lining the deck. People hurry to claim their spot in the shadiest places and there is a constant scraping of chairs being shifted as the sun moves across the sky. When Molly settles she tells me endless stories from her past. I've always been a good listener and I enjoy her company. At times, I find myself talking about my own life and I like the way Molly can accept anything and everyone. How has she become so confident and bold? Were her own parents the same, adventurous and free-thinking? Is it because she's travelled and lived in other countries? Perhaps the grief of losing two husbands and missing the opportunity to have her own family has given her insights unavailable to others. Often, with little else to entertain my mind, I compare my life with Molly's.

Growing up in a small country town, with old-fashioned parents and without brothers or sisters. The only people I mixed with were people the same as us. I smile to myself at how I once thought everyone in the world lived like we did, thought the same thoughts. Perhaps finding out about my adoption was not a curse after all, but an opportunity to learn and grow and see the world.

Sometimes, in the evenings after dinner, we go to the lounge. It's a beautiful room: lush crimson and blue carpets, tapestry-covered chairs grouped in sets of threes and fours around small elegant tables, wood-carved panels on its walls. It's quieter in here.

Prudence Talbot-Hamilton, the English woman who is on her way to join a friend in Hong Kong, sometimes volunteers to play piano. This arouses the interest of the English and Australian passengers, but the Chinese often retire early to their cabins. Lily, however, adores these occasions – she is taking piano lessons in Melbourne. Her father loves music and has encouraged her to study hard.

One evening, a few weeks into our journey, Prudence asks Lily to play, and because it is Lily all the diners stay. Wong Bao and Lam Ming are smiling when Lily makes her way to the piano.

As Lily sits, she turns to me. 'Knill, play with me.'

For a moment I can't move, but I also can't leave her to play alone if she needs me. We sit together on the wobbly stool, joking a little, and I can feel her nervousness beside me, mine too.

'What about Piano Concerto No. 1 by Tchaikovsky?' Lily asks.

We are playing without sheet music and hope to get it right. Our shaking hands trail across the ivory keyboard until we gain composure. Lily's perfect face is serious as she moves her slender hands along the scales. She is easy to play with and we anticipate each other's movements. Quickly, I move from reality to a state I love most, the special place where playing brings an inner vitality that I can never explain. Single notes form emotions that somehow transcend spoken words. Our shoulders touch as we lose ourselves in the rhythm and harmony of Tchaikovsky's well-known classic. We finish with a well-timed crescendo and smile broadly at each other. The relief! Prudence and Molly cheer loudly, alongside the other diners. Lam Ming's eyes shine with tears. An Meng claps softly, looking thoughtfully at the two of us. He sees me noticing him and holds his hand to his mouth as he coughs.

Some evenings Lily and I sit on deck, talking, a few other passengers nearby. All of us watching the night skies as the ship moves forward. I love the feeling of the ship then, the wide ocean ahead and the soft lapping of the water along the beam. The deck is hosed and swept, the ship made new again.

Occasionally, I wander off alone and explore the vast expanses of the ship. From the top deck, with its amazing ocean panorama, to the scullery and work spaces of the crew below. The engine room attracts me, but passengers are not allowed access. I peer through the glass panels and watch the men at work. It's dirty work and there's always an atmosphere of urgency. Sometimes on deck, I chat to the English-speaking sailors about how many sea journeys they've clocked up. Their lives are so different to mine. I don't like being idle and at times I envy them.

We are becoming concerned by An Meng's health: he retires early and is starting to spend much of his day resting. He is looking pale and has become more exhausted as the journey has gone on. Our Cantonese lesson today was short, ending with me fetching a glass of water for him.

'He is sicker than he tells us, I think,' Lily says as she sips green tea. 'And I am not sure that he's eating.'

An Meng has waited for a long time to return to China, she tells me. He has been homesick for as long as she has known him.

'Why did he come to Australia?'

'He first worked for my father's family in Canton. He was very young then. When my father came to Australia he promised An Meng that when he became a qualified lawyer he would pay for An Meng to come too. And, true to his word, An Meng joined him in Melbourne. He was my father's main support when my mother died. He is family to us.'

Although Lily has told me much of her life, this is the first time she has talked in detail about her mother dying.

'Your mother. That must have been hard for you and your father.'

'Mother died in childbirth and the baby – my little sister – died two days later. I was only three years old then. I can't remember much about it. My father's family in Canton wanted him to return home with me. They were very worried, saying that he couldn't take care of a little girl and be successful at law.'

'How did he manage to raise you on his own?'

'Oh, he wasn't alone. An Meng and Mrs Khoo helped us.'

'Who is Mrs Khoo?'

'Mrs Khoo cleans our house and cooks for us. She also looked after me when I was little. She was like a mother to me.' Lily looks away, her eyes glistening. She picks up her teacup again. Its colours remind me of the cup my mother left for me.

'Did Mrs Khoo come out from China to help?'

'No, there are many Chinese people who have settled in Australia. They need work like anyone else, and when my father advertised for a housekeeper she applied. She's been with us ever since.'

'Why did your father stay in Australia then?'

'He wanted a future, wanted to send money back home, to families in Canton, including his own family.'

'Will he ever go home to stay?'

'Not now. Twenty years away from home is too long and he is successful in Melbourne. And I have never lived in China. My father knows that the life in Australia is the only one I know. He stays for me, Knill.'

The closer we get to Hong Kong, the more my apprehension kicks in.

'There is much English spoken in Shanghai,' Lily says, trying to calm my worries, as we stand at the rail looking out to sea. Whales were spotted off the ship's starboard this morning and we have been watching for them, hoping they will return. Lily has been to China four times and speaks Cantonese and Mandarin so she has none of my concerns.

'What about in Canton?'

'Uncle's family in Canton are not so good with English but An Meng and Uncle will be with us. He will help you, and so will I.'

'And your uncle's coming to Shanghai?'

'Yes, he will have it all arranged. And there you will meet your father.'

Something catches my eye in the water – is it the whales? No, just the crisp white tip of a wave.

'What about An Meng? Is he well enough for all this family visiting?'

An Meng is looking paler than ever and walking with a pronounced stoop. We are doing everything we can think of to make his journey more comfortable. The ship's doctor, a serious-faced Chinese gentleman, has been diligent in visiting him each day. An Meng is resting in his cabin, and Lily has promised to describe the whales to him if we see them.

A cloud passes over Lily's face. 'Let's hope so.'

'I'm lucky to have you travelling with me,' I tell her.

'You worry too much, Knill, but I think I understand. Chinese ways are very different to Australian ways.'

'That would be an understatement.' I enjoy making Lily smile. 'There is something else that's nagging at me. Lily, do you believe that Fong Choon is my father?'

She places her hand beside mine on the rail. 'You have a way about you that is Chinese, Knill. When I first met you, I knew you were connected to us in some way. I can't tell you for sure that Fong Choon is your father, but your honourable nature is more Eastern than Western.' Her dark eyes flicker intently as she speaks. Then I realise that I've been staring at her for too long. I can feel my face colour slightly, as I look back to the sea beyond her delicate hands.

'It still might be a mistake.'

'My father is sure that you are Fong Choon's son.' Lily's hand flutters in the air for a moment as if she might place it on my wrist. But she doesn't. 'But you do worry and doubt like a Westerner, Knill.'

'Whales ahead,' one of the deckhands calls.

We look in the direction of his outstretched arm and see the surface of the ocean breaking. Two large blue whales arch their enormous backs to the sky and then dive forward in a lolling motion. Lily grabs my arm with joy. Breathless, we stare at the sea and wait for them to resurface.

But before the whales return, Molly appears on deck and calls to us. 'News from below: Hong Kong is only two days away.'

32

Nothing could have prepared me for arriving in the sludge-laden waters of the Hong Kong harbour. The strange odour. The cacophony of sound, which is disorientating and intriguing at the same time. Rotting vessels and flat-bottomed junks floating side by side mass below us, a chaotic array of bamboo and timber. Hundreds of sampans bumping against each other, so tightly packed that the edge between land and sea is barely visible. Men, holding their bamboo poles in the still water, shouting to each other across the jammed waterway, paying little attention to our ship as it inches its bulk to the throbbing harbour edge.

I pull back from the railing and the spectacle before me. What have I agreed to? But there is no going back. A deal is a deal.

Lily crosses the deck to me, seemingly unaffected by all the activity. She's seen it before, I guess.

'The ship doctor has advised that we get An Meng off the ship and home as quickly as we can.'

'What's the urgency?'

Lily brushes her hand across her eyes. 'He's dying, Knill, we have to get him home.'

'Dying!'

All the colours and smells around us swirl together. The ship suddenly pitches and I grab the rail. It is only then that I realise it was not the ship swaying, but me. An Meng dying. Lily's eyes are wet with tears, but she is filled with a quiet, determined energy.

'He became short of breath overnight. We have to move quickly. We must get to Canton first, then Uncle will help get him home.'

To get to Canton, we must take a barge up the Pearl River. It is a six-hour trip.

As we make our hurried plans, the ship berths and the sea-weary sailors open the large trapdoors for the massive task of unloading.

In the tiny bunk below deck, An Meng's dark eyes are sunken in his small face and his fine body is papery and withered. The old man preserves his energy. He is dignified and still as he waits for us to assist him. He's aware that he has the river journey and then an overland trip before him. He only wants to be home. Lily gently fusses around him, packing his belongings and preparing him to go ashore.

I help An Meng to move slowly from his bunk.

'Take it easy, An Meng. Let me do all the work. We'll be out of here soon.'

We painstakingly climb the steep stairs to the deck. An Meng requires help from me to stay on his feet; towards the top I carry him the last few steps.

'Thank you,' he whispers and leans his weight against me.

Lily and I exchange looks of concern, then we struggle along the deck. A crew member takes An Meng's weight from the other side and eventually we manage to disembark. We then become part of the swarming of people on the ground. There is frantic activity everywhere and pungent cooking aromas drift around us.

People mill across the dock, their shrill voices filling the air. I find it hard to differentiate between heated arguments and general banter. I watch closely, trying to make sense of what's happening around us. Lily is questioning a couple of men about the Pearl River barge. The conversation takes a long time. The men appear to be bargaining, waving their hands about, nodding and talking across each other and Lily. It's difficult to tell if they're friendly or annoyed. I'm about to leave An Meng's side to go to Lily's aid when, without warning, the men move towards us. Lily follows them.

'What was that about?' I ask.

'They have agreed to take us to the barge dock. They wanted too much money initially, so I had to haggle until they agreed on a reasonable amount.'

'Are you sure about them? I'm not sure we should trust them. We have a frail old man with us – we make easy targets.' I glare at the men who are watching me intently.

'It's going to be all right, Knill. They always argue over payment – it's the way things are here.' She touches my arm to convince me to let them past. Lily looks tired but she knows what she's doing, or at least I hope she does. Without another word, our luggage and belongings are bundled onto a dirty oil-caked cart. The men continue to watch me.

'I wish they would stop staring at me,' I say.

'You look different – they don't see many Westerners. They mean no harm.'

'What's so different?'

'You wear different clothes and your language is particularly strange to Chinese people. You had better get used to it.'

'I'm still not sure I trust them.'

'Don't concern yourself with minor things now, Knill. We have a bigger problem to worry about. When we arrive in Canton and Shanghai, there will be people who speak English. Fong Choon speaks very good English.'

'You're right. Let's concentrate on An Meng.' I realise I'm acting foolishly. I need to support Lily, not question her judgement. I throw myself into helping manage the problem of getting An Meng on the barge.

An Meng is aware of his dependence on us. He is too ill to carry out his duties and feels humiliated that he's causing such a fuss.

'Not want to give you trouble.'

'Hush. No trouble, An Meng.' Lily is by his side and holding his hand, I can see tears welling in her eyes.

'We will get you back to Hiyang soon,' I tell him.

The old man nods. He turns his head towards Lily and I notice a faint glistening at the edges of his sunken eyes. We all know there isn't much time to waste.

33

The cart men, with their skinny pigtails trailing down their backs, grip the handles of the luggage cart and heave it forward. They crisscross and weave amongst the throng of people and rickshaws.

Our trunks bounce and lurch as the men forge their way to the barge dock. An Meng, Lily and I follow in a rickshaw, its spindly wheels clacking along the uneven surfaces. The road is part of a communal space, people walking, riding and talking in groups. Despite this, we move swiftly, the driver skilfully dodging everything and everyone in our path.

The area around the barge ramp is home to whole families. Business and family life are intermingled. Tiny children play in the dirt alongside stallholders selling their wares, and women cook over small open fires, smoke swirling above them. They pause to watch us being pulled along.

The rickshaw narrowly misses hitting a man carrying a long bamboo pole across his shoulders. His tattered clothes barely conceal his nakedness. The pole sags heavily, with a large shallow dish tied at each end. The dishes are filled with blackened chestnuts; they still smoke from the cooking coals. A man shouts to the chestnut hawker and some sort of disagreement flares between them. The hawker quickens his step. Several other men join in the argument. The hawker retreats fast, with an increasing number of men in pursuit.

An Meng slumps against my shoulder in the rickshaw. The sticky humidity is affecting him. He is sleeping and waking in fits and starts. Will he cope with the barge journey?

The rickshaw comes to a standstill and we are ushered out. I carry An Meng to our luggage and sit him against one of our trunks. Lily is paying the men for the transport. It's warm and airless by the river, and there's no shelter or shade. Adding to our dilemma, there is no vessel or barge in sight. Lily hurries off to make enquiries and returns frustrated.

'The next barge isn't leaving until evening. There will be a queue.'

'We have to get An Meng out of the sun.'

We move two of our trunks against a wall and I lift him across to the small pool of shade. An Meng sleeps. I place my jacket behind him and ease his head against it. Lily tries to give him more water.

Getting on the barge is difficult. The long wait on the river dock has exhausted An Meng and his breathing is now short and laboured. Lily has engaged two young men who have been able to find a stretcher for him. Between the three of us, and with many exaggerated hand signals, we get An Meng onto the crowded barge. We have secured a small area for him to rest. We place thick items of clothing under the stretcher to form padding on the hard deck. An Meng looks tiny, childlike. My eyes smart at the sight. He takes a few sips of water from Lily but shakes his head when she offers him food. He closes his eyes and we know he is very weak.

The barge moves slowly forward.

'Are you all right, Lily?' She is pale, and dark shadows appear under her eyes.

She brings her fingers to her eyes. 'Yes and no,' she says.

The evening brings a gentle cool breeze out on the water and a sense of calm. We are relieved to be finally on the move.

Taking turns to watch An Meng, we doze sporadically, surrounded by jumbled boxes, luggage and other sleeping people. A couple of hours into the trip, I am awake whilst Lily sleeps, and I watch the dark sky above us as the barge eases its way down the inky river.

An Meng wakes and reaches out for me. I duck down towards him in an instant, straining to hear what he says.

'You…look after…Lily.'

'I will,' I say. Anything to reassure him, though he must know she will be looking after me more than I can look after her.

'She is…good girl.'

I take his hand, and soon he falls back to sleep, his face more peaceful.

The night turns cold and Lily wakes. We put on extra clothes to keep warm and cover An Meng with a blanket that Lily smuggled from the ship, whispering so no one else wakes.

'It is so beautiful,' I say to her, pointing to the starry sky above us, the black river around us. She smiles, and soon joins An Meng in sleep. But I can't sleep. Even now, I still must pinch myself to believe that I'm sitting on a barge heading up the Pearl River. Ted comes to mind and a warm flood of affection washes over me. I wish he was here now; he would know what to do. He is always good in a difficult situation. I dropped a letter in the ship's postal box this morning before disembarking. I will write again when we arrive in Canton. I fall asleep.

When I next wake, I guess we have about two hours to travel before we arrive at Canton harbour. The night sky has clouded over. Without the stars it is darker.

An Meng hasn't moved. I inch closer and watch him for a few more seconds then quietly get to my feet. The old man is still. I touch his arm, his hand, and then finally try to rouse him. I swing around to Lily; she sleeps on. I turn back to him and place my hand on his chest. He isn't breathing. His face is gaunt and pale, his mouth gapes open and the narrow line of his jawbone juts forward. I realise he is no longer with us.

I look up, sending him on his way.

'*Lou pang yau*, old friend,' I whisper. 'You'll be home soon.'

I stand slowly, take a deep breath, then move across to where Lily is sleeping. She stirs as she senses movement next to her. Her eyes spring open and instantly she guesses something is wrong. I bend down to her.

'It's An Meng.'

Lily is swiftly at the old man's side. She touches his face for a second, then looks disbelievingly at me. Her eyes travel back to the still form of An Meng. Her face contorts as she weeps silently. I wrap my arm around her shoulder, and she leans against me. I feel the tremble of her body. We stand together in a comforting embrace, with An Meng's body lying at our feet. I can only begin to understand what this must feel like for Lily. She has known him for most of her life and he loved her like his own child.

No one has noticed what's happened; luckily most are still sleeping or dozing. The two lads Lily hired to help stretcher An Meng on board are also still fast asleep. I try to collect my thoughts quickly.

'We have to get the stretcher ready to leave the barge. Will your family know what to do, Lily?'

'Yes, Uncle will help us sort it out. You are right, Knill, we must get him home.' Her voice breaks. 'The funeral is most important.'

'We have to pretend that he is still alive – that way we can get him off the barge without any fuss.' I'm concerned what would happen if the barge operators knew there was a dead person aboard.

'The boys will help, as long as they get paid well.'

We straighten An Meng's body on his stretcher, then, discreetly, Lily pulls the blanket higher to cover most of his face. We sit guarding his body as the first silver rays of morning light appear in the sky. The passengers around us begin to prepare for arrival in Canton. Lily and I stay until most have disembarked before we attempt to leave. The two young helpers wait patiently to resume their duties of carrying An Meng's stretcher. Faces averted, they say nothing. However, we suspect they know exactly what has taken place.

34

'How long will it take for him to get here?' I ask, after Lily has sent a rickshaw rider with a message to her uncle.

'Within the hour, I think. He and his family originally lived a few streets away. But he has a new house now closer to the city. There are many new modern colonial properties in Canton. His is one of them.'

'Why did he move?'

'They lived like many other Cantonese families, in small houses close to each other. Uncle's business is now very successful and so with it have come the trimmings of wealth.'

'Are they happy living in a new area or do they miss their old neighbourhood?'

'I don't think it's like that. You see, Uncle likes to display success for others to witness. A new, larger house is proof that he is moving up in the world.'

'Does your uncle have another name?'

'It is Ah Sheng, but everyone calls him Uncle. When I began to call him that as a small child, he liked it. And now everyone follows suit.' *Uncle*. I can do that. It is still strange to my Australian ear to call Chinese people by their full name, but it is customary, Lily tells me, and I will get used to it. It is different for Joseph and Lily, who have been in Australia a long time and have anglicised their names.

As we wait, Lily cranes her neck towards the road leading to the dock. The young men who assisted us sit cross-legged close by but avoid eye contact with us.

Within half an hour, Uncle arrives, climbing out of a shiny black car – a Buick. A truck with an open tray pulls up behind the car, and three young men step from it.

Uncle is a bustling, red-faced man wearing small wire-rimmed glasses. 'Li Ling,' he calls, coming towards us with outstretched arms.

He welcomes Lily with affection and glances over her shoulder at me. She cries hard then, and Uncle rubs her back as he hugs her. His three sons look away. Lily composes herself, wipes her eyes and turns to me.

'Uncle, this is Knill.' She then introduces me to her cousins, Ah Jian, Ah Qing and Ah Houjin. They stand back, not sure how to act towards me. Especially under the circumstances.

'*Fun ying heui*. Welcome to Canton,' Uncle says, shaking my hand.

'*Néih hóu*,' I say.

Uncle turns to An Meng's body and bows with his hands together in front of him, a small still moment. Then he instructs his sons to lift the stretcher onto the truck.

'What is going to happen, Uncle?' Lily asks.

She has allowed Uncle to take over responsibility for An Meng. Standing beside her, I feel her trembling as she watches the stretcher being carefully placed in the truck.

'The driver will take An Meng to Hiyang today,' Uncle says. 'You two come with me.' He gently places his arm across Lily's shoulder. 'We will go to Hiyang in two days for the funeral.'

We start to collect our luggage and Ah Houjin, the youngest of the brothers, quickly steps forward and gives me a generous smile before lifting our trunks into the boot of the car. The two older brothers hover in the background and watch as their father gives orders. Lily is holding her hand across her forehead and it's clear that the pressure of the last twenty-four hours is starting to show.

Uncle arranges for the two helpers to be paid and buys them a barge fare back to Hong Kong.

I shake hands with the pair; they look surprised, but they smile politely. We made a good connection despite the language barrier. As they leave, they turn and wave.

Uncle drives us through crowded streets. People swarm across the roadways, and rickshaws swerve and pick their way through spaces that seem impossible. The morning sun bounces off the fronts of old buildings, which form a wall of endless windows and shutters. The noise is like Hong Kong – the sound of China.

We arrive at Uncle's house and his sons, who travelled from the wharf by rickshaws, are already there. Lily looks exhausted but has a way of remaining calm and gracious with her relatives. Food and drink is offered and then a chance to rest. Our trunks have been taken to rooms on the first floor.

'Are you feeling unwell, Lily?' I ask as we climb the stairs.

'I need to rest and some time to think about An Meng. I must also write to my father. He will be shocked.' She blinks back the tears that have been lurking all day. As we stand together on the landing, Lily turns to me and places her hand on my arm.

'I am grateful you were with me, Knill.' She smiles and then quickly walks to her room. The feeling of her touch fades slowly.

In my room, I find gilt-edged wall tapestries and a bright multicoloured rug that dominates the floor. Puffed pillows sit, welcoming, at the bedhead and a silk quilt in vibrant colours drapes the bed. The room reminds me of Robina's account of Fong Choon's house in Australia, with its big bed and exotically coloured quilt. On a table close to the bed sit tiny teacups and a teapot.

I'm conscious of and appreciate the special treatment that I'm being given as a guest in Uncle's house but I'm not so sure that Uncle is pleased that I'm here. He spoke to Lily on the drive from the wharf but excluded me from the conversation by speaking in Cantonese most of the time. Need I worry? I brush it aside. It is nothing compared with the sadness Lily is carrying with such dignity. Growing up in Australia, a world so different to the one her parents knew, can't have been easy. Losing her mother as a young child under those circumstances is unimaginable. And now she has An Meng's death to grieve. She is so strong and capable and yet An Meng asked me to look after her.

In the quiet room, the last twenty-four hours can be released for me also. A hot, swimming feeling of tiredness and sadness washes over me. For An Meng, who did not live to see his village and family again. And for Rhoda, who looked, deliriously, for her lost daughter.

35

It's unseasonably warm as Uncle, Lily and I set out for Hiyang. I'm hot in my suit, and hope it gets cooler as we drive into the countryside. Mountains appear ahead. They line the broad landscape like muted pieces of a jigsaw. Terraced, lush market gardens emerge as the road climbs towards the village. Smaller gardens along the roadside are tended by the families.

The workers bowed over the fields trigger a childhood memory – an old man named Ah Fat, a Chinese market gardener who lived in Castlemaine. He had a good voice and was prone to singing. He could be found most days stooped over his perfectly spaced rows of carrots, cabbages and onions. I went there often with Ted to buy our vegetables. What happened to Ah Fat? I must ask Ted about him in my next letter.

The sun disappears behind a cloud, but a sullen humidity hangs low as the mountain range nears. The sultry day stretches before us and the narrow winding road slows our progress as Uncle carefully manoeuvres his black car up the steep rise. It becomes obvious that Uncle's driving experience is minimal, and the new car is creating tension for him. I'm surprised at just how quickly the scenery is changing. There is no comparison between the dense, busy Canton streets and the rugged mountainous terrain that is beginning to enclose us.

Hiyang is a welcome sight. The village is dotted with small houses hugging clearways and built at odd angles into the rugged hills. The villagers watch as we pass.

'The kids look scared,' I say to Lily.

'The villagers don't see many cars and the children run away from them.'

Some of the children scamper to their houses, to the safety of adults, but their small faces peep from stone door-ways as we pass.

'They know why we are here. The village is already in mourning for An Meng.'

Uncle waves to a group of people standing by the road-side as he parks the car. 'We can walk from here. The road is too narrow for the vehicle.' Uncle seems relieved to be abandoning the car to walk up the narrow road ahead.

We come to a house belonging to An Meng's relatives: his brother, two cousins and three nieces. The nieces appear to be about the same age as Lily and me. Their eyes dart between Lily, Uncle and me, as if not sure what to do next.

'*Néih hóu*,' I say as they nod towards me. I wish I'd been a better student for An Meng, had learnt more than a few words of Cantonese. But Lily nods her quiet approval, as they all gather around, speaking rapidly.

'They are welcoming you, Knill. They appreciate that the son of Fong Choon helped bring An Meng home to them.'

'They know Fong Choon?'

'Yes, of course. He has connections with this village.'

'Does he come here?'

'Sometimes. The family have just told Uncle that he was here yesterday to pay his respects.' Lily looks at me cautiously.

'He was here yesterday? Why didn't he wait?'

'Knill, don't ask questions, it's not the right time. Fong Choon has his own way of doing things, no one questions him.'

It's becoming clearer that I have much to learn but I hold my tongue for the time being.

'An Meng's family is honoured that you are here today,' Lily says.

So that is why Uncle insisted that I come to the village. My link to Fong Choon holds some sort of significance, both to Uncle and to the villagers. I nod respectfully and hope I don't make mistakes. I'm thankful for Lily by my side.

An Meng's coffin lies in the courtyard. It is simple, wooden, with a curved lid that brings to mind the humps of a camel. Colourful bowls of fruit and rice sit in front of it.

Lily touches my arm. 'An Meng's relatives have covered mirrors and some windows with red paper so that the reflection of the coffin is not sighted.'

In the corner of the room, I notice the first of the red paper. 'Not sighted?'

'It can cause bad luck or death to another person in the family.'

It's a sad day for Lily – the saddest of days. However, gone are her tear-filled eyes. She is walking taller and appears determined to see this through for An Meng and his family, who fuss over her and treat her with fondness. My admiration for her grows daily.

Mourners begin to gather and prepare for An Meng's last ceremony.

'The people in the white mourning robes are his relatives,' Lily explains.

Lily is also given one to wear. She puts it on and one of An Meng's nieces helps her tie it at the back.

The family, in their white flowing clothes, burn incense at the foot of the coffin. Thin trails of smoke drift skyward.

'It is a sign of respect to light incense for the deceased,' Lily whispers. 'Would you like to light one?'

I step forward with her and take a stick of incense.

'An Meng would smile to see you do this, Knill.' I think I see tears at the edge of her eyes but she turns away.

'It's you he would be so proud of, Lily.' We both blink and step back from the coffin.

Relatives and neighbours quietly burn joss paper, and the remnants float upwards, burning black before dissolving into white ash. A Buddhist monk is chanting a prayer for the dead, over and over, a melody that rises and falls, and lingers. I'm mesmerised by the beauty of it. After that, flute-like music wavers in the background. Some of the mourners wail and cry as the coffin is finally led away to a hillside cemetery. The journey to the cemetery is slow. More incense is burnt and An Meng's family walk at the front of the procession with their hands resting on his coffin. Lily walks with them and Uncle and I follow. At the site of An Meng's final resting place, a low table laden with food sits in front of his grave. Lily tells me that food is considered a powerful link with ancestors and the gods.

Finally, An Meng is laid to rest. He would be glad, I think, this quiet man, to be buried here, in soil he knows so well. His quest to be home brings Castlemaine to mind and the landscape I know better than any other. The cricket ground, crackling and dry in the summer heat, and yet as kids we flocked there after school to hit balls and stir up mini dust clouds until teatime. Playing tiggy in the back-yard with Will and Eugene, and Rhoda calling from the back door to be careful of her garden beds. Rabbiting with Ted in the bush, setting traps in the evening and going back the next day to check the catch. Sometimes when we were there I'd pull leaves from the lower branches of the eucalypts just to crush them in my hand and inhale the sharp exhilarating smell of the bush. I think of Rhoda's funeral, the roses on her coffin, the hymns echoing through the little church. The importance of being where you belong.

One of An Meng's nieces hands me a white towel.

'To express thanks to the mourners,' Lily whispers.

Afterwards, there is a banquet to honour An Meng. An abundance of food. The more food, Lily tells me, the more esteem there was for the deceased. I have no idea what some of the dishes are but the aroma is mouth-watering. We haven't eaten since breakfast time.

Lily and I move between the banquet tables, where large bamboo steamers hold an array of steamed buns. Light and fluffy, they are filled with sweet meats, chicken and pork. There are bowls of large duck eggs, a luxury in the village. The tiny corn cakes are delicious and I go back for a second helping. Laughing at me, Lily tells me they are a secret recipe. Transparent noodles and bamboo shoots are piled high on oval platters. The last dish to be brought out is rice: white, fluffy and plentiful.

The family and villagers seem proud to be partaking in this special feast. They are, however, subdued and I understand that the state of mourning has begun.

The family are deep in conversation. Lily tells me they are reminiscing about An Meng, his parents, and those before them. At times, I see them watching me, and they smile and nod. My eyes keep returning to the hill where the cemetery sits higher than the village. The peaceful quiet is occasionally interrupted by a lone birdsong that breaks through the still landscape.

'A hard day for you, Lily.'

'I'm sad that An Meng was unable to see the beautiful valley of Hiyang one more time. How he would have loved to look up to the mountains and to cherish the sunset once more in the land of his ancestors.'

'Yes,' I say, and squeeze her hand. It is warm under mine.

'At least he is home,' she says. 'An Meng is finally home.'

36

The sky darkens over Canton the following day and takes on a veiled appearance. There is relief in having carried out An Meng's last wishes but we are tired. A full day passes, in which Lily looks pale, another night, and then we wake with more energy.

Over breakfast of steaming noodles and plates of sizzling pork and chicken and delicious small white dumplings, Lily tells me that we will soon be going to Shanghai. We must wait a couple of days for Uncle to be able to leave his business to travel with us.

'Tell me about Uncle,' I say.

Uncle remains a mystery to me. There are times when he is friendly and engaging; at other times he scowls over the smallest detail.

'Aunty Bai Chen died five years ago. She was a wonderful person and I loved coming to see her. The boys and

Uncle miss her, not that they talk about her much. I think it makes them too sad.'

'Uncle moved to the new house after your aunty died?'

'Yes, one year after.'

'A new start?'

'Maybe. Uncle's business is based in the centre of Canton near the old wall, not far from here. I think Uncle wanted to live closer to his work and, as I have told you, it's a step up.'

We drink several cups of light-coloured tea. At first, I found the Chinese tea bitter but now I'm surprised to find how much I enjoy the brew.

'What is this business of his?'

'He employs over twenty men to carry out contract road building and cleaning. The men sweep and water-spray the city roads in the new Canton area. Uncle is paid well by the new regional council, who make important decisions for Canton city.'

'And the business is large enough for Uncle to have his sons work for him?'

'Yes, Ah Jian and Ah Qing work in Uncle's new office. They manage the contracts and employ the men. They also supervise the workers. They ensure that the work is done to the satisfaction of the city hierarchy.'

'For someone who is successful, Uncle doesn't look like a happy man.'

'Uncle has many worries and is known as the family grump.' Lily smiles now, but explains that he works very long hours and that he's often tired and anxious. His sons are similar and mostly serious, except for Ah Houjin.

'I like Ah Houjin,' I say. 'I've seen him laughing and joking with you and his brothers.'

'Yes, he is fun, but he teases his older brothers. They get a bit tired of his antics. So does Uncle.'

'At least one family member has a good sense of humour.'

'Poor Ah Houjin – always the clown. But he's the one who tells me what is going on in the family. I worry that Ah Houjin will get into trouble with Uncle, if he's caught gossiping to me.'

'Has he told you anything about Fong Choon?'

'He told me that Uncle is still unhappy with Fong Choon because he left Canton and made his home in Shanghai.'

'That was a long time ago.'

'Yes, but many people rely on Fong Choon in Canton. Uncle is one of them.'

'I'm finding this all a bit difficult to follow.'

'It must seem odd, but that's the Chinese way, Knill. You will soon start to work it out.'

Lily's smile to me is sweet. She is different in China too: she's outgoing and laughs more. I like it that she trusts me enough to discuss the family. It makes me feel less alone somehow.

It seems a long time since I left Australia. In fact, it's only ten weeks, but it might as well be ten years. What's happening back home? What are Will and Eugene up to? More evenings at the pub? More of the things they know and love? And Ted? It's hard to think of him alone in Castlemaine.

'Come, Knill,' Lily says. 'You look as if you are thinking too hard. I must show you something of Canton.'

37

We take to the streets of Canton in a rickshaw. We are pulled along the dusty road by a swarthy runner. Considering the cool weather, he's lightly dressed; the legs of his trousers flap around his spindly shins. When he smiles he exposes blackened gums, devoid of teeth. His eyes reveal a hard existence. How long has he been dragging people around Canton? Yonghan Road stretches before us, the hub of shopping and local activity.

'It's the modernisation of Canton,' Lily calls from my side. 'There used to be an old marketplace next to that wall. It's been demolished.'

The newly paved street is throbbing with people. I'm reminded of ants swarming and crisscrossing nests in the Australian bush. Carts are being pulled along and rickshaw owners stand in groups to the side of the road waiting for fares.

Lily wants to go to a department store recommended by Ah Houjin. It has only recently opened. 'We can walk from here, Knill. There are things to see along the way.'

We start out on foot. I follow Lily closely, not wanting to let her out of my sight for fear of losing her amongst the crowd. She swings around, her face relaxed and free. It's the happiest I've seen her since we arrived. Despite the immense sadness of An Meng's death, there is now a sense of relief settling over Lily. Ensuring he was returned to his village for the funeral was a difficult task. With this accomplished and his life honoured she is feeling less responsible.

A narrow street unfolds ahead of us. It's choking with banners and signs covered in colourful Chinese symbols. Storekeepers stand languidly beside their wares. Hundreds of fabric shoes are packed tightly together in containers and shelves of boxes are piled higher than the makeshift display stands. Bowls and teapots are stacked to wobbling heights on rough planks, threatening to collapse at any time. The smell of spicy food being cooked is as strong as at the Hong Kong port.

Above the shopfronts, large sails of fawn canvas wave on bamboo rods, forming a massive moveable canopy along the narrow street. An open gutter runs crookedly along the blocks of grey stone that provide a walking path. At times, we are jostled when the crowd thickens or the walkway narrows as laneways intersect. Lily takes the crowd in her stride.

'Not so fast, Lily. I don't want to be lost in one of these laneways.' I'm trying to joke, but the truth is I feel hopelessly out of place. I'm the outsider here, a strange face in a crowd of familiar faces. All my life I've felt different, but not this different. The nuances of China are lost to me, even if I have a thirst to know.

The noise is deafening. Words are all around me but I'm in a sea of silence. To hear but not comprehend is an isolating experience. I am watched. No doubt the locals wonder what this tall stranger is doing accompanying a petite Chinese woman. They gape and comment as we walk by. Our smart Western clothes make us stand out in the crowd. Lily ignores any reactions from the Cantonese. On previous visits to China, she was accompanied by An Meng on excursions like this, or sometimes her uncle.

'Today is a free day,' she says. There is laughter in her voice. Uncle is busy with his business and her cousins are occupied at their office.

'Bloody noisy place, Lily.'

'This is real China, noisy but happy.'

At the end of the street we find the department store. It's three storeys high with large ornate stairways. More orderly than the street, less busy. I'm intrigued to see that they sell hundreds of lines of pottery, rows and rows of brightly coloured pots, cups and teapots. There is a full floor of fabrics: bright silks, satins and printed cotton on long rolls. Shoppers swarm around the displays, talking in the piercing voices that I'm becoming accustomed to. The language tones are expressive, but for the ears of a non-speaker the words remain a mystery. The shop attendants whisper as we pass. Lily is not concerned. She's having such a good time, smiling and nodding as she inspects the rows of clothing, purses and slippers. Soon we have several parcels, including a teapot to take back to Australia for Ted. As I'm paying for Ted's present, I catch sight of a stand displaying hundreds of tiny perfume bottles. Every imaginable colour and shape is on the stand. Whilst Lily is occupied with beaded purses, I buy her a surprise gift. An opaque squat green bottle with a bronze atomiser at the neck and delicate pink embossed flowers at the base. Now I'm the one to feel excited, and I slip it into my coat pocket.

Lily decides that we should visit a teashop for a traditional Chinese tea ceremony. To reach the old tearooms we climb a flight of rickety stairs. I must duck as I follow Lily, and she giggles at me when I bump my head on the low doorframe. I grin back at her and hold my brow in pretence of having injured myself.

'*Néih hóu.*'

A shy young attendant ushers us to a table by an open shuttered window, stealing quick glances at us as she waits for us to be seated. I'm getting used to these subtle and sometimes not so subtle looks. The Cantonese are curious but polite, and when they see that I've noticed them watching me, they quickly turn their heads away.

Archaic and unadorned, the teashop is filled with a delicious spicy aroma. Lily orders tea and dumplings. Soon the attendant comes back with a tray and begins the ceremony.

She pours boiling water over the cups and upturns them before filling the teapot with water. The tea is then ceremoniously poured from container to container until the colour is considered ready. We watch in silence until we are permitted to taste the special brew.

'What do you think, Knill, do you like the tea? It's made from camellia. The locals say it is the best tea in China.' Lily watches closely as I sip the red-tinged tea from the tiny cup.

'Chinese tea is worth travelling to China for.'

Lily smiles at me, and drinks her tea.

'There are many ceremonies here,' I say, gesturing to the teapot.

'China is an old country,' Lily says. 'With lots of old ways, both good and bad. Change is slow.'

I wonder what Lily's life would be like if she lived here. The same? Would she feel free to sit with me in a tea parlour?

'I would have to comply with Chinese traditions,' Lily says when I ask her. 'It's different in Australia – my father encourages me to be strong about what I think and believe. I can be myself.'

'In what way, Lily?'

'He says that smart people should seek an education. He thinks I should study law and work alongside him.'

'Would you like to study law?' Lily never ceases to surprise me with her revelations.

'Yes, but it's difficult if you're a woman, more so if you are a Chinese woman!'

'Does that mean it can't happen?'

'No, but it will require me to fight with those who are prejudiced against women.'

'In China?'

'Not just China, Knill. Australia also has strict ideas about the roles of women. And that does not include being a lawyer.' Lily laughs.

'They make it hard?'

'It's hard to get admission to law school in Melbourne. Women can apply, although few do. Even if they complete their studies they find it difficult to practise.'

'But you could practise with your father.'

'Yes, but I have to be accepted to study first.'

'So, you have already applied to study law?'

'Yes. I'm waiting to hear if I'm to be admitted.'

The food arrives, but it takes me a moment to pay attention. I'm still taking in what Lily told me. Then I notice the strange-looking object placed before me. It is nothing resembling the dumplings we ate on the ship and at Uncle's house. This is large and bulbous and inside is a steaming clear soup.

Lily tells me to push my ceramic straw through the top of the dumpling and suck up the soup. 'These are my favourites.'

I pull a face, attempting to hide my trepidation. 'And they are my favourites.' I point to the almond cookies on the counter of the teashop. But I drink the soup, which is strange at first and then delicious.

We eat seconds and sip the fragrant tea, ordering the biscuits to add to our feast. I purchase a box to take home to Uncle.

'Now,' Lily says. 'You must see the Bund River.'

I love the Bund, with its wide expanse of murky water flanked by old Canton buildings on each side. We wander along, laden with Lily's parcels, Ted's teapot, the almond biscuits and the secret present. I can't remember a day I've enjoyed more. And Lily is the happiest I've seen her. But after we have been walking for some time, Lily checks her watch and her mood changes.

'It is later than I realised. Uncle will be angry if we are not at home when he returns from work.'

'Why will he be angry?'

'He thinks we should not be out alone without a local guide. He feels responsible for me when I'm in China.'

'But that's ridiculous. I'm with you and we are adults, aren't we?'

On the way home in a rickshaw, Lily is tense beside me. Nothing I say seems to help. Back at Uncle's house we find him home and in a rage.

'Where have you been? Gone so long.'

'Uncle,' Lily says, 'we've been to Yonghan Road, just shopping.'

A heated argument begins instantly. Once again, when any real discussion occurs it happens in Cantonese, so I find myself watching but not understanding. Uncle is not going to be calmed easily. He's waving his hands in the air and shouting. He bellows and protests at Lily and scowls at me as if to say I'm to blame. Just when he appears to settle, the yelling resumes.

I move between him and Lily. 'I don't know what you are shouting about, but you should stop now.' My voice is louder than intended.

Uncle storms from the room.

Later in the evening, Lily explains that Uncle is struggling with the responsibility of looking after us.

'He is worried that my father will hold him responsible if anything untoward happens to me. He is also concerned that you and I should not spend time on our own. He's old-fashioned, Knill.'

'He doesn't approve of me because I'm not Chinese?'

'Maybe, but it's not considered correct for young people of different genders to spend time together without a chaperone.' A blush makes its way across Lily's delicate features.

'But we are not doing anything wrong, Lily.'

'No, but it's the custom, Knill. You will soon understand Uncle. He is often tense, but he means well.'

'His yelling is ridiculous.'

'Yes, but he's under pressure. You have to remember he also carries the heavy burden of caring for the son of Fong Choon.'

'I don't want him to feel any responsibility for me…I'll tell him so tomorrow.'

'But it is expected. It's the custom.'

I have not given thought to the idea of having a chaperone, until now. It seems it wasn't such a problem to be alone together on the barge when An Meng died, but now a mere social outing has caused a major upset.

38

The shadow of the liquidambar falls across the verandah, shielding the house from the harsh afternoon sun. Ted sits wearily on the bench in the shade and smiles as he remembers the fuss that Rhoda made about having a liquidambar planted in the first place. She had wanted it closer to the house and he had wanted it further out.

'They grow to become massive trees, Rhoda.'

'It will be years before it's large enough to be a problem.'

But Ted won that argument, one of his few victories. He normally gave in to Rhoda's way of thinking. But that day he stood his ground and insisted the tree be planted further out. The hole was dug and in went the small tree. Today it's a monster, with its glorious branches as wide as the front of the house and its lush green foliage towering above the roofline.

He looks up to see the postman at his letterbox.

'Hot day on the bike, Ray?'

'It's a stinker.'

Ted collects two letters and goes back to his shady seat as Ray pedals off. The church newsletter – he opens it, looks at it briefly and then stuffs it back in its envelope and fans his sweating face with it. The other letter sits beside him on the bench until he notices the overseas stamp. His shaking hands rip at the fine envelope. Instantly, he has forgotten the heat and the postman pedalling up the hill.

January 1922

Dear Ted,

I've never been away at Christmas before. It must have been sad without Rhoda this year; still I know that Uncle Stan and Aunty Kate would have jollied you along. We were getting ready to land so the celebrations were basic, and anyway not all people on board celebrate Christmas. I'll make up for it next year.

In my last letter I mentioned that An Meng was sick. Ted, he became seriously ill and died just after we left Hong Kong. It was a terrible time, particularly for Lily as the two of them were like family. We attended his funeral in a small village outside Canton. I could never have prepared myself for that experience. I went as a guest of Lily and her uncle. I wasn't at all familiar with the Chinese customs, but I felt an odd sort of belonging on the mountainside of that small village. The ceremony was emotional and moving. It made me think a lot about the day we buried Rhoda, Ted. Sometimes I still can't believe it. I'm sure there are times when you feel the same.

Lily and I have been exploring Canton together. It is an amazing place, loud and colourful. Sometimes I pinch myself to believe I'm here.

We go to Shanghai tomorrow. At last I'll meet the man who says he is my father. Well, he might be my birth father but not my real father, Ted. You will always hold that place for me.

I've heard things about Fong Choon, but will reserve my judgement until I meet him. Everyone, it seems, knows about this man. Makes me feel nervous. Lily tells me to make up my own mind. I suspect she's right. She has excellent judgement. Lily also says that I have Chinese ways. I laugh when she says that. She is probably just being polite.

I will write to you from Shanghai and let you know about the meeting with Fong Choon. I trust you are well. Please pass on my greetings to Uncle Stan and Aunty Kate. I will send a letter to Will and Eugene as well.

Yours sincerely and with love,
Knill

Ted reads the letter again, slower the second time. He folds it and puts it back in its envelope. There is something about Knill that sounds different. All this talk about China and an 'odd sort of belonging'. The shade from the liquidambar is now falling long over the house and garden, the heat of the day is dissipating. Ted sits on the bench for a long time going over Knill's comments in his mind. Although reassured by Knill's letter, he holds a silent fear. What if he doesn't come back? What if his sense of belonging only grows? Still, he's finding his way in the world, Ted thinks. And, if finding his way in the world isn't enough, he sounds like he's mightily smitten with this young Lily person.

39

The train stops unexpectedly for long periods of time without any apparent reason, sometimes at small stations, sometimes in the middle of nowhere. People mill around at the stations: some alight and others board, but many simply crowd around the train. I've learnt, since coming to China, to watch and wait, and sometimes the reasons for things become obvious, though often it is Lily who ends up enlightening me. However, she is also unsure why the train is stationary. As we wait, Uncle sleeps, grunting loudly at intervals. This amuses two small, wide-eyed children sitting across the aisle, who giggle with each of Uncle's snores.

The seats are narrow and uncomfortable. Small windows are dotted along the inside wall of the carriage but provide little exposure to the outside world and add to the feeling of being closed in.

The trip to Shanghai is tiresome and Uncle is particularly testy. When awake he speaks curtly to Lily and ignores me.

'What's today's problem?' I ask, when Lily and I are buying snacks from the hawkers at one of the stations.

'Uncle is worried about his meeting with Fong Choon.'

'He's worried! What's he concerned about?'

'Uncle would say…everything!' She throws back her head and laughs.

I like it when Lily makes fun of her family.

'Uncle and Fong Choon often disagree on business matters. They usually sort it out, but it upsets Uncle. He says he's getting too old for all these family matters.'

'Fong Choon sounds difficult too.'

'Oh, it's not just Fong Choon, it's also my father who Uncle gets upset about.'

'So why does he agree to their requests? It seems odd that he continues to be involved in things that worry him so much.'

'Uncle feels indebted to my father and to Fong Choon because they both gave him money to start his business.'

'So they expect him to pay it back by doing as they ask? Is that how it works?'

'Yes and no, I suppose. In China, paying back is expected, and that often includes being loyal and carrying out favours.'

I nod but I don't fully understand Lily's explanation. I can't differentiate between cultural differences, family patterns and secrets. The train rattles on. Uncle snores. Lily reads. And with each mile I come closer to meeting my father.

In Shanghai, we are staying at the Astor Hotel, set on the north corner of the busy Bund and Waibaidu Bridge. Uncle tells me that we will be here for five or six days, depending on Fong Choon's arrangements. I have learnt to be patient with Uncle, not to ask too many questions, otherwise he becomes flustered and cranky. I'm just pleased to be in Shanghai at last. The hotel caters for Westerners as well as wealthy Chinese travellers and it is clearly expensive. Under normal circumstances, I would never be able to afford to stay here, but I immediately adore the Astor, with its grand and towering corner facade of sand-colour brick, full views across the Bund, and arched ground-floor windows. I've never seen such grandeur and elegance before.

The hotel provides a welcome distraction for me. Instead of worrying about Fong Choon, I admire the grand black marble steps leading to myriad passages and hallways. The timber walls lined with gilt-edged paintings, imposing and bold. Chinese wall hangings which grace the high walls above the timber panels. In the long corridors, the smell of cigars and tobacco.

In my room stands a high bed with a heavily embossed canopy on three sides. White pillows are stacked high at the head of the bed. My luggage has already been taken up, and I hang my clothes in the wardrobe, admiring the intricate carvings on the doors. Shutters open to reveal a bath and wash facilities. It's possible to bathe and view the Bund at the same time. The Salvation Army boarding house comes quickly to mind. 'Shanghai,' I whisper, exhaling.

The scene below the window transfixes me. The weather-beaten barges move without a ripple along the wide brown stretch of water. Smaller boats, with cargo packed at unstable angles, mark the river. The piercing voices of men, shrill whistles from the barges, the quick calls of the street traders below, and the modern sound of the throttles of motor cars rise to meet me as I stand watching. This really is the sound of China.

There is a gentle tap at my door. 'Knill,' Lily calls. 'Will you post a letter for me? It's to my father.'

'Of course.'

I close the shutters to a view I promise to explore later and prepare to return to the bustle of the foyer.

At the large mahogany desk I hand over Lily's letter to be posted. As soon as it leaves my hand I hear a familiar voice.

Molly Lau Hong, wearing a crimson silk dress and a matching woollen coat, is surrounded by assistants and a large number of trunks. Other guests watch as she shouts instructions for all to hear, sending the hotel porters into a flurry. It is a spectacle to enjoy. After long minutes, she catches sight of me.

'Knill McMillan, I thought I might see you here. Where is your lovely companion?'

I'm embarrassed to have the attention of the loudest woman in the hotel lobby, but pleased to see someone I know. I move towards her.

'Lily is also here,' I say.

'Excellent. We can have tea together after I get this wretched luggage sorted.' Molly adjusts the rings on her fingers, then turns her attention to seeing that her boxes and cases are being carried upstairs. She waves to a young porter struggling with her oversized trunks. 'Careful, one at a time.' She clucks annoyance before turning back to face me. 'Tea at four, here in the foyer, Knill?'

'Yes, I'll ask Lily,' I say. 'But I must tell you that she has suffered a terrible blow since arriving. An Meng died the day after leaving the ship.'

'He died!' Molly's eyes widen.

I fill Molly in on all that has happened, so she won't blunder and hurt Lily with a cheery question as to An Meng's whereabouts. 'And then we made our way here,' I finish.

'Mm, you and Lily.'

'And her uncle.'

When Molly has finished asking questions and commiserating, she moves off to the clink of her glass beads as they swing across her bosom. I'm aware of others watching her as she flounces across the foyer. It seems the news of An Meng's death has barely touched her. But why should it be otherwise?

Molly is late to tea. Lily, looking rested, is wearing a pale blue dress with a small stand-up collar. A soft cashmere shawl is wrapped around her shoulders and her hair is pinned up in a tight knot behind her neck. Uncle is wearing a newly pressed suit and has taken time arranging his hair. It's parted finely on one side, which accentuates his receding hairline.

A few minutes after four Molly rushes down the stairs, now clad in flowing green silk, and floats across the room to us. She makes a fuss of Lily and nods to Uncle when I introduce him.

After we order tea, Molly says to Lily, 'Condolences on your loss. Knill informed me earlier.'

'Thank you,' Lily says. 'It was unexpected.'

'What did you do in Hong Kong?' I ask Molly, aware of how keen Lily is to change the topic of conversation. She is still finding it difficult to speak about An Meng's death.

Molly is happy to oblige and entertains us with stories about her Hong Kong social life and dinner parties, which were full of what Molly describes as 'fascinating people'.

Uncle's demeanour towards Molly is cool but polite. He joins in when necessary, but he clearly doesn't enjoy her company. Molly does not draw breath and gives little time for anyone else to speak. Lily continues to graciously listen to Molly's endless stories, but Uncle drifts off into his own thoughts and worries. Molly glances sideways at him, pulls a funny face and winks at me. If Lily sees this rudeness she pretends not to notice and places her cup back on the tray with a dignified smile.

Why exactly, I wonder, had I been pleased to see Molly again?

Right now, I wish that I could invite Lily to come walking on the Bund with me. That we could leave Uncle and Molly behind and, in the middle of noisy China, find some quiet.

40

Sleep is evasive; the muted sounds of Shanghai hold it at bay. When it finally comes, I dream.

Ted and Rhoda seem far away, their voices too faint to hear. I try to reach them, but my legs are heavy and I can't step forward. Coloured lights flash around me: bright, swirling reds and greens. I speak in a language I don't own. I am powerful as the owner of this foreign tongue. People admire me; they laugh and talk to me. Then the gentle sound of a violin drifts in. It drowns out my euphoria, as if chastising me for my boldness. Humbly, I allow the music to dominate. A tall, graceful woman in the distance waves, the slightest of gestures. I remain still as she moves towards me. Her face and long falling hair are familiar. I call to her but she fades and is gone.

Awake, I try to hold the vision of the woman's face. It escapes me, slips away to someplace irretrievable. The dream unsettles me. It takes me back to the time in Sydney, looking for Eliza. My questions. What would she be like? What would she think of me?

Restless, I throw back the soft bedcovers and pull open the shutters. I must immerse myself in the present not the past. The dark Shanghai night surrounds me. I stare into the night space, and it's then that I notice a flickering light in a window a few rooms down from me. It's Lily, standing by the window in her nightclothes. She looks as if she's crying. I consider going to her when she steps back into the room and the light disappears.

When I wake, my thoughts instantly return to Lily. I dress quickly and hope to catch her before breakfast. She is in the lobby, making her way to the door. I run to catch up with her.

'Lily. You're going out?'

She looks tired, her eyes duller than usual.

'For a walk,' she says, turning to go.

I'm not sure if I should follow.

'I'll walk with you?'

'If you like.'

I sense she wants to be alone but I persist. It's early and still cold. Lily is wearing a warm coat and gloves. I'm not dressed for outdoors but it doesn't matter. We walk in silence in the direction of the river.

'Are you unwell, Lily?'

'I'm well. Why do you ask?'

'I saw your light on late last night.'

Lily shrugs and keeps walking. I glance across at her and see that her eyes are shining. She is looking ahead, almost away from me. I place my hand on her arm. She stops still and we face each other on the cold Shanghai footpath.

'Lily, there is something wrong.'

Tears appear on her cheeks and she closes her eyes to compose herself. She flicks back her hair and takes a deep breath.

'There is so much that makes me sad.' Her voice breaks a little. 'Every time I come to China there are family problems. Father has no idea how difficult it is for me to come here and act politely, as if their behaviour doesn't upset me. They confide in me and sometimes I feel responsible to keep the peace.'

People are moving around us on the footpath. A nearby hawker watches us as he flips over his charred corncobs. Smoke rises from his fire and the inviting aroma permeates the air. A man selling chestnuts chants his sales pitch to others nearby and we stand motionless.

'I thought you enjoyed coming here.'

'Yes and no. But this time it's extra hard.'

'You mean because of An Meng?'

'Yes, of course, but there are other things too.' Lily begins to walk again. I fall in beside her.

'What other things?'

'Sometimes when I come to China I think about my mother and try to imagine her here with me.'

'I had no idea…'

'I miss her but I can't remember her.'

'Does your father know about this?'

'That's the problem. Father doesn't talk about her, it upsets him. Stay strong, focus on the future, he says.'

'Funny he thinks that, Lily. Because the past is why the two of us are here.'

The cold air stings our faces but it's energising to be out of the confines of the hotel. As we walk, my arm brushes Lily's shoulder. She's shivering.

'Is there something else, Lily?'

She doesn't answer but after a moment she stops again.

In her eyes I see many things I am not sure of. Confusion and pain and…something else. My heart does a slow flip in my chest as I see her, really see her. The gentle curve of her face. Her warm dark eyes. What is in her eyes I know is in mine also. What do I say? What can I say? What must I say?

Lily saves the moment. Her expression says – *not now*.

'We should get back soon, Uncle will be looking for us,' Lily says.

'Has he been difficult again?'

'No, but let's not give him a reason.'

The tantalising smells from the food peddlers reminds us that we haven't had breakfast. Lily is smiling again.

'I tell you all my woes, Knill. Thanks for listening.'

'I'll always listen to you, Lily,' I say as I wrap my arm around her shoulder and pull her to me.

Uncle tells me that the meeting with Fong Choon is set for the following day. Finally, I will meet the man who has brought me halfway around the world. It will be at a restaurant near the Peace Hotel. Lily and Uncle are to join us for lunch but I'm to arrive earlier than the others so that we can meet alone. Fong Choon has everything worked out in fine detail.

'Why can't we meet at Fong Choon's home?' I ask.

'Fong Choon is very reserved, a formal man, and he always entertains people at restaurants,' Uncle explains. 'He rarely invites anyone to his home.'

I turn away from him and shrug my shoulders. 'I'm not anyone. Apparently, I'm his son!'

41

Early the next day, despite the bitter cold, I sit beside the Bund and watch the morning light filtering across the muddy water. I like Shanghai; it's different to Canton. Here I have time to think. I just want today's meeting with Fong Choon to be over, but still I don't feel prepared.

Rhoda's death flashes into mind, as it often does. Usually I fend it off, but today it won't stay away. I can't think about my mother without sorrow. What happened to her that early morning? Was it all too much? The way I reacted? Or were her own ghosts overwhelming her? I almost can't bear to think about her loss. Having a child and giving her away, and then adopting me when probably all the time she wanted her own daughter. And to think that Ted was unaware of the whole damn thing.

Did Eliza want me? She did at first, I know. But did her longing increase or diminish over the years? At least if she did die in the Sydney fire her sadness died with her.

In the park, elderly men are lined up and moving in unison. They move in a trancelike state, swaying from side to side, a few paces backward and then forward again. Gracefully, they imitate large birds with swooping, landing actions.

'Tai Chi. They do it every morning.' The clear voice of an Englishman breaks the silence. 'Ancient exercise – oldest form in the world, they say.'

I swing around to face a man who looks so much like Eugene it's uncanny. I'm thrilled to think that someone has spoken to me in precise English, and stand up from the bench.

'Knill McMillan,' I say.

'Anthony Millar. Are you Australian?'

'Yes, from Melbourne.'

'Been here in Shanghai long?'

'No. Arrived a couple of days ago.'

'China can be a strange place until one gets used to it.'

We chat on as the men continue their morning ritual. Anthony comes from Cornwall and works for the Bank of England.

'I've been in Shanghai for six months,' he says. 'What brings you here?'

'Family. I'm meeting my father here.'

It feels such an easy explanation, I'm surprised how simple it sounds.

Today, I meet my father.

42

Crimson and green dragon heads perch high on pillars beside the restaurant gates. The late morning chill hovers. Nearby, an old woman softly sweeps the dirt path with branches of flax. Her slow action is typical of the Shanghai people. A sinewy dog is lounging by the roadside. Its eyes follow me as I enter the grounds. I know the sweeping woman is watching me too.

Inside the gates is a lush, manicured garden, with a small murky pond tucked between the walkway and the restaurant. Waterlilies float idly at the edges. The tranquillity of the place is calming. I pause for a moment and breathe deeply. Familiar garden scents drift across my path. Variegated conifers and clumps of peonies, plants I know by name. Rhoda talked nothing but gardening when I was growing up and we spent countless hours looking at pictures in gardening books.

I arrive at a red door framed with purple miniature orchids in moss-covered pots. I hesitate for a moment, but I tell myself I need to do this now, it's what I've come to China for.

Despite the cold day my hands are clammy; I wipe beads of sweat from my forehead. The door opens and an attendant wearing a white tunic over black trousers ushers me into a lavish foyer. Another attendant comes forward and they bow excessively. I feel my face redden. It's obvious they are expecting me; their submissive behaviour makes me feel foolish. Averting their eyes, they escort me through an archway with crimson curtains tied back with gold toggles. A grand dining room stretches ahead. My heart races.

Then I see him. Standing tall across the room. Time slows as he moves towards me. Dressed in a dark suit and tie he looks almost out of place amongst the Oriental trappings of the restaurant. He extends his arm to shake my hand. I am conscious of my wet palms as I grip his strong hand. Fong Choon and I look at each other awkwardly but with immense curiosity. I can't take my eyes from him. He is real now. I take in the angular face and the dark penetrating eyes. I study the lines of age that have started to spread across his forehead, and his thin, greying, receding hairline.

'*Néih hóu,* hello. It is a pleasure to meet you, Knill. I have often wondered if it would ever happen.' He smiles as he watches me intently.

I search for my voice. '*Néih hóu.* Yes, a pleasure to meet you, sir.' I step back, but my eyes remain fixed on his face.

There is no doubt in my mind that I'm in the company of a very accomplished man and I find myself deferring to him.

'I understand you had some doubts about coming to China?'

'Yes.' My mouth is dry and I am mumbling. I wait for Fong Choon to take the lead in the conversation. I'm uncertain as to how I should address him. Is it wrong to say Fong Choon? I certainly can't call him Father.

'You have shown a great deal of character by coming to China to meet me.'

'Joseph Ah Sing was persuasive: you should give him the credit.'

Fong Choon laughs at my remark and I exhale as if I have just passed some test. I continue to search his face, looking for familiarity, looking for myself.

The attendants approach. They speak to Fong Choon, who appears to be ordering or giving instructions about the meal. They scuttle away, eager to please. Are they always nervous in Fong Choon's company or is it just today? Perhaps they too understand the importance of the occasion.

Fong Choon turns back to me. 'Have you been well looked after on your journey?'

'I've been in good company.'

'You were surprised to hear I was looking for you?'

'I didn't know you existed.'

'You are employed by the railways in Melbourne?'

'I resigned to make this trip.' I feel a little less over-whelmed now. I notice that Fong Choon tends to ask a question rather than comment on my replies. He's clearly in control.

'Please, sit.' Fong Choon points to the round table that seems to be set for too many people. 'You helped Lily when An Meng died?'

'Lily and I managed it together. It was sad for An Meng that he never made it home.'

Fong Choon nods in agreement. 'Thank you. Your efforts were appreciated by his family in Hiyang.'

He tells me briefly about his own two children in Shanghai. They are younger than me. I learn that his wife died a long time ago. Until this moment, I hadn't given much thought to his children or his wife. I hadn't asked Lily or Uncle for details about his family. I should have, but my focus had been on meeting the man who claimed to be my father.

'You will meet them soon,' Fong Choon tells me.

Almost on cue, two people arrive through the archway. They greet their father quietly. He nods and they stand awkwardly beside the table. They stare at me as I get up to meet them.

'Knill, let me introduce my son and daughter. This is Fong Wan and Fong Pen-Lee.'

They wait for me to speak. I can feel the knot in my stomach and the sweat under my suit jacket. My mouth is dry and my tongue is sticking to the roof of my mouth. To meet not only my father but two half-siblings is too much. I clumsily shake hands with Fong Wan. His features are similar to those of his father, and mine, for that matter.

'Hello, Knill,' Fong Wan says. 'I hope your journey has been satisfactory. It is a long way to come, especially to meet people you didn't know existed.' His English is perfect.

'Thank you. The journey was fine. And I sure didn't know you all existed, you have that right.' I smile at Fong Wan, uncertain how to interpret his comment.

Fong Pen-Lee watches but says nothing. She is slight for her fifteen years and flawless. Her hair is cut short and modern. She nods in acknowledgement of me but shows no warmth or friendliness. An awkward moment follows. Am I not welcome by Fong Choon's children? Of course, I have no idea how long they have known about me. My guess is they only discovered they had a half-brother when it was confirmed I was coming to China.

Several minutes later, Lily and Uncle arrive. I sigh with relief. I'm even pleased to see grumpy old Uncle as he walks to the table. Fong Choon smiles at Lily; he seems fond of her. His greeting for Uncle is a firm handshake and a businesslike nod. He then quietly suggests where we should sit. Uncle is placed between Fong Wan and Lily, and I am next to Fong Choon. Lily is seated across from me next to Fong Pen-Lee, whose sour demeanour changes remarkably as Lily squeezes her hand. Lily flashes me a reassuring smile. I still remember the feel of her as I put my arm around her shoulders.

The meal takes forever. Just when I think it's coming to an end, yet another enormous plate of food arrives. As the special guest, I'm expected to take the first serve of each plate that is brought to the table: small delicacies, tiny cabbage rolls piled high with a tart-tasting mince; shiny fried squid; beautifully wrapped rice rolls in neat rows; flat turnip cakes; and small dumplings. Despite Lily instructing me in how to use chopsticks in Canton, I am self-conscious and careful, especially with the others watching me so intently. I have no hunger and force the food into my mouth as the others feast with pleasure. I have no idea what Fong Choon is thinking about me. I want this formal lunch to be over as soon as possible.

No sooner are the previous plates cleared than more arrive: duck, tofu and pork dishes. They are steaming hot and garnished with spring onions, ginger and nuts. A large tureen of shark fin soup is placed before us. I can tell by the exclamations that this is a specialty. The soup is followed by bowls of white rice. I sit with my anxiety, my poor chopstick technique and an overfull stomach.

Fong Choon is quiet during the lunch. Since the arrival of the others, his friendliness towards me has turned to something more formal. Fong Pen-Lee talks to Lily and excludes everyone else from the conversation, but Lily occasionally glances at me with an encouraging smile. It becomes clear that there won't be any talk of Fong Choon's time in Australia today. Still, perhaps I'd hoped for too much at our first meeting; this is a conversation to be had between the two of us in private. But there's something not right in this family. Is it my presence that is affecting everyone? What do they think I want from them? After all, it was Fong Choon who summonsed me to China. I do understand the shock it would have been to Fong Wan and Fong Pen-Lee to suddenly find out about a half-brother who lives halfway across the world. I'll give them time to get used to me, I guess.

Occasionally I catch Fong Choon watching me. When this happens he slowly turns back to his food. Do I look like him? Do I feel any connection to him? I find it impossible to follow the flow of the conversations across the table or to concentrate. The volume and tone of their voices is disorienting. At times, they use English to accommodate me, but mostly they lapse into Cantonese.

'Tell us about Australia. What part are you from?' Fong Wan asks, but he doesn't seem to want to know.

'Victoria. Your father knows it well.' I can't resist this not-too-subtle barb and I watch as Fong Wan glances uncomfortably at Fong Choon. The older man does not respond.

'I don't know very much about your country at all,' Fong Wan says.

'Well, I'd rather hear about what you're doing in America.' I attempt to move the conversation to safer ground.

'I completed school this year. I'm going to begin studying medicine at the University of California…'

Fong Choon allows Fong Wan to carry the conversation and seems content to listen, though I can tell it makes Fong Wan nervous. By the time lunch ends, my temples are aching from the tension of concentrating on the strained relationships, food customs and stilted conversations. I can't make much sense of any of it.

43

My headache vanishes in the river air and, instead of retreating to my room at the Astor, I sit in the lobby, watching and thinking. The grand pillars in the hall are decorated with ornate vases of pink cherry blossom and its faint perfume drifts across the room, contributing to an air of giddy luxury. I marvel at the number of people who arrive and depart the hotel, all focusing on travel and business plans. I wonder what it's like to live like these people – they wear expensive clothes, have an entourage of assistants and travel around the world spending the sort of money that most people can only dream about. What would Rhoda and Ted think of it? Nothing good. I, too, have little admiration for the way of life being enacted before me; I see a falseness and a lack of fulfilment in it. Molly is a fine example, always busy shopping and socialising but doing nothing of substance.

A sudden discomfort hits me, and I twist in my chair as I realise there's little difference between me and the people I'm criticising. One of Rhoda's favourite sayings was that people in glass houses shouldn't throw stones. After all, I'm allowing Fong Choon to pay all my expenses. And I'm spending time socialising and being waited on by others. It doesn't feel right. This is not who I am. The sooner I conclude matters with Fong Choon the better. I want to go home and lead a normal life.

And there is Molly, bustling down the stairs towards me. I send her a silent apology for my thoughts about her. I'm hoping she has time to sit with me. I need to talk to someone about the lunch or I will go mad. Lily was whisked off by Pen-Lee to go shopping. And Uncle, despite his annoyance, dutifully accompanied them.

'Let's have some tea, I'm parched,' says Molly.

'I'll be in that. I could do with some different company.'

'Do I sense a disgruntled Knill?'

I laugh and instantly feel more relaxed. We order oolong tea before I tell Molly about the lunch.

'It's as if I'm just someone here on business.'

'Perhaps for him family *is* business.' Molly is unusually serious. 'And about Pen-Lee – she's only fifteen, Knill. You have to expect that she won't know how to act around a new big brother.'

'You might be right about that.'

'When do you see your father again?'

'Tomorrow. He's sending a car to take me to his house. I'm not looking forward to it.'

Molly pours herself some more oolong.

'Knill, I know it's none of my business, but I have heard some things about Fong Choon that perhaps you should know.'

'What have you heard?'

'There are people in Shanghai who believe he lives a strange life. He apparently travels between Hong Kong and Shanghai often and he's secretive about his personal life.'

'How do people know this?'

'Well, you know how people are…'

How could I not? I smile as an image of Rhoda flashes through my mind. She was always curious and surmising about others.

'It seems when Fong Choon's wife was alive they only attended a few formal functions together and she was rarely seen outside the family home.'

'Is that so unusual?' I ask, wondering where this is heading.

'It is understandable because Fong Choon's wife was ill, but it seems that she lived an isolated life for many years before her health problems became evident.'

'What were her health problems?'

'Some people say she suffered from melancholy and erratic behaviour. She was often unpredictable and had servants with her at all times. Sometimes she would shout and call out to people she didn't know, other times she would take to her bedroom for weeks on end.'

'What about her children – who looked after them?'

'The servants, I guess.'

There is a pause as we sip our tea. I have been so focused on Molly's words that the noise of the hotel receded. It returns now and, with it, my sense of fatigue.

'Who was Fong Choon's wife? Did she have any other family?'

'Apparently she was the daughter of a Canton businessman who lost his fortune through bad management and a gambling addiction. No one seems to know much about her.'

'At least Fong Choon would have had enough money to care for his sick wife.' I'm thinking of the two children, my half-siblings. They lost their mother too. So many lost mothers.

'What else did you hear about Fong Choon?' I ask, recovering from my thoughts.

'He is known to donate large amounts of money to local charities and receives many favours in return.'

'The Chinese are big on favours, I gather.'

'It seems he has very few close friends. No one really knows what goes on in his life.'

'Maybe he likes to keep to himself. There's no crime in that.'

'No, there certainly isn't, Knill. But what I've heard fits with your experience today. It seems that Fong Choon doesn't give much away about himself.' Molly leans back in her chair and observes me.

I suddenly regret revealing so much to Molly and I'm uncomfortable hearing gossip about Fong Choon. After all, I've barely had time to get to know him. But what she said churns over in my head as we drink our tea. Fong Choon is a complex person and it seems that everyone has a view about him. Perhaps he doesn't want to get to know me at all. Molly is uncharacteristically quiet. I stare into space, my own thoughts swimming, blindly drinking the sweet tea.

'I hope I haven't been too forthcoming. Knill, it's nothing more than common knowledge in Shanghai circles.'

'I just need time to think. It's been a lot to take on board.'

Instead of feeling better after the talk with Molly I feel more confused than ever. Difference is all around me: food, customs and language. I'm frustrated by not understanding the language and having to rely on others to explain what's going on. Right now, I would trade the Astor Hotel for being at home in Australia. My familiar job, my cousins and people I can talk to. I miss Ted with a swift and sudden ache. I'm tired of feeling and looking like the odd one out. And meeting Fong Choon has offered no relief.

44

I tidy for dinner with scattered thoughts leaping through my mind. Uncle is already at the table when I arrive.

'Hello, Uncle.'

'Big day for you, Knill,' Uncle says. 'Lunch was a success.'

I guess he's relieved that one of his duties has been discharged.

'I'm not sure what to make of it all.' I take the chair next to him.

'Fong Choon likes you. He's happy you are here.'

'How do you know that?'

'Oh, I can tell when matters do not please him. All good today, Knill.'

'Thanks for making all the arrangements.'

Uncle looks up sharply, but he's grinning widely. 'Ha, that is what I do. Arrangements and more arrangements, they never end.'

I like this man when he isn't so stern.

I look around for Lily and am pleased to see her coming through the door. She is looking harried; it's been a long day for her too. She is wearing a blue floral blouse that I haven't seen before – I guess it's new – and her hair is falling loosely over her shoulders. She smiles and sits across from us.

The house-waiter hovers in anticipation of our orders. I decide to skip dinner. The thought of another meal after the extravagant lunch is too much. I order tea instead.

'Sick?' Lily asks.

'No. Weary.'

A rare frown appears on Lily's face as she looks from me to Uncle. He looks at her as if to say *I didn't do anything*, which makes me laugh and the tension eases.

'Has something happened?' Lily asks after dinner, when Uncle is out of earshot, heading for the stairs.

'Nothing specific, just the whole thing is starting to become difficult. Stepping around Uncle's moods, Fong Choon's family. I guess I'm a bit tired of it all.'

'Tired of it?'

'It seems to me that no one says what they are thinking. I don't know why I can't just have an honest talk with Fong Choon. After all, he wanted me to come to China.'

'You are too impatient.'

'I thought that once I met Fong Choon I would feel relieved. Instead I feel like I've done something wrong. He's secretive, Fong Wan's aloof and Fong Pen-Lee is downright rude.'

Lily touches my hand across the table. She looks perplexed and I am suddenly sorry for adding to her burden.

'You have to try to not be offended. They don't understand what it's like for you. They only know what it's like for them. They didn't know you existed until a few weeks ago.'

'That might explain why Fong Wan and Fong Pen-Lee acted the way they did.'

'Knill, I think the situation is very complicated for the family. They feel pushed aside by their father and his attempts to find you and bring you to China.'

'Complicated is a good word for it,' I say, feeling less annoyed.

'They also have their reasons for being cautious. They are not a very happy family, much sadness and many troubles.'

'So I believe.'

'What do you mean?'

'Just a few things Molly said.'

'She shouldn't be commenting on other people's lives.' Lily flicks her hair to the side. 'Knill, let's walk the worries of the day away.'

I glance at my watch; it is a quarter to seven. We need to get our coats if we are to go out.

'I'll meet you by the front door at seven?'

As we are about to climb the stairs, a porter calls, 'Mr McMillan, a letter for you – just delivered.'

I open it in my room, my pulse quickening when I realise who it's from.

Dear Knill,

Your arrival in Shanghai is complicated. My children
do not understand the significance of the event. I
would even guess that they are displeased. I worry
that my children do not appreciate the opportunities
they have and their privileged existence. Each day
is taken for granted and they show little interest in
those less advantaged. I sense you may be different.

I have a suggestion for you that I wish you to
consider. I would like to take you to visit some very
special people with me. Tomorrow, when you are
collected from your hotel, bring overnight luggage. I
will explain more when we speak.

Yours truly,
Fong Choon

Is this Fong Choon inviting me to meet him on different
terms? Today, when we finished lunch, he told me he
would send a driver tomorrow. I was to visit him at his
house for tea. Now, it seems there is a change of plan.

This letter has taken the sting out of the day. I feel my
composure return and realise it's something to do with the
longing to be acknowledged.

I pull on my thick overcoat. Lily's waiting by the
entrance and waves as I stride down the stairs to meet her.
I take the last few steps two at a time.

45

The driver scoops up my bag and we head into the freezing morning beyond the door of the hotel. The driver doesn't speak English, but his grin is reassuring as we drive to the north of Shanghai. The streets are wider but just as hectic. We are heading out of the city when the car turns abruptly into a driveway. Gates swing open with the help of two men who appear from nowhere. Chinese jasmine climbs erratically along the top of the fence. Our car moves forward into a courtyard, on the other side of which is a large building. I soon realise this isn't a private residence. I look around, hoping to see Fong Choon.

Washing hangs from bamboo poles attached to makeshift timber frames. Two lazy dogs lie motionless underneath them. Several people rugged up against the cold are walking around the enclosure. The driver nods a familiar greeting, and a man nearby waves. Apart from the people and the dogs, the washing lines and the jasmine climbing on the fence, the yard is bare. No trees, no garden beds, not even a path to what looks like the back entrance to the building. The car stops, and the driver jumps out and opens my door. As I step from the Citroën, Fong Choon appears. We shake hands, the dogs stir, and everyone in the yard turns to watch us.

'Hello, Knill.'

'Good morning…What is this place?'

'I will explain. Come with me.'

I follow him into the building and down a long corridor. The air is gamy and stale. Then I hear them – people calling and moaning. One door is ajar, and I steal a fleeting glance into a room as we pass. Beds are jammed closely together along a wall. At once I understand that we are in some sort of hospital.

We enter a room at the front and Fong Choon motions me to sit. Three shabby chairs sit at the edge of what was once a beautiful crimson rug. The fringe of the mat is frayed. The walls are white-washed like the outside of the building. There is no heating and the room is cold.

'Thank you for coming today, Knill. I know you must be wondering what this is about.' There is little expression on his face.

'I need to be told why I'm here. Since I've been in China, I've been expected to respond to instructions, and I've tried to, but…'

'Yes, yes. Things will become clearer, Knill.'

'I hope so.'

'I thought you might like to know about the businesses I'm involved with.'

'Yes, I'm curious. Is this a hospital?'

'We do our best for the sick but it's never enough.'

'We...is this your hospital?' Is this possible? That my father owns a hospital? Why not?

'It's not exactly my hospital, but I do provide money for people to work here and look after the patients. The building belongs to me but as you can see it is in need of repair.'

'Who runs the hospital?'

Fong Choon explains that the hospital is overseen by a charitable hall, a group of businessmen who give some of their time and money to the needy. Despite the work of the charities, poverty and illness is a huge problem in Shanghai and across China. It is more than he or the charitable halls can address. The hospital relies on relatives and volunteers to feed and nurse the sick. One doctor is paid to come daily, but his services do not stretch far enough.

'I thought there were many doctors in Shanghai?' Molly once mentioned the well-trained Chinese doctors who flock to Shanghai to practise.

'You are correct, but they only work with people who can pay for their services. The people here have no money and must rely on charity. Sadly, many perish in bad circumstances without help.'

'How often do you come here?' I can't quite put all of this together.

'Every week, as well as another location. You will see later this afternoon. I have duties here. Come with me.'

Down the corridor, a thin woman wearing a long skirt and faded tunic shuffles towards us. She speaks to Fong Choon discreetly, not wanting me to hear. He nods and places his hand on her shoulder. She moves on without a sound.

'Her husband is very ill and is expected to die soon. They have no children and no one to help them. She is sad but also worried about what will happen to her when her husband dies.'

'What will happen to her? Surely there is someone to help.'

'She can stay here for as long as we can keep her, but there are many like her, without money or family to assist. Unfortunately, we can't help everyone.'

There is weariness on Fong Choon's face and, unlike yesterday, his body is slightly stooped. The room we enter is stark and bereft of comfort. Narrow beds, all of them occupied, are haphazardly arranged along both sides of the room. Makeshift bedding is bundled beside them. I assume family members keep a vigil with their relatives. Everyone looks up at us. They greet Fong Choon and wait in turn to speak as he moves around the room. I walk behind him, conscious of being a stranger, perhaps even unwelcome amongst these people. A frail man with sores covering his scalp weeps openly, clutching at Fong Choon's arm as they talk, as if he is pleading for something. Fong Choon calls someone who looks like he may be a helper or an orderly, and he attends to the patient.

In the next dormitory, the same scenes repeat themselves, the same arrangement of the beds, the anxiety of those attending the sick, the obvious lack of medical treatment. Fong Choon remains unruffled. He continues, room after room, a few comforting words and a gentle pat on the arm to a crying relative when needed. This is not the man that I met at lunch; instead he is full of compassion and care.

We are back in the front room with the frayed mat. Tea and food arrives, carried in by an elderly woman wearing a blue tunic top over long black pants. She flashes us a warm smile as she leaves the room, but I realise too late I haven't responded. I'm still reeling from the sight of so many sick and dying people. I have many questions about this hospital. And I'm also unsure why Fong Choon is exposing me to this part of his life. I can't eat, but I swallow the tea thirstily.

'What happens to these people?' I ask.

'Many die. Some survive. We help where we can.'

'So many sick people. And poor. It must be difficult to come here.'

'Sometimes, yes. And at times I'm deeply troubled, but we must always try.'

'I'm not sure I understand all this, Fong Choon.'

'You will, Knill.' He stands up, and I follow him to the waiting car. 'Be patient, there is more to see.'

46

The road narrows as we drive east from Shanghai. We pass villages of tiny thatched houses and dwellings surrounded by tall bamboo foliage, brilliant purple vines winding over the rooftops. Outside the villages, dense plantations of rice jut against the skyline. Despite its lush greenness, the landscape is harsh for the workers. Wrapped in thick clothing against the stinging cold, the workers in the paddy fields are stooped almost in half as they move along the furrowed lines.

'It's so cold for the people to work,' I say to Fong Choon.

'Yes, very cold, but they prefer it to the harsh conditions of summer.'

Fong Choon remains silent for most of the journey. I get the impression that he isn't in the habit of discussing anything in front of his driver. Still, I've decided that I am entitled to ask more than I'm being told.

'Where are we going?'

'To Nan Chi – to an orphanage for abandoned infants and children.'

'An orphanage?'

'There are many children in China without anyone to care for them.'

'What about their parents?'

'Often the parents cannot afford to feed them, sometimes children are left abandoned, and occasionally children just arrive by themselves. There is a lot of poverty outside the big cities and towns.'

'They can't afford to feed their children?'

'Like we saw this morning, Knill. Poor people are desperate people, they do what they have to do.'

I'm struck by how profound it must be to give your child away because you can't afford food. That is so unfair. Then I think about how unfair it was for Eliza to be forced to give up her baby. Not for the sake of extreme poverty, but for the sake of family shame. Is that why Fong Choon is interested in these causes? Because of Eliza…and me?

'It won't be long before we arrive,' Fong Choon says.

'What's your connection with the orphanage? Does it belong to you?'

'Not exactly. As with the hospital I give money and time. It is expected of people who have success in business to give to those less fortunate. When we get there, stay close to me. The children will flock around, but just follow my example.'

The car stops outside a shambolic group of huts. There are people everywhere and groups of children dressed in ill-fitting clothes, some barefoot. The older children, mainly girls, carry the little ones, some no older than a few months. Toddlers wander aimlessly behind them. The arrival of the car causes the group to rush forward. They push and jostle for front positions. Soon the car is surrounded. There are no smiles, just kids desperate for attention.

As we leave the car, the children grab at my arms and legs. One small boy has hold of my coat sleeve. There is little chance of getting him to release his grip. Others swarm close to me. Walking without tripping is impossible. I notice that Fong Choon doesn't give the children any attention, although they crowd him and try to grab hold of his clothing. He walks straight ahead, ignoring them. Reluctantly the children move aside for him.

'Follow me, Knill,' he calls from several paces ahead of me. 'If you stop, they think you are going to give them something.'

Despite the cold, my shirt is damp with sweat. I can feel the desperate twisting motion of the little boy's hand as he clings to my sleeve.

'Let go, please.' I look pleadingly at him. His black eyes widen and stare back at me. He holds on with determination. I tug him towards a low-roofed dung-coloured building. Two men and a woman run out and start shouting at the rabble. The smaller children back off, but the others ignore the threats. The boy on my sleeve is immovable.

The adults bow to Fong Choon and he speaks briefly with them. They turn their attention to me and again wave their arms to disperse the swarm around me. The children reluctantly back off. But the little boy remains. Fong Choon enters the doorway and turns to see me trying to tug my coat away.

'One has to admire persistence, Knill.'

Fong Choon looks at the child and asks his name. The boy answers quietly. A conversation follows, during which the boy relaxes his grip on my arm.

'What's going on, Fong Choon?'

'The child is telling us that he is six years old and that he was brought here against his wishes. He comes from Shanghai where he has many brothers and sisters. His name is Little Tong and his mother is sick and his father is dead. His family has no food and his younger sister died last week, here in the orphanage.'

'This little kid should be with his family.'

'As I have told you, Knill, there is much poverty.'

'But this kid needs to be looked after. It's no wonder he's almost yanking my arm off.'

Fong Choon runs his hand over the child's head and asks him to let go of me. The child obeys but does not move away. He stands so close to me I can feel his tiny body leaning against my leg. I place my hand on his shoulder. He looks up, his black eyes darting between Fong Choon and me. A discussion takes place with the adults who are fending off the other children. It is clearly about the boy. Soon the child is led away. I begin to protest but Fong Choon hushes me.

'The boy is very intelligent and shows potential. I have asked the carers to get him washed and dressed. We'll take him back to Shanghai with us,' Fong Choon says.

'Who's going to look after him?'

'A school for boarders. The school masters will see that he is cared for and that he gets an education.'

'What about his family?' My arm still tingles from Little Tong's fierce grip.

'When he is settled in school it can be arranged for him to visit them.'

'I hope so, he can't be kept apart from his family.'

'I give my word he will see his family.' Fong Choon looks me directly in the eye. It's the first time I realise that his eyes are like my own. 'Come, now we have other matters to attend to.'

I take a deep breath as I follow Fong Choon through a small door and into a large dormitory. The room contains cots and beds occupied by children. Fong Choon greets them by name. Lying in one cot is an emaciated girl, wearing a thin cotton dress and a nappy. An old blanket is partly covering her. Her limbs are rigid, her hands are cupped tightly. She smiles crookedly at Fong Choon as he approaches.

'*Néih hóu,* Mai.' Fong Choon softly touches the child's head, then turns to me. 'Mai was found abandoned when she was no more than a few weeks old. She has been here for about ten years.' Fong Choon moves on to talk to the children in the adjoining cots. My feet are heavy on the bare boards. I look back at Mai and smile timidly at her. What world have I entered? I've seen poverty back home but nothing like this. The Astor Hotel seems a lifetime away.

'How can you bear to witness these awful circumstances without doing more?' I ask him as we leave.

'I do as much as I can, Knill.' A hint of weariness enters the older man's voice.

'But this can't be acceptable, Fong Choon?'

'No, not at all, but we try to do what we can. If we did nothing it would be worse. At least some of the people and children are being looked after.' Fong Choon looks at me for a long time. I'm silent under his stare.

'Coming here has upset you, Knill?'

'I've never seen anything like this. It's…it's dreadful. And I'm surprised that your business is looking after the needy. Surprised in a good way.'

'This is only a small part of my business, Knill. The other part allows me to do this,' Fong Choon replies. 'Come. We should eat and rest before we continue our journey.'

I begin to think that I'll never understand the complexities of this man's life. Shark fin soup and his family terrified to fall out of his good grace. And this.

47

Little Tong, scrubbed clean and changed into ill-fitting but clean clothes, is silent and looks frightened on the journey back to Shanghai. I smile at him and he peeks at me from beneath his long hair. His hand grasps the doorhandle and it then occurs to me that the boy hasn't been inside a motor car before.

In Shanghai, we take him to the school as Fong Choon promised. The small boy hesitates as the heavy door of the car is opened. He looks wide-eyed at me. I get out of the car with him and take his hand. Fong Choon talks kindly to the boy as we lead him to the school building. He's just a frightened kid trying to survive. I can't imagine being alone at such a young age. I marvel at his guts – could this have been me if I'd been born in China?

The shadows of evening light are falling when our car enters the gates of a large house surrounded by a bamboo fence. Ponds with arched lattice bridges flank each side of the driveway and narrow lamp-lit paths wind casually between thick, drooping Banyan trees. Two men wander amongst the trees, one sweeping and the other carrying a hessian bag to collect the last unwanted leaves and twigs of the day. Fong Choon nods to the men and they grin willingly in return. He then turns to me. 'This is my home. You will stay here tonight.'

The house is colonial in style. It reminds me of drawings I've seen in picture books – English mansions, tall and grand, with stately window boxes and ledges. I collect my bag and follow Fong Choon without a word, half-expecting to see Fong Wan and Fong Pen-Lee, but there is no one other than the two of us and the servants. My body aches with tiredness and my head swirls as I try to make sense of the life of this man who has claimed me as his son. All its contradictions.

'We can eat later. First it's time to bathe and rest.'

'Thank you.'

Fong Choon looks equally tired and I suspect he's looking forward to the rest as much as me.

'The house servants will see you are settled in your room and they will call you for dinner.' Fong Choon moves slowly towards a staircase. I wonder if this is how he lives his life – attending to his community duties, his business, and at night returning to a silent household. I can't help but feel sorry for him, a powerful but sad man. Where are Fong Wan and Fong Pen-Lee?

The gentle knocking of the house servant wakes me a couple of hours later. I wash, dress and follow him down the staircase and into the dining room.

Fong Choon is seated already and looks refreshed. He nods to me. 'Did you have a good rest?'

'Yes. Thank you.'

The food arrives at intervals. The aromas are tangy and inviting. I'm pleased that the table is set with English cutlery as well as chopsticks. I know I will never manage the small intricate food with anything but a fork. A duck dish comes first, shiny and crisp, served with a concentrated soy vinegar, shallots, ginger and peanuts. The next dish is a mystery; the sauce is strong-smelling with black swirls of oil floating across the surface. Fong Choon explains that it's eel, a favourite in China. I tentatively try it, with Fong Choon smiling at my caution. It's delicious. Rice arrives to signify the end of the meal.

Moving to the grand formal sitting room, Fong Choon sits across from me with an expectant air. I am hopeful that this will be the discussion I came halfway across the world to have.

'We have time to talk now, Knill. You must be wondering why I asked you to come with me today?'

'I have many questions for you. Not just why I'm here today. I need to know what happened in Australia. About you and Eliza.'

'Tonight, we talk about the here and now. The matters of long ago can wait.'

I breathe deeply; this man infuriates me with his air of control and yet, somehow, I resign myself to waiting until he's ready to discuss the reason I'm here. Right now, it's clear he has other ideas.

I sit back in the cushioned chair as Fong Choon tells me about his factories in Shanghai and Hong Kong.'

'What do you make?'

'Oh, china and pottery, many different types. Orders come from all over the world. Well-established businesses, Knill. They have been in operation for a long time. First my grandfather, then my father and now me.'

'And these businesses are very profitable?' I'm starting to see why he can do his charity work.

'Yes, and of course that means more requests for help.'

He explains that the more he does in the community the more requests come to him each year.

'I am getting older, Knill, and I'm not always well. My heart is a trouble now. I need someone to help me manage my affairs and to work alongside me. It is a big responsibility to ensure that these places are all managed well. I must be confident that the family continues to support the poor. That was my father's wish and it's also mine.'

'Is that why Fong Wan is studying to be a doctor?'

'My children do not express interest to take on the work that has been done over the generations. Fong Wan has some sympathy for the causes but he is also very keen to stay in America when he finishes his medical studies.'

'I see.'

I'm surprised to hear that Fong Wan wants to leave China for good.

'It is becoming a problem, Knill.'

'Can you employ someone to help take some of the load off your shoulders?'

'No, Knill, that is not the point. You see, it's very important for one of my own family to continue the work. That's how it's always been.'

His family. Fong Wan and Fong Pen-Lee. It's understandable that Fong Wan wants to finish his studies, but why can't he return to China after that? He is the obvious choice to take over his father's affairs. Fong Pen-Lee is still too young and it's more likely she will eventually marry and have her own family. Fong Choon is silent and lost in thought, but eventually he stirs, sitting upright.

'I have something important to ask you.' There is urgency in his voice.

'What is it?'

'I want you to delay your return to Australia and stay in China. You are my firstborn; you can learn to run the family business.'

'What! Stay in China and run your business?'

'Yes, it's an offer for you to consider. You could stay for an extended time, see if you like living in China and then make up your mind.'

'But I'm a foreigner. I know nothing about the place, let alone your business.'

'You would learn quickly.'

It's then that I realise Fong Choon is serious. Very serious.

'I can't even speak the language. How can I possibly be of assistance without understanding Cantonese, Mandarin or the local dialect?'

'There is a language school in Shanghai. You can learn the basics.'

Fong Choon's face is still and solemn. I can feel him scrutinising me for a sign or a response. I run my hands along the soft fabric of my chair as I contemplate the possibility.

'I can see you are giving my request some thought, Knill.'

'I'm honoured and surprised by your offer. I need time to think about it further.'

A stunned silence has fallen over the room. I can't believe Fong Choon's request; it complicates everything. Just a few days ago I was anticipating meeting the man who claimed to be my father. I don't know this man, and likewise he hardly knows me. And yet he wants me to stay and help run his business. What is behind this offer? Is his interest in me merely in terms of my being of assistance to him?

As if reading my mind, Fong Choon says, 'I suppose you are wondering why I'm asking you to stay in China, after such a short time?'

'Yes, I am.' I don't know what else to say.

'I think that you have the character to carry out my work beside me.'

'I'm not sure how you come to that conclusion.'

'After seeing your curiosity and compassion towards the people at the hospital and the children at the orphanage today, it seems a natural solution. The kindness you showed to Little Tong. You notice enough to ask questions. Fong Wan and Fong Pen-Lee will not come to the hospital or the orphanage with me. They avoid the poor.'

'Perhaps when they are older…' I'm not sure how to respond to Fong Choon when he criticises his own children, especially to me.

'Fong Wan is not so young, he is nineteen. It's a question of character and values.'

Did Fong Choon intend this all along? Did he invite me here to entice me into a family role? Is that why he looked for me in the first place? If I'm to be honest, I'm flattered that he sees me as someone who can rise to the job and help him run his companies. But there are a thousand doubts in my mind as well, and confusion as to how I feel about him drawing me to China with this purpose.

I want to ask him about my mother, but I hold back. Despite his politeness, Fong Choon controls the direction of the conversation. Even his silence is powerful and not easily interrupted.

But I try again.

'Can we talk about the reasons I'm here, Fong Choon?'

'What do you mean, reasons?'

'It was a big risk for you to ask me to come here in the first place. You must be certain that I'm your son.'

'Not as big a risk as you might think. I know you are Eliza's son and I know I am the father of her child.'

For a short time, I can't respond. Fong Choon has just told me that he is my father and yet his face is without emotion. I collect my thoughts, take a breath and follow suit.

'And your health, what do the doctors say?'

'The doctors say there isn't a cure and that I should avoid stress and worry.' He laughs.

'And do the doctors say you have to work less?'

'Yes, yes, all of that.' Fong Choon waves his arm in the air.

The house boy arrives with a silver tray stacked with cups, saucers and a teapot. As he places the teacups on the table. I freeze. The vibrant blues and greens swirling around grey dragonflies dance before me. The cups are identical to the one Eliza sent with me when I was taken from her. I look up to see Fong Choon watching me. We stare at each other in silence.

'You have seen these cups before, Knill?'

My mouth is dry and a burning sensation begins in my throat. 'Yes.'

'Do you know where the cups came from?'

'From you, from your…house in Australia.'

'Yes, that's right, but they originally came from Canton. They were made for my family.'

I sit still. The lump in my throat prevents me from talking as I sit in the same room as my father.

48

Fong Choon slumps on his bed. He sighs as the full impact of his day with Knill floods over him. This young man has impressed him beyond expectations. There are many things that he should say to Knill, but how does a father tell an abandoned son why he left it so long to find him?

There are some matters too hard to discuss. The time in Australia when he was called back to his homeland is one of them. He quivers with guilt at the very thought of Eliza, all those years ago, expecting his child and being ostracised by her family. He knows there is nothing that will stop his timeless love for her and there is nothing he can do to change the past. He also knows that he's tried hard to make up for the past. Now the most remarkable of all things has happened and the circle is complete. His son, his and Eliza's son, is here in China. If Knill agrees to stay it could change everything. If he decides to go back to Australia, then life remains the same and must be accepted.

Over twenty-one years ago, Fong Choon was called back from Australia because of difficulties in China. Family matters and difficult connections. Not knowing that Eliza was with child, he married his wife to appease family, both his and hers. Then the children were born. He knows he wasn't the best husband or father. He's not proud of it. Family business was demanding, his wife's illness was confusing and problematic from the beginning of the marriage. Somehow his life had taken a path that was laid out for him but not by him.

The last days have stirred memories that he's managed to put aside for many years. He sometimes thinks that he buries himself in his community work as a way of easing the eternal guilt that follows him. That he does good in the hope that it might counteract all that he has done wrong.

Resting back on his pillows, his thoughts turn to the young man asleep across the landing. His eyes are moist as he allows himself to feel the pride and the anguish together. Who would have imagined that his Australian son would be such a fine young man? What must it have been like for Knill to be adopted out and forced to live a life that was not his own? Does Knill hate him for abandoning him and his mother? Fong Choon is weary but sleep does not come. He knows his new-found son deserves an explanation about the past. There is also something else that Knill should know, but Fong Choon stands to lose too much if that's revealed too soon. He picks up his pen.

Dear Knill,

By now you have guessed that I am not good at talking about matters that are personal. This letter is to express my gratitude to you for coming to China to meet me. The decision to come so far to meet a man claiming to be your father took considerable courage and trust. I thank you.

I would like to explain what it was like for me in Australia all those years ago and why I came back to China, unaware that your mother was with child.

In Australia, I loved working for the Chinese Protectorate. I met many good people. Being in your wonderful country opened my eyes to new ways of thinking and my views on life became different to those of my contemporaries back in China. I was treated well in Australia because I was an educated Chinaman. But, despite educated Chinese being treated well, the colonialists did not accept marriage between the Chinese and their own. So, Knill, you can see how difficult it would have been for your mother and me, even if I had stayed all those years ago. It is about this very matter that I feel guilty and dishonourable. As you know, your mother was left with a very difficult situation and as a result you grew up in a family not related in blood. I will always feel shame for the situation I caused for you, Knill.

When I came home to China, I intended to return
to Australia and your mother. But in Canton, family
matters were complicated, and I was pressured into
working and then quickly marrying. The matters do
not require an explanation here as the honour of my
family members must be upheld.

Discovering years later that I had a son in Australia
was a shock. I decided that I should attempt to find
you. It has taken many years to do so. Meeting you
in the past week has been something I only dreamed
of until now.

Knill, I understand that my request to you to stay
on in China comes unexpectedly. I have no right to
pressure you regarding this matter but if you take
time to consider the possibility I will be grateful.

Yours faithfully,
Fong Choon

He slowly folds the letter and slides it into a small envelope.
He seals it and props it carefully on the dresser next to
his bed.

Fong Choon reaches for his jacket.

49

My room is at the front of the house, overlooking the garden. On one wall, a painting hangs in a gilded frame, capturing bright cherry blossom and delicate birds set against a mountainous background. It reminds me of Hiyang, which gives me a pang for Lily, and for An Meng, and the quiet time on the ship. Things seemed more simple then. I fall asleep thinking of the evening I played the piano with Lily.

Sometime in the night the sound of a car being started wakes me. I go to the window. The house boy is closing the car door and Fong Choon is at the wheel. He moves off and the servant disappears inside the house. I watch the empty driveway for some time before I return to bed.

The next morning, the car is back in the driveway. I didn't hear it return and can't imagine why Fong Choon would go out late at night. In the breakfast room, Fong Wan and Fong Pen-Lee are just finishing as I arrive. Fong Choon is in the garden, talking to the men who were sweeping the paths the evening before. I scoop congee into a small dish, eat two small sweet buns and wash them down with scented tea. Fong Wan says hello briefly and hurries off. Fong Pen-Lee also leaves the dining room but as she does she turns to me and nods. I can't decide if she smiled or not.

The driver is waiting by the car to transport me back to the Astor. Fong Choon arrives in the passageway, greets me formally and then hands me an envelope.

'We will speak soon, Knill.'

The Shanghai streets slip by as we drive. I open his letter, read it twice, curious about this man who can write what he cannot say. It's as if he owes me something more than I understand.

Back at the hotel, I look for Lily. I need to talk to her. I find her in the lobby, sitting by the window reading the book Molly gave her on board the ship: *Are Women People?* written by someone called Alice Duer Miller, a few years back. Molly told us it caused quite a storm at the time. Lily hasn't seen me yet, her lovely face is bent to her book. My relief is palpable; I feel a relaxing all through my body, yet my heart beats a little faster. I've missed her. Lily looks up, catching sight of me, and I see my expression mirrored in her smile.

I ask if she will go to the Bund for a walk with me.

'Perfect. Uncle has gone out,' says Lily.

'All is well with the world then,' I say.

Shanghai drifts around us. Tall buildings, smartly maintained, and old modest dwellings almost squeezed out of existence vie for the waterfront space. Rugged up in our overcoats and gloves we cross the road to the walkway. The dark clouds hover and we hope the rain holds off.

Lily moves at a brisk pace and I'm happy to oblige. We walk for what seems a long time in the drab winter light before she suggests we rest for a while. We sit on a bench beneath a cherry blossom tree, bare and dormant in its winter state.

It's a relief to confide in Lily. Detail by detail I tell her about the visit to the hospital and the orphanage.

'I am surprised that he took you on such a tour. You have been privileged, Knill.'

'It wasn't what I expected either.'

'Very few people have insight into the charitable aspects of Fong Choon's business. I'm sure that Fong Wan and Fong Pen-Lee have never visited the places you were taken to.'

'Fong Choon said that Fong Wan isn't interested in being part of the business and wants to stay in America.'

'Yes, that's true. Fong Wan has always made that clear to his father.'

'That's why he wants me to stay in China and assist him with the work.'

'He asked you to stay here. In Shanghai?' Lily stares at me, her dark eyes wide. 'You can't do that!'

'Yes, I know. It seems ridiculous.'

'I can't believe this. It is most unexpected.' She stands, takes a few steps to look out over the water, then comes back and sits down again.

'I've been wanting to talk to you so much. It all seems a bit odd.'

'A bit odd? Knill, it's crazy!'

'Yes. He hardly knows me. If I were to consider this request—'

'We leave Shanghai in three days. You're not seriously thinking about staying, are you?' Lily's expression is unreadable, and I feel her drawing away from me.

'No, of course not…there are too many things I don't understand about him.'

'What things?'

'The way his children behave towards him. And the things Molly said about him leading a secretive life. You have always kept your family secrets, Lily. But please tell me. I need to know. Especially now.'

Lily is shaking her head, clearly upset. Finally, I realise she is angry, though with Fong Choon, not with me. I don't think I have ever seen her in this state before. 'There are many stories about him,' she says. She hesitates and looks across the water before turning back to face me. 'It's said that Fong Choon lives a double life, at least that's what the family whispers are about. It is also the reason why Fong

Wan prefers to live and study in America and why he is dismissive and rude at times. Fong Pen-Lee is the same. She will not forgive her father for her mother's sadness.'

'What's this double life you talk about?'

Lily looks away from me. Small drops of rain fall on my face but I ignore the change in the weather.

'In China, it's not so unusual for men to have other relationships outside their marriage. They call the other women "concubines". Mostly a blind eye is turned and it is managed in a discreet manner.'

I immediately think of Fong Choon leaving the house in the car. Suddenly it makes sense. I'm aware that Lily is waiting for me to speak.

'If it's not unusual why do they resent him?' I ask.

'Just because society turns a blind eye doesn't mean a wife does or the family.'

'So Fong Choon's wife knew about this.'

'Yes, when she was alive she was distressed and shamed because of the other women in his life.'

'Other women! There was more than one?'

'No one is sure, but Kuan-Yin became very suspicious – at least that's what the family say.' Lily looks down at her feet.

'What happened to her?'

'She was sick for many years. Countless physicians were consulted to diagnose and treat her illness. Sometimes she went away or was hospitalised for months on end.'

'Who looked after Fong Wan and Fong Pen-Lee?'

'Live-in nannies and house staff. Kuan-Yin was a good mother when she was well. Fong Wan and Fong Pen-Lee loved her. They were also very loyal to her.'

'It must have been hard for them.'

'Yes, I think so. They were often subjected to their mother's claims that their father was a dishonest and hurtful man. As a result, Fong Wan and Fong Pen-Lee have carried on their mother's anger towards him.'

'It's starting to make sense.'

'Yes. And when you arrived in Shanghai, Knill, you were yet another reminder of their father's other life.'

I can feel Lily's piercing eyes watching me now.

'Even though that happened well before he met his wife.'

'Fong Choon had already promised to marry Kuan-Yin before he left for Australia. It was to be an arranged marriage.'

'So when he was in Australia he was already planning to marry someone back here?' I pick up a stone at my feet and throw it out into the water.

'I can see you don't like what you're hearing, Knill.'

'It's a big mess.'

'Fong Choon's children believe that he was to blame for their mother's ongoing melancholy.'

'They all gossip about him, but no one confronts him. Everyone has a story of disrespect, but he helps them all financially.'

'Yes, that has been a problem.'

I look across the murky river, trying to reconcile all my father's contradictions. Could a man who is so kind and compassionate towards the poor and needy be so scurrilous in other ways? The two characteristics are not compatible. Or are they? People can have many sides to them. I think of my own parents and how Ted and Rhoda kept my adoption from me and yet, at the same time, doted on me and gave me their best.

We sit silently under the tree. Mindlessly, we watch as people, many of them young children, gather nearby. A frame and curtain are erected for a puppet show. The squeals of the children indicate the start of the performance. A scraggy puppet appears, nodding and thrashing about in its colourful ancient finery. The children's voices drop to a murmur as a child puppet pops its shiny black head next to the scraggy character. Then the two stick figures move along the confines of the puppet box. They dance and sing. The children squatting on the ground sing along in high-pitched voices. Lily is smiling at them, but I know she is lost in her own thoughts, as I am.

When the show finishes we walk away in silence.

'You are not the first person to be confused by Fong Choon,' Lily says in her thoughtful way. 'He is a mystery to many people. Even Uncle doesn't know some of his business contacts.'

'Business, charity, family and this other life of his, all separate. A chameleon.' I take Lily's arm.

'I'm glad you haven't taken after your father, Knill.'

50

Uncle is pacing in the foyer of the hotel. He pounces on us as we walk through the door.

'You two, never here when I need you.'

'Where's the fire?' I say.

'We have been walking, Uncle,' Lily says. 'What is wrong?'

'Fong Pen-Lee is here. Refusing to go home. She wants to speak to you both. She won't talk to me.'

Uncle then launches into Cantonese, a long speech, with Lily reassuring him at the end of it. He sighs and sits heavily in a chair by one of the pillars. By the look on Lily's face, there's trouble ahead. Uncle has quietened but looks pale. All this worry can't be good for him. I follow Lily up the stairs. Looking back, I see Uncle with his head in his hands.

Fong Pen-Lee's face is swollen and blotched from crying. She seems much younger as she sits timidly on the edge of Lily's bed. The things Lily told me earlier have made me realise what a rough time Fong Pen-Lee and Fong Wan had as kids.

Lily crouches beside her and I sit in one of the chairs. Then Fong Pen-Lee is on her feet, wringing her hands. She speaks in English.

'I don't want to live in my father's house anymore. I'm not going back. Fong Wan will soon leave for America and I will be there on my own. I won't stay there. I won't.'

Lily goes to her and puts her arm around her shoulders. I now understand why Uncle is in a state. Lily raises her eyebrows at me. I am right out of my depth and hope Lily can persuade Fong Pen-Lee to return home.

'Does your father know you are here?' says Lily.

'No.'

'Has something happened at home?'

'He's never home. I'm there all the time with the servants and my tutor. I hate him.'

'Fong Pen-Lee, we'll come to your father's house,' says Lily. 'We can talk to him.'

'No.' Fong Pen-Lee is shaking her head and crying again. 'I want to come to Australia with you.'

I find Uncle sitting at a small table in the tearoom. I tell him the purpose of Fong Pen-Lee's visit. His face turns a purplish red and he is unable to speak for a moment. I'm guessing that he thinks Fong Choon will blame him in some way for Fong Pen-Lee's actions. Uncle's reaction to Fong Choon continues to baffle me.

'I think we should talk about the family,' I say to him, sipping my tea.

'Family is private business,' Uncle says, clearly angry. 'Problems from the past. You would not understand.'

'You forget, I also live with problems from long ago.'

Uncle falls silent.

'No point in bottling it up.'

'Ba…you not understand.'

'No, you're right, I don't understand, but it's no fun being dropped in the middle of it.'

'A long story.'

'Can you let me in on it?'

I catch a glimpse of amusement on his face. 'You Australians have a funny way of saying things.'

'You mean we call a spade a spade?'

He looks slightly bewildered but doesn't enquire about the spades. 'Always problems,' he says and his protracted sigh hangs in the air.

'And family secrets,' I say.

'Ba. You have hit the hammer on the nail.'

'You mean, hit the nail on the head.' We both laugh.

Uncle becomes serious again. 'One big secret…Fong Choon's wife was my sister.'

'Your *sister*?' Lily has never mentioned this.

'Our father was a businessman in Canton, who lost all the family money. Gambling took over his life. The Chinese like to gamble but not like my father, he was not able to say no.'

'And not so lucky?'

'Sometimes, but then he would lose all his winnings. He kept gambling – no one could stop him. When he died, there was no money left for inheritance or to pay his debts.' Uncle is sitting with his hands crossed in his lap. A quiet moment hangs between us. I sit still and refrain from jumping in to fill the silence. I learnt as a kid not to fill the air with useless chatter. Ted used to say, 'Think before you speak, and likewise give others the chance to do so.' Unlike Rhoda, who had no tolerance for any gap in conversation. I feel a warmth sweep through me as I think about them now.

'Big story,' Uncle says.

'Sounds like big trouble.'

'You guess well.'

The tearoom is almost empty now. The clatter of teacups and people murmuring to each other have gone. The winter afternoon shadow darkens the long windows and only the faint sound of the stallholders on the Bund can be heard. I ask for more tea and turn my attention back to Uncle.

'Fong Choon. He saved the family's honour, cleared the debts and gave me money to start my business. Without him we had no future. The families agreed on the marriage before he went to Australia. My sister had hope of a good future with him. When he returned from Australia he was different. Evasive and troubled. But a promise is a promise and he married Kuan-Yin. Ba, her hopes were soon dashed.'

Uncle's family always struggled with the shame associated with this time. He says he felt that he never really succeeded in his own right, despite his hard work and profitable business. By his own reckoning, he is indebted to Fong Choon and always will be.

Then I realise that Lily's father is in the same position. Fong Choon's wife was his sister, too. Fong Choon is not only a client of Joseph's but also his brother-in-law. And, just like Uncle, Joseph is indebted to Fong Choon for supporting the family when their father was ruined financially.

'Uncle, these things happened many years ago. You can't live your life repaying your father's financial or moral debts forever.'

'It is the honour of it, Knill.'

'Do your children know about these matters? Does Lily?'

'They know that Fong Choon helped me once and that is why he asks favours.'

'But they don't know that Fong Choon's wife was their aunty?'

'No. Joseph and I decided not to tell them. Our sister, she was always sick, not right in the head, more shame on our family.'

'And Lily and your sons don't know that Fong Wan and Fong Pen-Lee are really their cousins?'

'No. It's only in recent times that we've had contact with Fong Choon's children.'

It all begins to fall into place. The secrecy has been an attempt to hide the shame of Kuan-Yin's illness and their father's gambling debts. Fong Choon has had his own guilt and remorse. A marriage he never wanted and, in later years, the news of a son in Australia. Fong Choon's wealth, it seems, gave him an opportunity to assist Kuan-Yin's family. Uncle's role in accompanying Lily and me over the past weeks has been an expected 'favour'. Joseph did the same by sending Lily to support me on the journey. Who is to know if the expectation of repaying favours is held by Fong Choon or by Joseph and Uncle? I feel a strange mixture of empathy and pity for Uncle and conflicting emotions towards Fong Choon. He has managed to keep those around him reliant on him or in debt to him.

Why has he asked me to stay on in China? Does he want me to become dependent on him too? Any ambivalence and doubt about my decision to go home is now erased. Uncle is contemplative. It is as if there's been some relief in sharing his story.

'Perhaps you are right, Knill. I can't continue to pay back for my father and sister.' But the slow shake of his head indicates that he's not so sure.

We shake hands and walk together to the staircase. He must talk to Fong Pen-Lee. Uncle's gait reflects the lifting of a burden – perhaps. Unlike Uncle, I'm clear about my next step.

51

The dream is vivid and lively.

I'm standing amongst a crowd of travellers on the ship. Leather suitcases piled at odd angles along the wooden floor. Children shriek and run, whilst their parents wait anxiously to disembark. Straining, I get a glimpse of Ted standing on the dock. I hail him.

'Come down, come down,' Ted calls back to me.

He's small and frail, his face craggy and his hair slicked thinly across his near bald head. A navy suit jacket drags low on his shoulders, his familiar hat is absent. Behind Ted, throngs of people jostle and push for a vantage point. There is a party atmosphere to it. They are waving and calling from the dock, parting colourful streamers, tangled and thick, which have fallen from the ship railing.

I see Rhoda in the crowd, a wispy, shadowy figure walking towards Ted. She wafts in and out of the floating streamers with ease. She looks calm as she moves past Ted without as much as a glance. Ted continues to call me.

Behind the revellers on the dock, I catch sight of a tall, serene woman standing motionless. Her long hair falls thickly across her shoulders as she clutches her coat firmly against her lean body. There is a look of nervous expectation in her stance, as if she is waiting for someone she's unsure of. I raise my hand to wave to her. I call but no sound comes from my mouth. Someone stumbles in front of me and cuts across my line of vision. The woman is lost to me. I scan the sea of faces below. She is gone…

I try to get to the front of the line but the passengers are edging and shoving towards the gangway. The noise is deafening; it swirls around me. When I finally reach the front of the line, the dock is empty. I call loudly. But Ted, Rhoda, the serene woman and the other revellers have all disappeared.

I run across the deck and peer over the other side of the ship. There are many more people, different people. Fong Choon is there, standing tall and straight. Lily is nearby; she smiles and waves knowingly to me. Uncle stands by her side as if waiting for something to happen. Chinese dragons, a sea of red, green and gold, weave in and out of the crowd, creating a festival atmosphere. Then firecrackers blast upward. My eyes follow the path of the powder-filled rockets. Bursting, they spew out thunderous flashes of colour and sound and then fall quickly away to small rays of light. All faces stretch skyward. Then the noise and colour stop. When my eyes return to the crowd, Lily, Uncle and Fong Choon have disappeared. I shout Lily's name into the vacuum. There is no answer. I run along the silent, empty deck and continue calling out to Lily and Ted, but it is to no avail.

My own voice startles me awake. I sit bolt upright in my tossed bed. As the dream fades, it leaves a stark reality in its place. As I look around the room my eyes come to rest on a ginger bowl in shades of orange and red. The small lid on top sits slightly askew, as if it doesn't match, or doesn't quite fit. Am I the lid? I think in China I am.

I have an ache to return to the wide sky, the sharp air and most of all to sit on the verandah with Ted. And then there's Lily. I can't imagine myself being in China without Lily.

I will meet with Fong Choon for a final time to tell him about my plan to return home and to talk about his letter and Eliza. I think I'm entitled to an honest discussion with the man who claims me as his son.

52

I wait for him in the large sitting room with its heavy gold and green embroidered curtains. On a long table near the doorway sit identical urns, decorated with butterflies around the rims. They remind me of the family cups.

I appreciate the letter he wrote, but I'm not sure how to respond to it. It was personal and seemed honest and yet there was something I felt he was holding back from me. But I may never know. There are many questions about Fong Choon's personal life that I would like answers to.

However, there is one thing that I'm sure about. I'm not going to be part of the family secrets and manipulation. By paying back the money he gave me for my trip and expenses, I'll ensure that I don't fall into the same trap as Lily's father and Uncle. I will not owe Fong Choon anything. There is no way I'm going to be part of this flawed dynasty.

Fong Choon enters the room quietly. An aura of calm surrounds him. It is this aspect of him that intrigues me most. I wonder if it is the key to his family's deference to him. He smiles as he sits down, motioning for me to do the same. He looks tired, with dark circles below his eyes, and shoulders that are slumped.

The house boy enters with a tea tray. I glance at the traditional cups and watch as the tea is slowly and meticulously poured. Fong Choon shows no impatience towards the servant and nods to him politely when he finishes his duties.

'I read your letter,' I say.

'Now you know what happened all that time ago.'

'Not exactly, I was hoping you might talk with me about Eliza.'

'First things first. Have you given thought to my request, Knill?' Fong Choon quietly sips his tea and I realise there will be no discussion regarding Eliza.

'Yes.' I place the fine china cup on its saucer. 'I've given it some thought.'

'And your decision, Knill?'

'I cannot stay on in China.'

'Is there a particular reason for your decision?' Fong Choon remains expressionless but places his cup on the table.

'I have a life in Australia, Fong Choon. I don't belong here.'

I try my best to explain what the experience has been like for me since learning that I was adopted. I tell Fong

Choon about the many emotions and feelings that I've endured since coming to China.

'I feel like a clumsy tortoise in a fish pond. Not belonging is very familiar to me. I don't want to make it worse by trying to fit in here.' I feel my emotions rising and cough to regain composure.

'Then there is nothing left to talk about.' Fong Choon's expression is guarded and unreadable. Have I hurt him? He will never reveal that to me.

'I think there is. I want to know about my mother and the time you were in Australia.'

'You read my letter, Knill. There is nothing more to tell. I came back to China.'

'You never thought of her again?'

He draws a deep breath and looks away. 'I was very much in love with your mother. It was a terrible shock to hear years later that she had given birth to a child, months after I returned home.'

'But you didn't try to find her?'

'I was told she had disappeared. By then I had responsibilities here. There is nothing more I can say on the matter.' Fong Choon straightens in his chair and for a moment I sense there is something he is not telling me.

'I also want you to know that I intend to repay my expenses in time,' I say.

'That won't be necessary, but I'll leave that to you.'

'There is something else that I would like to discuss.'

'What is that?'

'Your daughter, Fong Pen-Lee, wants to go to Australia with Lily.'

He leans back in his expensive chair. As he does, he rubs his thin hand along the polished armrest. His dark eyes take on a grey tinge as he sighs loudly. He is silent. I wait. After a long pause, he begins to speak.

'I have been concerned about my daughter for some time. She is a very angry young person. Fong Pen-Lee has similar traits to those of her deceased mother. She blames everyone else for her sadness, including me.'

'Perhaps she is just sad. Losing your mother when you are so young is tricky.'

Fong Choon continues as if I haven't spoken.'My wife's moods were often erratic, and the children learnt to recognise for themselves when she was sick. Fong Wan did not worry as much as Fong Pen-Lee and got on with whatever he had to do. But Fong Pen-Lee has always been problematic. I worry that she will end up like her mother.'

'We are all ourselves, and even if our parents influence us we are not them.' I know I'm speaking out of turn, but I don't care anymore.

Fong Choon doesn't respond; instead he claps his hands together. 'This is unexpected, but yes.'

'You give your permission?'

'Yes. My daughter has my permission to go to Australia. Uncle can make all the arrangements.' Fong Choon then stands up, which makes me follow. He attempts to shake my hand.

'Before you leave, I have one more request. Will you see Fong Pen-Lee and assist her with her arrangements?'

We are the same height and meet each other's eyes.

'Are you telling me how to manage my daughter, Knill?'

'No. I'm asking you to have a discussion with her and send her to Australia with your blessing. And it isn't Uncle's job to make her arrangements, it's yours.'

For the first time, I see hesitation in his expression, but I still don't fully understand the range of expressions that flicker across his face. I can tell, though, that he is thrown by my bluntness, but I'm not backing down. I wait for his reply.

'Tell Fong Pen-Lee to come home. I will send a driver. In accordance with your wishes, Knill, I will make sure the necessary arrangements are made for her. I will give her my blessing, providing she agrees to come home to China in two years' time.'

'Thank you, Fong Choon.' Breathless, I shake his hand.

'I wish you a good journey back to Australia. It has been an honour to meet you.'

He turns abruptly and leaves the room. As he does I catch a glimpse of his face: he's furious.

53

Anxious faces greet me at the hotel. Lily and Fong Pen-Lee are waiting for my return. Fong Pen-Lee, since her arrival at the Astor, has changed towards me. She is polite and accepting; there has been no sign of her earlier sullen ways.

Sometimes, her limited English can make for some amusing conversations, but Lily comes to the rescue for both of us. I'm starting to like this young half-sister of mine.

'What did he say?' Lily asks.

'He said yes.'

'I can go to Australia?' Fong Pen-Lee shouts.

'Yes, but you are to go and see him first. His driver is here. After all, he is your father and you owe him some respect. Leaving on bad terms is not a good start to your journey.'

'Yes, I'll go now. Thank you. Thank you, Knill.' She runs up the stairs to collect her coat.

'Will your father approve of Fong Pen-Lee returning with us?' I ask Lily.

'Yes, I think so. Providing Fong Choon has given his permission. We were concerned that he would not allow Fong Pen-Lee to go to Australia, which is why we suggested that you put the request to him.' Lily cheekily winks at me.

'I guessed as much.' I grin, pleased that Lily thinks I have influence over Fong Choon.

Fong Pen-Lee has plans to study English in Australia. Lily hopes her father will find work for her in his legal practice in Melbourne.

'There is too much work for me alone. Especially now that An Meng is no longer with us, and if I go to university,' says Lily.

We stand on the street, waving to Fong Pen-Lee as she's driven away.

'Are you all right, Knill?' Lily asks when the car has turned the corner and vanished from sight. 'You seem... calmer.'

'Yes,' I say. 'I think I finally am.' I smile at her. 'And what about you, Lily?'

She tucks her hand under the crook of my arm. 'I am pleased we are nearly at the end of our visit.'

Since the conversations with Uncle and Fong Choon, I'm discovering a new sense of calm. I'm able to think clearly about my life and where I belong. The gut-wrenching sense of rejection I experienced after discovering my adoption has eased. I'm now able to appreciate Ted and Rhoda for their efforts in raising me; they were good parents. Eliza remains a mystery to me and her life is the missing piece of the jigsaw, but I know I must live with not knowing.

Coming to China has changed me. The small-town lad with small-town ideas doesn't exist anymore. My connection with my biological father has been one of ambivalence but it was a useful encounter in other ways. I think about the lessons learnt from Fong Choon. How to stay respectful, how to trust your own instinct and, above all, how to live with mistakes and uncertainty.

I turn my thoughts to going home.

54

Spirits are high at the Astor. Molly is leaving for Europe and is holding a party to celebrate. People are laughing, the atmosphere is festive, everyone is dressed in evening clothes. Even Uncle looks happy. Perhaps it's because we are returning to Canton in two days' time.

Fong Pen-Lee is smiling; she has met with her father and, according to Lily, it went better than expected. Fong Choon has arranged an allowance for her while she is away. He has, however, placed a firm condition on her being allowed to travel to Australia. She is to study English and work hard before returning to China. Fong Pen-Lee has agreed to her father's request.

Music and laughter fill the dining room, Molly's melodious voice often the loudest of all. Uncle is talking with two men at the end of his table. The food arrives to shouts of gratification. Do these socialites ever do anything but dine and gossip? Still, tonight nothing can annoy me or distract from the excitement and relief of the forthcoming journey to Canton and then home. I smile and laugh along with the others, wondering where Lily is. Her seat, next to mine, is empty.

It's then that I see her; she's wearing a gown made from shimmering cream satin embossed with large pink roses trailing from her neckline. Small buttons made from the same material follow the line of the roses. I stand and watch her as she approaches.

'Lily, you look…you look beautiful.'

She smiles one of her confident Lily smiles and I step back and bump into a passing waiter. She laughs, and we sit down. I recover enough to hand her the small perfume bottle I purchased in Canton. It's wrapped in green tissue paper with a white ribbon.

Lily gently unwraps it. 'You surprise me, Knill. It's so delicate, I love it.'

People are all around us, talking and laughing. The light from the chandeliers shines on Lily's black hair and it reminds me of the first time I saw her in her father's office, when she was sitting close to a lamp and her hair was aglow.

'It's to thank you for getting me to China. I would never have managed here without you.' I fidget, and Lily smiles shyly.

'You don't have to thank me, Knill. You've helped me understand my family in ways that I've never contemplated before.'

'Are you looking forward to going back to Australia, Lily?'

'Oh yes. Australia is home for me even though I enjoy being in China.'

I take her hand. 'Will your father approve of our friendship when we return, Li Ling?'

She smiles sweetly at her Chinese name. 'Just friendship, Knill?' She squeezes my hand.

I want to kiss her, but I can't. Not here.

'I hope it can be more, much more,' I say.

We join the revellers in the main ballroom. Tonight, we are to enjoy ourselves.

Later, when Uncle has retired for the night, Lily and Fong Pen-Lee suggest we go for one last rickshaw ride along the Bund. Outside the Astor, the rickshaws are lined up. As we step into the cold, clear night, a rider approaches us.

'I drive you, sir?'

We laugh as we squash together in the hooded seat. I put my arm around Lily's shoulders, and she returns my gesture with a quick smile. Fong Pen-Lee is squeezed in the opposite corner. We place a rug across our knees. I hope the rider's able to manage the weight of three people. I've seen rickshaw riders transporting groups of people all over China but still I wince when he pedals for the three of us.

Soon we are heading across the bridge onto the road beside the Bund. The night lights of Shanghai are splendid.

Magical. And the night shadows camouflage any areas of decay and poverty. As the rickshaw moves past the grand houses and hotels, I visualise the streets behind the modern facade: the tiny laneways that shocked me on my discovery tours. I imagine people crouching over their small fires, cooking rice and chestnuts, the ragged children drifting between family groups and the men squatting in small circles, talking and smoking. I think about the privation I saw with Fong Choon and speculate as to how such poverty can exist behind the new opulence.

The now familiar smells of Shanghai waft around us as the chill breeze of the night envelops us. I smile as I imagine trying to explain Shanghai to Will and Eugene at home. Fong Pen-Lee is the most relaxed that I've seen her. She laughs and jokes with Lily, her face glowing in anticipation of her time ahead in Australia.

I lean back in my seat, feeling a flood of relief when I think about the journey ahead: Canton, Hong Kong and then Melbourne.

'What are you smiling about?' Lily teases me.

'Home, I was thinking about home.'

The rickshaw slows to allow several cars to drive by and Fong Pen-Lee continues to talk excitedly as we move along. I join in the silly banter when I can.

Several cars move past the slow rickshaw, then Fong Pen-Lee suddenly tugs at Lily's arm and points to a black Citroën as it draws beside us. Fong Choon sits alone in the comfort of the leather seats. He stares ahead, ignoring the traffic around him. We watch in silence as the vehicle moves on, then as it carefully leaves the road to enter a wide driveway. By the time the rickshaw pulls alongside the entrance, we see Fong Choon entering the house.

55

Fong Pen-Lee calls to the rickshaw driver to stop. We look at her in bewilderment.

'What are you doing?' Lily asks her.

'I'm seeing what he is doing here,' Fong Pen-Lee replies as she jumps down from her seat, her sullenness returning. Lily follows her, giving me a questioning look over her shoulder. I step down from the rickshaw as Lily asks the driver to wait.

'This is not a good idea,' I call to them.

Although I want to stop Fong Pen-Lee from acting foolishly, I'm equally intrigued as to why Fong Choon is visiting this large residence, so far from his own.

Lily is speaking to Fong Pen-Lee in Cantonese.

'She just wants to have a little peep to settle her curiosity,' Lily tells me.

'We need to be careful. It's not our business, you know.' But we follow Fong Pen-Lee.

The entrance is darker than we expect. Tall overhanging trees provide privacy to the house. In the moonlight, the beautifully maintained gardens sprawl ahead of us. We creep towards a lamp-lit window at the front of the house.

We all know we shouldn't be doing this. It feels wrong and yet the exercise has taken on a life of its own. Lily is quietly telling Fong Pen-Lee that there is nothing to see, in the hope that we can retreat. She can only be thinking how much trouble it will cause if we are caught spying on Fong Choon. Lily knows enough about the way the family functions to understand the repercussions. She now speaks sharply to Fong Pen-Lee, but the young woman doesn't heed her tone. I'm aware of how Lily is feeling but now I also want to get a glimpse of the inhabitants of the house.

We stand huddled together, peering through the front window from behind the tree-lined path. Keeping our distance, we strain to see as shadowy figures come into view. Fong Pen-Lee, intent on securing a better vantage point, tiptoes closer to the house. Lily gives her a look of caution, which she ignores. Lily and I creep behind her, our eyes fixed on the glow emanating from within the house. The light is closer now, and we can see the outline of the room beyond. A sharp noise nearby startles us. We freeze guiltily. Then Fong Pen-Lee inches ahead.

'We have to go back,' Lily whispers.

Fong Pen-Lee doesn't respond. I smile weakly at Lily, trying to hide my mounting interest in what is before us.

I am, however, concerned that Fong Pen-Lee's careless approach might be noticed. I tap her on the shoulder and motion to her to return to the trees. At the same moment, there is movement inside the room. Fong Choon comes into view. A woman moves to stand beside him. Fong Pen-Lee steps forward, scrutinising her father and the stranger. Her hand flies to her mouth. Then she turns. She is sobbing as she runs past Lily and back down the path. I sense, but don't see, Lily hurrying after her.

As I move to the window, a familiar but disorientating sensation sweeps over me. My eyes do not leave the tall woman beside Fong Choon. The old photograph flashes before me as I stare into the face of Eliza.

56

I watch for what seems an eternity although it's only minutes. Then I follow the path back to find Lily and Fong Pen-Lee, who are waiting for me by the rickshaw.

'I've seen her before,' Fong Pen-Lee tells us.

'Where have you seen her?'

'At my father's house. Only a couple of times but I know it's her.' Fong Pen-Lee looks down at her feet.

'Go back to the hotel,' I tell Lily. 'I'll meet you there later.'

'No, Knill. You must not confront him. There is nothing to be gained. We leave so soon. Can't you just let it be?'

'I have to do this.'

'There is nothing you can do about it.'

'Lily, it's Eliza. I'm sure it's her.'

Lily gapes at me and steps towards me. 'You must be mistaken, Knill. How could it be?'

But she helps Fong Pen-Lee to climb into the rickshaw. She places her hand on my arm before telling the driver to go back to the hotel. 'Be careful,' she says.

'It's not me who needs to be careful.'

A servant in soft slippers peers around the heavy door. The loud knocking at night has unsettled her.

'I want to speak to Fong Choon.' My voice is clear and loud; it echoes in the still of the night.

'Sorry, sir, no visitors.' The woman attempts to close the door, I step forward.

'Tell Fong Choon I want to speak to him now.'

'You wait here.'

The servant steps back into the hallway and as she does I push the door open and step into the large hallway.

'Who is there?' I hear Fong Choon's stern voice as he walks from the front of the house. He stops abruptly when he sees me. He holds me in his stare for several seconds. The housemaid looks from face to face, waiting for Fong Choon's reaction. Annoyed, the older man waves her away.

'I think there is something we need to talk about,' I say.

'What are you doing here? This is a private house and you have no invitation. We have said our goodbyes, Knill.'

'Who lives in this house, Fong Choon?' I step forward, coming closer to him.

'That is no business of yours.' He shifts to block the entry way, then I hear footsteps coming from the front room.

'Fong Choon, who is it?' The tall woman emerges, clad in a green dress, the fine fabric shimmering as she moves. The neckline is scooped elegantly across her shoulders and the frock hangs long to just above her ankles. Her hair is pinned back from her forehead and falls thickly down her back. I look at her eyes and I know it's her.

I feel light-headed as I watch them. Fong Choon's shoulders sag as the woman looks to him for an explanation. He hesitates, and the woman quickly steps towards me.

'Who are you? What do you want here?'

'I'm Knill, and, and…I'm looking for my mother.' I can't take my eyes from her face.

'Your mother? Well, who is she? Is that an Australian accent…?' She swings around and looks at Fong Choon, who then steps forward. Before he can speak, the woman turns to me.

'Did you say your name is Knill?'

'I'm Knill McMillan from Australia. Are you Eliza?'

'Yes, I am Eliza but how do you—' Then, as if shot, she staggers forward. Her eyes search my face.

Fong Choon is quickly by her side and takes her arm. She flicks him away.

'Scarffe?'

'Yes. Well, I was Scarffe, but my name is Knill now. Are you…are you Eliza from Majorca?'

We stare at each other for what seems a long time. Fong Choon stands still beside Eliza. She then slowly turns to him.

'And you knew that my son was in China?'

'Yes.'

'When were you going to tell me? How dare you, Fong Choon...' Her voice is quiet but firm. She looks towards me again.

'I think we should discuss this later,' Fong Choon says.

'No, we need to discuss this right now,' says Eliza.

Fong Choon collects himself and takes a deep breath. 'I arranged for Knill to come to China. We met and I offered him a chance to stay in China and become part of the family business.' He glances awkwardly at me.

'You did all of this without telling me?'

'You would have put a stop to it.'

'You had no right to do this, Fong Choon.'

'I had every right. He's my son and I eventually found him in Australia. He doesn't want to stay here so there is nothing more that can be done.' Fong Choon looks angry and agitated.

'But he is my son too.' Eliza shakes her head and looks at me again.

'You would never have allowed me to find him, Eliza.'

'He has a family of his own and...' Eliza trails off. After a long moment she suggests we sit in the drawing room.

Somehow, the three of us move to a room with large chairs and thick rugs. Eliza, who is now sitting on the edge of a chair, continues to stare at me. Fong Choon's face is crimson, and the servant is peering from a doorway down the large hallway. He waves her away.

'I feel I owe you both an explanation,' Fong Choon says, still on his feet.

There is silence as Eliza and I look up at him.

'Eliza, I knew you were reluctant to find Scarffe. You always believed that he would think poorly of you. You also believed that it was in his best interests to let him get on with his own life.'

Eliza is watching me again, her face stony as he talks.

'But I always believed he had a right to meet us.'

'I'm sorry you have to hear this, Scarffe,' says Eliza faintly.

I sit as if in a scene from a film, watching actors talk about someone else's life.

'I arranged for Scarffe to come to China. I was under the belief that once he was here you would gradually relent and agree to meet him.'

'And when were you going to tell me, Fong Choon?'

He turns, nods to her before he faces me.

'When you decided to return to Australia, Knill, I realised that I had made a mistake by not telling Eliza.' He turns back to her. 'I came this evening to tell you what I had done and to plead with you to meet your son before he returned to Australia.'

'And if Eliza refused, would you have let me go home without knowing?' I ask.

'Yes.'

A tea tray arrives and the servant pads out quietly. Fong Choon drops into a chair. Eliza ignores him, I suspect she is holding her tongue, for now. She watches me, though, as her eyes flicker in the soft lamplight above her chair. There is warmth in her face and for a split second I experience a glimmer of something familiar stir within me. I can't speak, cry, shout or laugh, instead I simply look at her. Every line in her face, her dark defined eyebrows, the outline of her lips, the way her hair falls behind her, and her eyes, most of all her eyes. The image of the girl in the photo rises in my mind; I know it so well. It's now replaced with the older version sitting across the room from me. Eliza, the woman I thought I would never meet.

Part three
April 1922

57

The three men don't realise they are at the dock to meet the same people until I introduce Will and Eugene to Joseph, Lily and Fong Pen-Lee. We are in fine spirits and thrilled to be home. Lily is overjoyed to see her father. They hug each other and laugh as if the rest of us are not there.

'Li Ling,' says Joseph, 'it's so good to have you back home, my daughter.'

'Oh, Father, I've missed you.'

The bond between daughter and father is a strong one, anyone watching can see that. Then Joseph turns to me and shakes my hand.

'Was it the experience you hoped for, Knill?'

'In many ways and more. Thanks to you, Joseph. You were very persuasive.'

We laugh.

'Father, I have invited Knill to come for lunch tomorrow. We have matters to discuss with you.'

'Yes, yes, of course.' Joseph looks surprised by Lily's request – as do Will and Eugene – but today he lets nothing interfere with the pleasure of his daughter's homecoming.

'Oh, Knill, I almost forgot to give you this.'

Joseph pulls an envelope from his inside pocket. It has his business stamp in the left-hand corner. Briefly, our eyes lock. A look of understanding, excitement even, passes between us. I take the letter and pocket it.

Will raises his eyebrows at Eugene. They don't miss much.

'Then it's arranged. We will see you tomorrow, Knill. You have the address,' says Lily, breaking a moment of awkward silence.

As they leave, Lily turns hesitantly and waves. I watch them for a moment, realising that being home will make a difference to the way Lily and I are able to relate to each other. Over the last months we have become accustomed to daily contact. On the ship coming home we were together constantly.

Now, as she leaves with her father and Fong Pen-Lee and I with my cousins, it feels like a wrench between us. I love Lily and she me. I've never been this sure about anything else before.

'Sounds like there's a story to be told, Knill,' says Eugene with a grin. 'And not just about meeting your father.'

'Stories, all right. Stories you will hardly believe,' I say, as they help me collect my trunk and bags, but I'm still thinking of Lily going home with her father.

We head for the tram and instantly I'm back. The sounds and smells of Melbourne, the rattle of the trams as we rumble along the familiar route, the grinding as they pull to a halt to collect passengers, the unique drawl of the Australian accent. I think of Ted and how much I'm looking forward to seeing him. Leaning back in my seat, I take it all in. There's so much that I've never appreciated before.

'Pleased to be home, Knill?' says Will. 'We were a bit worried you might have stayed away longer.'

I tell Will and Eugene that there was an opportunity for me to stay. They listen with wide eyes as I tell them about Fong Choon and Eliza. For once, the two of them are dumbstruck.

'And what about Lily, Knill?'

'What about Lily?' I fox. We all grin. 'For god's sake, let me talk to her father first.'

In Collingwood I find my room as I left it. Somehow, it seems from another time. It's been four months since I left for China, but it feels much longer.

Before going to the pub for a homecoming beer with Eugene and Will, I unpack. I place Ted's teapot on the dresser and hang my clothes in the wardrobe. The envelope from Joseph is still in my coat pocket. I open it, read its contents, and sit down to collect my thoughts. Then I know what I must do. Being decisive is a skill I've mastered since going to China. My writing pad and envelopes are where I left them, and I have time to write the letter before we leave. I borrow a stamp from Eugene and post it on our way to the pub.

58

Lily opens the door and touches my arm lightly, nodding towards her father. 'It is just us,' she whispers. 'Fong Pen-Lee is sleeping.' Joseph looks up from his book and gets to his feet. The house is small and welcoming. On the wall, two large paintings depict rural Chinese scenes, and on the mantelpiece sit framed photographs. There is a photo of a small girl aged about three with a smiling woman. Lily and her mother, probably not long before her mother's death.

'Welcome to our home, Knill,' says Joseph. 'We have much to talk about, I believe.'

I glance at Lily and her smile reassures me. This might not be as difficult as I first thought. I'm nervous of the man standing in front of me who commands all of Lily's respect.

'Sit down, please.'

We all sit in separate chairs and Joseph doesn't waste any time getting to the point.

'I hear from Lily that the two of you have formed, well, let's say, a strong friendship.'

'Yes. And…and with your permission, Lily and I would like to marry.'

Joseph stands up from his chair, walks to the window. 'You should know – and I've told Lily this – it's not always easy to marry outside your culture.'

'But Knill isn't outside of our culture, Father,' Lily says. 'He is half-Chinese, you know that.'

'Hear me out,' Joseph demands. 'Knill, you have been raised in Western culture. I know that in recent times you have discovered your Chinese origins, but there is still a big difference between you and Lily.'

Lily jumps up and waves her hands at her father. 'That is so unfair. We are more alike than you think. After all, I was educated in Australia.'

'Yes, yes, but I'm just making it clear about the differences. Sometimes it's others who can make difficulties for you. People can be cruel and judgemental about mixed marriages.'

Lily slumps in her chair and glares at her father, shaking her head at me as if to say, *Don't listen to him.*

But I know that we can't not listen. He's a powerful man. He's Lily's father and I know she loves him. I also owe him my respect.

'I'm not refusing the idea of the two of you being married, but I want the facts to be before us. You must know what you are letting yourselves in for.'

'Sir, I understand what you are saying. I've thought of the differences and I know that not all people will approve of our marriage but should that be reason to not marry? We love each other. I love your daughter, sir. If I've learnt anything since I first met you, it's the importance of knowing where you belong. And I belong with your daughter.'

Joseph nods and walks the room. Lily leans across from her chair and places her hand on my arm. We are silent, waiting for him to speak again.

'I have a request for you both.'

'What is it?' says Lily.

'I will give my permission for you to become engaged on one condition. That you, Lily, wait until you have completed your law studies. Only then will I give my permission for the two of you to marry.'

We look at each other. There are tears in Lily's eyes.

'But I haven't even been accepted at university,' Lily says. 'I may never be.'

Joseph goes to the mantelpiece and reaches for an envelope that is tucked in behind the photos. Smiling broadly, he places it in her hand.

59

The leaves on the liquidambar are turning a golden yellow, and the April days are shortening. The afternoon sun is dappled across the verandah as Ted places the tray with his new teapot from China, cups, and a plate of Aunty Kate's fruit cake on the old metal table. I sit on the bench that's been here since I was a kid. Ted pours the tea.

The bond I feel with Ted is stronger than ever. It wasn't until I met Fong Choon and Eliza that I realised that it is Ted who knows me best. It was Ted and Rhoda who raised me, moulded me and made me who I am today. China might have broadened my thinking about family and connectedness, but this is my home.

Over the next few hours, I tell Ted about An Meng's death, meeting Fong Choon and the shock of finding Eliza. Ted laughs when I tell him about Uncle being on hot bricks with worry most of the time.

'Poor bugger, sounds like he was bending over backwards for everyone and still getting it wrong. He must have been glad when you left.'

When Ted hears about Fong Choon's offer for me to stay in China, he shakes his head in disbelief.

'And I didn't see it coming,' I tell him. 'And Lily couldn't believe it. But, you see, it turned out to be a strategy to get me to stay longer.'

'Because of Eliza?'

'Yes. Fong Choon had arranged for me to come to China without her knowledge. He thought if I was there long enough, she would change her mind and embrace the idea of meeting me.'

'He got it wrong?'

'Yes, he did. She was convinced that I'd never forgive her for giving me up as a baby. Prior to my trip to China, Fong Choon wanted Eliza to come to Australia to meet with me. She flatly refused. I think that's why he was so angry when I refused his offer to stay. Fong Choon told me that Eliza doesn't get out of bed on the fourteenth of November.'

'Your birthday.'

'In his defence, I believe he wanted to help Eliza feel less guilty and burdened by what happened all those years ago.'

'And perhaps he really did want you to stay and learn how to run his businesses.'

Ted sits quietly, his teacup still in his hand. I know it can't be easy having to hear of all this. And yet he's told me that he wants to know all the details about what happened in China. The afternoon sun fades as the shadows of the trees creep over the house.

'I think it's time for a beer,' he says. 'Stay here and I'll grab a bottle and a couple of glasses.'

I can hear him opening the icebox and then the ping of a top coming off the beer bottle. He comes back and resettles on the seat. He pours two glasses with an expert hand and passes one to me.

'What happened when you went to Eliza's house that night?'

'Ha, it took quite a bit of sorting out. Eliza is the one person who doesn't feel indebted to Fong Choon. But after all the fuss there was a strange relief. Especially when I told Eliza that I'd been looking for her back in Australia. Once she knew that I'd searched for her it somehow made a difference.'

'And she was in China all that time?' Ted shakes his head.

'Yes, for over ten years.'

'And everyone back here thought she'd died in that Sydney circus fire?'

'She was there when the fire happened, but she and another seamstress escaped. They were new to the circus, they knew no one, so they just looked for other work and places to live.'

'Then she disappeared?'

'She didn't contact her family and friends so in a way I guess she did. You see, she carried enormous shame for having given up her baby. Even if she had no choice at the time, she always believed it was her fault. After the fire, Eliza worked for several Sydney families as a seamstress. Years later, she sewed for the wife of a Chinese business-man. He happened to know Fong Choon. He contacted him in China and Fong Choon persuaded Eliza to travel to China to meet him again. He paid her expenses and made the arrangements.'

'What the heck has she been doing all this time in China?'

'Eliza and Fong Choon are committed to each other. They resumed a relationship but live in separate houses. Eliza has nothing to do with Fong Choon's family. They both feel guilty for past events and so they've put their time into making amends in other ways.'

'Making amends?'

'Eliza has earned her keep in China, Ted. She works with abandoned babies and mothers who are destitute. She set up several houses and an orphanage in Shanghai. She speaks both Mandarin and Cantonese.'

Ted tops up my beer glass and I'm pleased it's him sit-ting beside me. There's a comfort talking with Ted on the verandah I played on as a kid.

Meeting Eliza was the last thing that I'd expected. I'd given up any idea of her being alive. When I walked through the door of that grand house in Shanghai and met her for the first time, it seemed like I'd known her all my life. The tilt of her chin, the way she flicked her hair. And the eyes – those eyes that I knew so well from the old photo-graph. I still recall how she looked at me when she first saw me.

Ted and I sit with our own thoughts for some time until he breaks the silence.

'Will you see Eliza and Fong Choon again?'

'Fong Choon is trying to persuade Eliza to come to Australia for a visit. Eliza hasn't yet agreed. She's stubborn. She says she needs time to consider returning to Australia, even for a visit. However, she has decided to write to her brother Michael and her friend Robina.'

Ted doesn't say much, but I know he's taking in every detail. He turns to me slowly. 'And you, Knill. What's it meant for you?'

I know he's hanging on every word I'm saying.

'I'm not the same anymore, Ted. I've changed since that day I found the box on top of the wardrobe. Sometimes I can't quite believe all the things that have happened. Rhoda's death knocked the stuffing out of me. It wasn't until later that I realised how much she meant to me. I was selfish for a while; all I wanted to do was find out who my other parents were. Leaving you to go to China was hard and I felt guilty. Thank God you somehow understood why I had to go.'

Ted hasn't moved and my view of him seems frozen in time. Then he blinks and nods, as if giving me permission to continue.

'Meeting Fong Choon was difficult. I had no idea how to act. I now know that he felt just as confused and had almost considered not going ahead with arranging for me to go to China. Finding Eliza was monumental. I still get goosebumps when I think of seeing her through the window. Funny, but I knew immediately who she was.'

'It worked well for you, didn't it?'

'It was something I had to do, Ted.'

'What now, Knill?'

'A job. Once again I need a job.'

Before I caught the train, I went to see Artie, and I tell Ted that Artie is retiring and asked me if I wanted to apply for his job. I filled in the application before I left the office. It'll be a step up for me and better pay than the clerk wages I'd been on before going to China.

I am hoping against hope that I get the job as I want to start paying Fong Choon back. We continue to talk about work and what it will mean to be head clerk if I'm successful.

Then Ted turns to me.

'And what about Lily? You sure talked nonstop about her in your letters.'

'Yes, there is something important to tell you about Lily, Ted.'

A warmth spreads through me. It has been so difficult to wait to tell Ted, but I wanted the story of Lily and me to not get mixed up in the story of Fong Choon and Eliza.

'I've asked her to marry me and she's said yes.'

He lowers his glass of beer and places it on the table. 'Well. That's a surprise. Isn't it a bit soon? Are you sure you know what you're doing, Knill?'

'What do you mean?'

'Well, you might get some opposition – different background, all that.' Ted's expression is serious as he looks me directly in the eye.

'Lily's father says the same thing. But we love each other and have much in common. She is smart – smarter than me. She's wise and she's thoughtful and kind. I wish she and Rhoda…'

I don't finish my sentence. I'm not sure I can.

'And that's that.' Ted smiles. 'My father questioned me about Rhoda once – but she was the only woman I wanted. I can see you feel the same way.'

'It will be a long engagement. Lily has been accepted to study law at Melbourne University and we have agreed with her father that we will not marry until she's finished her degree.'

'Studying law? Sounds like she'll keep you on your toes.' Ted leans back in his seat.

'I know you will really like Lily, Ted.'

His smile deepens. 'It's about time you brought her to Castlemaine then.'

'She'll be here on Thursday.'

We sit in comfortable silence until the evening breeze picks up, telling us it's almost time to go inside. The front gate squeaks. We look up to see a woman walking down the path towards us.

Ted slowly places his glass on the table beside him as he stands. 'Rhoda? Rho…'

'Hello. Sorry if I'm disturbing you, but…I'm Hattie… Hattie McKenzie.'

We are both on our feet. Hattie is near the front steps now, and Ted is staring at her.

'Sorry, I thought you were someone else…' Ted says.

The colour has drained from Ted's face. He looks from Hattie to me and back again. I have not yet recovered from the shock of Hattie's uncanny resemblance to Rhoda. Her smile is wide and confident, I'm drawn to her clear blue eyes, which are just like Rhoda's. She's wearing a fashionable tweed jacket with a belt pulled tight around her narrow waist, teamed with a matching pleated skirt and polished tan high heels.

'And you're Knill?' Hattie shakes my hand. 'Thank you for the letter.'

'Hattie,' I say. 'I thought you were coming tomorrow.'

60

The next morning, when Hattie returns, Ted is composed. I suspect he had a restless night after the shock of seeing her walk up the path in the evening light. But, true to form, Ted is ready and prepared to welcome Rhoda's daughter to his home. To Rhoda's home.

'She would want you to have these,' says Ted.

He keeps looking at her as if he doesn't quite believe who she is and yet her resemblance to Rhoda is striking. He has set out some of Rhoda's special crockery on the kitchen table, along with an embroidered tablecloth that Rhoda meticulously worked on when they were first married. He looks at me as if to ask if it's all right that he gives them to Hattie.

'I couldn't take them, they look so precious,' Hattie says.

'If Rhoda were here she would be wanting to give you more than this, Hattie,' Ted says. 'You were never far from her thoughts.'

The gate at the cemetery is stuck. I push with my shoulder and it swings open.

'Brute strength,' Hattie says with a laugh. 'You know, I've been wanting to visit her grave, but something stopped me. If you hadn't contacted me I may have never worked up the courage.'

'How did you know that Rhoda died?'

'I was staying here in Castlemaine with my parents' friends, the Cuthberts, the family I stayed with last night after seeing you and Ted. Anyway, at the time they were talking about a local woman, Rhoda McMillan, who died after being found in a dam. I knew my real mother's name was Rhoda and wondered if it was the same person.'

'How did you know her name?' We stop by the old Presbyterian sign.

'My parents told me that her name was Rhoda James and that she came from Castlemaine. They weren't supposed to know but apparently the minister's wife let it slip in conversation when I was taken to them. Anyway, there aren't many Rhodas around and the age matched with the skimpy information I had. I guessed she had most likely married and would have another name.'

'So when you came to her funeral, you weren't sure if she was your real mother?' I ask.

'No, but somehow it seemed right. Though I didn't hang around for long that day – I felt that I shouldn't have been there. I remember you, though, Knill. So when your letter arrived, it confirmed that I was Rhoda's daughter.'

We arrive at Rhoda's grave and stand in silence looking down at the headstone. Hattie moves forward and gently places a small bunch of roses on the grave.

'Roses were her favourites,' I say.

'What was she like, Knill?'

I've never been asked that before. I think for a while.

'Rhoda was busy, talkative...sometimes too talkative, kind, and a bit of a worrier. Well, not just a bit, she worried about everything. I've since realised that she carried a large burden. Giving you away and then adopting me years later. Perhaps her guilt made her nervous. She was a hard worker and liked things to be just right. It almost seemed that if she could make her outside world perfect it would help her manage the events in her past that were imperfect.'

'It sounds so sad, and all the time I had a good life. She didn't need to be so guilty and worried,' Hattie says.

'Even so, there was so much good in her, and she brought so much good to the world. Ted and I, we loved her.'

'Yes, I see that.'

'Lately, I've been thinking a bit about how people cope when awful events happen in their lives. Especially when they can't change them. Like Rhoda and my mother, Eliza.'

The two of us talk for a long time. As we stand by her grave I can't help but wish Rhoda could hear Hattie saying that she is fine and that she holds no angst towards her. Would it have made a difference? Would she still be here if she knew that no harm had come to her daughter?

'And her garden? Tell me about it, Knill.'

'It was her favourite pastime – she loved it. She once told me that you can lose yourself in a garden, and she was living proof of that. Some days she would spend all day digging and tending her plants.'

'She knew a bit about it then?'

'Oh, yes, she was involved with the show committee and the gardening groups. She was considered an expert.'

'It's weird but I feel like I know her. I share her love of gardening, unlike my parents, who have no interest. And she was right, Knill. You can lose yourself in a garden.' Hattie bends down to brush away a stray leaf from Rhoda's grave.

'There is something else, Hattie…I'm not sure if you realise it but you look just like her.'

61

I tell Ted everything: how I found the details of Rhoda's daughter's birth in Reverend Dancy's book when I went to Bendigo in search of my own birth record. I kept the information to myself, intending to search for Hattie after I found Eliza. Then Lily's father came along and before I knew it I was on my way to China.

'Before I left for China, I asked Joseph to make some enquiries about Rhoda's daughter. I figured if he could track me down he might be able to do the same for her. I knew that she was adopted to a Mr and Mrs McKenzie, who lived in Maryborough. If I hadn't been going to China I would have looked myself.'

'So how did he find her?' Ted asks.

'The same way that he found me, except he contacted Robina in Majorca. I told him she had connections with Maryborough and sometimes visited relatives there. She enquired through her relatives and wrote to Joseph to tell him that they knew the McKenzies through the church. She also said they had one daughter, Hattie, who was about thirty years old.'

Again, we are sitting on the verandah, with the liquid-ambar casting its late afternoon shadow over us; a gentle autumn breeze drifts in. The familiar sight of the blue-gums towering against the sky remind me I'm home. I can hear the kids on the footy oval, calling for the ball. For a moment, I'm there with Will and Eugene, the three of us dusty and sweaty, all those years ago.

Ted's eyes are distant and I can tell he is thinking of Rhoda. He has invited Hattie to have lunch with him in two weeks' time, and already they are planning another visit to the cemetery, where she wants to see Rhoda's plantings.

'A piece of luck, Robina having connections.'

'Yes, but knowing Hattie's parents' name removed some of the difficulty. And then when I arrived home, Joseph presented me with the details of his findings.'

'And Hattie was happy to be found?'

'Yes. I only wrote to her last week.'

Ted rubs his hand over his chin and looks out to the road.

'Sorry we got the days mixed up, Ted. Hattie arrived a day earlier than I expected. I was going to tell you the next morning, to prepare you for her arrival…but there she was, surprised us both.'

'I just wish that Rhoda could have met her,' Ted says.

He stops then turns towards me and shrugs. Silence hangs between us until Ted takes a deep breath.

'She would have loved her. Hattie looks so much like her. Thank you for finding her.'

I turn away when I see him blink back tears. He goes inside to the icebox and returns with a bottle and two glasses. The sun dips below the line of trees and the cool air is the perfect temperature against my skin.

'Now when did you say Lily is coming?'

'Tomorrow, Ted. Tomorrow morning.'

Acknowledgements

Finding Eliza is a story that has taken a long time to tell. It's been a time of discovery and learning. I'm grateful for the many writers and mentors who have travelled parts of the journey with me.

Thanks to author and teacher, Dr Adib Khan, who opened the door to the literary world and who graciously allowed me to stumble awkwardly through. To Dr Jill Blee, for her historical expertise and teaching. For all the workshop participants and presenters along the way, including Toni Jordan, who made me think it was possible to complete this novel

To my wonderful writer friends and manuscript readers, Jane Vanderstoel, Annaxue Yang, Maureen Riches, Suzanne Gatz and Mary Melcherts, who shared in the doubting times as well as the fun times. Their valuable insights and reflections contributed enormously to the process

Thanks to Julie Postance for expert online publishing assistance and Alissa Dinallo for a beautiful book cover design.

Gratitude and thanks to my amazing editor Alison Arnold. Her professional editing, mentoring and project management skills made all the difference.

Andrew and Ben, it's been a long wait. Your love and encouragement has been so important. Thanks, Andrew, for the help with technology.

To Kevin, whose support has never waned, even when my enthusiasm did. Thank you for believing that I could write this book.

And to family members long departed, who gave me a strong sense that belonging is everything.